Home for a Christmas Wish

AN EROTICA FANTASY NOVEL

GEORGE BARRET

Contents

Acknowledgements

My thanks to all those who helped me out with this book.

Thank you, DieselJester, who humored my ideas at each point.

Thank you, StarLiAneChan, for the cover artwork.

Thank you, Rainy Graphic, for making the title look better.

Thank you, Stoham Baginbott, for your editing service.

Thank you, Hallmark, for all the fine fodder for this parody.

And thank you, my Luna,

I love you with all my heart.

Also by George Barret

Short Stories

"The Hero's Reward" – published in "Dukes of Harem"

"The Runaway Monk" – published in "Knights and Maidens"

Novels

The Sanguine Elf

For all who are searching for light in the darkest of times.

Chapter 1: An Act of Kindness

Being home sucks, Ray Adler thought, sitting on a couch by himself at a Thanksgiving party he'd been forced to go to with his parents.

The person throwing the party was a friend of his father's and next-door neighbor, Tim Waters, but being there only intensified the sting of why Ray was home at that time of the year. Ray sat on one of the multiple couches while the overlapping white noise of party conversations continued around him. His gaze never left the sight of the paper plate of deep-fried turkey slices, watery mashed potatoes, and green bean casserole. He wanted to eat but was under a thick cloud of dread knowing that someone was going to ask about why he was there. He decided to wait for the hammer to fall before trying to eat.

Maybe I'll be able to enjoy the food then, he supposed.

"Hey, Mike," Tim's voice called out to Ray's father while they sat together at the other side of the room. "You didn't mention but what brings Ray home for the holidays? He hasn't been back this way in years."

"It's because he *failed* as an adult," Mike answered.

Ray's eyes flicked upward towards the voice, and he found his father sipping a glass of whiskey while giving Ray a disappointed scowl.

The look was one that Ray remembered well because it had been burnt into many of his most horrible memories. One such memory was when he was a young boy, and he came home with a B on his report card. His father had that look prepared like a bug zapper waiting for the prey that was young Ray. As soon as he had stepped past the front door, his father demanded the card and Ray gave him the card with the dreaded letter on it. Upon seeing it, Mike Adler erupted into a bellowing tirade about how Ray needed to do better.

B's are for those who don't succeed in America! That's why A's are for winners because American's are winners!

Years later, sitting across from his father at that Thanksgiving party, Ray still felt like the young boy coming home with a B on his report card. A grown man of thirty reduced to feeling like a grade-school boy. All because of a look. A look that a son could feel his father making at him without having to turn his eyes to see, but seeing it only made it worse, like looking at a needle about to penetrate the skin.

Mike Adler was a man of an imposing height of six feet and four inches that dwarfed his son's five foot eleven. His height was only one part of his body's intimidation caused by his thick build from his chest to his bulging gut and his thick arms and legs. His skin was extra pale which always flushed into a deep red when he went into his fits of rage. Mike's age was an obvious sixty years from the evidence of his thinning white hair that was combed over his bald head along with the full whiteness of his thick and bushy circle beard. His hardened expression was deepened thanks to the thick gouging lines of age around his eyes and across his forehead. To top it all off, his eyes were a pale piercing grey and appeared to be sunken into his face.

It was from those eyes that Ray could feel the scorching contempt and cold disappointment that seared into the pieces of his shattered soul. He felt that each word of the sentence that his father spoke broke the pieces ever further. Ray's own depressing thoughts had mirrored his father's words since he'd been home, but it was another thing entirely when someone confirms one's own worst thoughts aloud. And to an audience no less.

"Mike!" Wanda, Ray's mother, who was standing next to Mike, snapped, slapping the man's shoulder. "He's been through enough as is."

Wanda Adler was three years younger than Mike and her overall appearance visualized someone who had been plucked out of a bygone age and dropped into the modern world. Her fashion of a shirtwaist dress invoked either an aesthetic of the 1950s or someone trying to make vintage look sheik. She had beautiful shoulder-length, wavy, brown hair that had streaks of silver and white. It was so well kept as if she spent half of the day on her appearance while spending the other half preparing to entertain a dinner party. Her heart-shaped face invoked worry and concern as she looked around the room and, in particular, in Ray's direction with her sweet green and motherly eyes, but Mike wasn't having it.

"It's the truth," Mike continued his inebriated tirade while listing off Ray's failures on each finger of his thick and calloused hands. "He lost his job, his apartment, and couldn't keep his relationship with his fiancé together. And what does he do? He moves back home just when I thought the nest was finally empty. And now like every damn millennial and Gen Z brat in this goddamn country, when things go wrong, he comes running home to *mommy* and *daddy*. Sickens me! This sort of shit never happened in our day! At least his older brother was smart and chose business. Not graphic design or whatever liberal nonsense they're teaching these days in those indoctrination centers they call colleges. Business is how you make it in America! Business and hard work! Not handouts!"

"That's enough, Mike," Wanda said reaching over to take his whiskey glass.

Mike pulled the glass away from her grasp. "Oh, I'm sorry," he said in his thick sarcasm, "I thought this was America. Isn't that right, Tim? Don't I get to say what I want? You know what the liberals always scream and whine about?"

"Damn straight," Tim chimed in. "Freedom of speech protects what you don't want to hear. God bless, America!"

All of the men and some of the women rose their glasses in their blind agreement to the statement while several called out, "God bless America!"

Hearing his father talk about how he failed made Ray feel like he was on trial for his own life with his father being the eyewitness to his failures with the dinner guests were the court audience calling for his punishment.

Guilty!

Guilty!

Guilty!

Ray couldn't stand the humiliation anymore. His own heart and mind did enough punishment to him for his own failings. He stood up from the couch with the plate of food in his hands and walked away.

"See what I mean, Tim?" Mike called out. "We raised a generation of pussies who can't handle the truth! You *failed*, Ray! Fuck your feelings!

Quit being a pussy and man up!"

Ray tried to soothe himself with the reminder of how his father was when he got drunk but the facts of his situation kept coming at him like the pain of sunlight through shut eyelids. The past was haunting him while the present was crushing him, and the future was threatening him. He walked out the front door and sat on one of the wicker chairs set on the wide brick front porch. After taking a deep breath, he glanced downward and did what anyone does in the face of failure; ruminate.

Everything was going well, he thought over his own life, *where did it all go so wrong? What did I do wrong?*

He looked at the food while it steamed in the cold air, but he couldn't eat it. Taking another deep breath, he brought his gaze upward to look at the Christmas lights. Some of the houses had them up, despite it being Thanksgiving, but others hadn't cracked open those boxes just yet. The ground already had a thin layer of snow on it.

It was the one thing that he missed about his life in the small town of Northview Valley, the way that everyone went all in when it came to Christmas decorations. Some houses just went simple with lights on the house and some on the trees and shrubbery, while others went wild with theirs.

The lights made Ray think about a house down the road that had all kinds of lights. The owner of that house would decorate the house, the bushes, and the trees, and would even bring out glowing figures of Santa, his reindeer, snowmen, elves, and candy canes. The "more is better" house, as his mother called it. But next door to that house there was a simple sign on the front lawn adorned in red Christmas lights that read "Bah

Humbug".

Tim Water's house, where Ray sat, was near the cross-street corner and thus gave the front porch a good view of it. Just down the street on the next street corner Ray caught sight of a disheveled man in brown dirty clothes, a scruffy white beard, and a red beanie that was growing threadbare. On the man's back was a red tattered backpack and in his hand was a piece of cardboard that was torn up at the edges, over folded, and a message written on it in desperate scratches of dried black permanent ink. Ray couldn't read what was written but he already made his assumptions of it.

Seeing the look of the man and feeling the cold reminded Ray of his own situation. If it weren't for the fact that his parents allowed him back home, he would have been homeless just like that poor man on the corner. The reminder and reality check made Ray look at the man, then down at his food and couldn't help but feel the pang of sympathy for him. Knowing that he wasn't going to eat the food himself, he got up and headed over to the corner.

The man on the corner was turning away from him with his sign hoping someone would see him not knowing who was coming towards him.

"Pardon me," Ray called out.

The man turned and without missing a beat or taking a pause he said, "Okay, I get it. I get it." He folded up his sign and waved his hand at Ray as if telling him to back off. "I'll move along from your nice neighborhood. No need to let a bum like me ruin your nice decorations even though it's still only Thanksgiving."

"Nah, that's not it," Ray said shaking his head and holding out the food to him. "Thought you might like a little food."

The tattered man looked at Ray, then down at the food, and then back at him.

"Oh, bless you, sir," the man said setting down his sign and reaching out for the plate.

Being close to him, Ray saw that the tattered man was thin possibly from eating too little due to whatever misfortunes had befallen him.

"You're much better than most of these rich assholes around here," the tattered man observed.

"Yeah," Ray said crossing his arms and trying to ignore the cold. "I may have come from this, but I'm not like them."

"Good thing. Money just makes you an entitled snot."

"If you'd like to sit, there's chairs over on the porch," Ray invited, holding his hand out towards Tim's home.

"Oh, bless you, son," the tattered man said holding the plate in one hand and the piece of cardboard in the other as he followed Ray.

The two came back to the porch and sat down.

"What's your story then?" the tattered man asked continuing to eat and not even caring that some bits of turkey and globs of mashed potatoes were getting stuck in his white beard.

"It's a pretty pathetic story," Ray sighed, turning down his gaze to the ground again.

"Well, I'm not gonna judge," he assured. "I mean look at me."

He gave further example to his point by holding up his sign. Ray gave it a glance to read what the man had desperately scratched in permanent ink: *Too honest to steal. Not pretty enough for porn. Any donations would be appreciated...*

Ray had to give a small huff of a laugh at the sign.

"Sounds a lot like me," Ray observed but he took a deep breath and began his sob story. "My life was going great for a while. But I lost it all. My job. My fiancé. My apartment. All of it."

"Shit, man." The tattered man breathed out a sigh, setting down his half-eaten plate. "I'm so sorry."

"Yeah...so, I have to suffer the indignity of moving back home with a pretty awful family."

"And around the holidays too."

Ray nodded while sniffling a little and hiding the fact that tears were only a few blinks away from spilling out of his eyes. But he held his eyes open, hoping that the cold air would help dry them. It was just a hard thing to have been on top of the world only six months ago and then to have it all fall apart as if it were made of playing cards.

"Hey, it's okay," the tattered man said, laying a hand on his shoulder. "I think you'll make it, kid. Just gotta keep a positive outlook on things. Each day is a new thing. So, something's gotta show up sooner or later."

"I know. Just wish that..." Ray sniffled once again, "Just wish that my life was better."

"I hear that, my brother," the tattered man said, finishing up the meal and setting the plate on the small table between the wicker chairs. He then got up, picked up his cardboard sign and stood in front of Ray. "Thank you for the food. And for this act of kindness, I hope to pay you back soon, but would you mind doing one more thing for me?"

Ray felt confused that the man would ask for anything else but given if it didn't involve him having to go back inside and face his parents, he figured he'd do it.

"Sure, what is it?"

The tattered man reached into his coat, pulled out a small, red envelope, and handed it to Ray. He looked at it and felt confused by it since it was stamped and only had the mailing address that read:

Santa

The North Pole

"Could you mail this for me?" he asked.

The situation was confusing to Ray but there was something about the tattered man that he wanted to do one other act of kindness for him. He knew of a mailbox that was right next to the mall. It was out of the way, but it was a good excuse to get away from the party, since he had no intention of going back for more verbal abuse.

He shrugged and said, "Sure. I'll take care of this for you. By the way, what's your name?"

"Nicholas," the tattered man said. "Happy Thanksgiving. And have a Merry Christmas as well. I hope that things do get better for you."

"And you too as well, Nicholas," Ray said standing up, turning towards the front door, he opened it, leaned it, grabbed his coat, and came back outside.

Yet, when he turned, he found that Nicholas was gone. Putting on the coat, he made a quick dash out to the curb but found no one. There was no sign of him. No tracks, no shadows, and no sign that the man was there.

"Wow..." Ray whispered and then shrugged. "Weird."

Once again, he looked at the red envelope and saw how pristine, neat, and clean it was. Even the handwriting was done with the most elegant of script as if it were done by someone who didn't belong in the age of emails and printed envelopes. He slipped it into his coat pocket and made his way towards the mall.

The town of Northview Valley was just big enough to have a shopping center like the Northfield Square Mall. To Ray, who had seen shopping centers that dwarfed it, it wasn't too bad by the town's standards since it was one of the few buildings that was more than one floor. Inside there that there were stores of various kinds from clothing to electronics, to books, to games, and even a few cookware stores. It was a place where Ray had a few good memories, such as the arcade back when it was a necessity to leave the house to play certain games.

Since it was just past six at night, there were cars in the parking lot for people who were camping out for Black Friday deals that would start the next day. It was near one of the entrances where there was a blue mailbox that had a thin cap of snow. Approaching it, Ray took out the red envelope and slipped it in.

Glad I could help, Nicholas, Ray thought before turning and heading toward his parents' home.

He came back to the street corner to look at the house where the party was still going. The windows were just big enough to look inside and see the various people eating, laughing, sometimes singing, but mostly drinking. This much Ray knew with the people that his parents hung around. No matter the time of year, the drinks of choice for that crowd were margaritas or whisky. With the time that it was, Ray was certain that everyone was past the point of tipsy if not full-blown drunk.

Not wanting to go back to the party and face his parents, Ray shoved his hands in his pockets, and made the walk home. All the while his mind kept wandering over his life and how he must have made a mistake somewhere. He had worked hard and thought he had made good decisions.

I did my best, he thought over and over again as if saying a prayer to a god of losers who might take pity on him and his plight. *I did my best. I did my best, didn't I?*

Once he got home, he went to a section of the dining room where there was an open bottle of Jack Daniels. He took it along with a glass that he filled with ice, went upstairs to his room, and started drinking.

"Happy Thanksgiving to me indeed," he muttered in a whisper that outclassed the bitterness of the whiskey.

And it wouldn't be his only drink of the night.

Chapter 2: The Reindeer's Bookshop

It was Cyber Monday. Four days had passed since Thanksgiving and the heart to heart that Ray had with the tattered man named Nicholas.

Lying in bed, Ray wasn't sure what time it was but then again, the passage of time didn't really matter. All he knew was that the sun was coming up and illuminating the snow outside giving a blue-white glow through the drawn blinds of his bedroom. Rolling onto one side, he brought up his phone, pulled up the photos, and began to scroll through the ones of him and his ex-fiancé, Angela Linke.

Every detail of her was etched, carved, and burnt into Ray's memory. She was considerably shorter than him with her height of four foot eleven. It was a fact that Ray always tried to tell her that he didn't mind that bout her.

You're not short, he often said smiling at her. *You're fun sized.*

The sentiment always made her laugh and smile in a way that was so bright in his memories that it would have been worthy of a toothpaste commercial. He couldn't help but stare at the pictures of her face with her shoulder-length blonde hair, sweet blue eyes, fair skin tone and round cheeks that he always loved to kiss. Then there was her curvy figure that was accentuated by her short stature. Ray remembered she was always so self-conscious about her looks from her height, her hair, her weight, and every other detail. To him, he loved every part of her from the outside in, but each detail had become a reminder of the wounds within him.

He went to a photo that was one of his favorites. It was one that he took of himself and Angela during their third anniversary when they went to probably the most expensive dinner they had. She was wearing a sexy red dress that accentuated all of the curves that Ray had intimate knowledge of. Then there was the way that she had her hair done and the make-up. It was one of the best times that he had with her, and then there was the night of incredible sex afterwards.

The memory of that night began the twist of pain in his heart that went down through his stomach and into his groin. It twisted further with the memory when it all came crashing down. He'd come home unexpectantly to hear moaning noises in the bedroom and discovered her bouncing up and down with his boss, Christian Strauss, underneath her in the bed that they shared.

A distraction was needed.

He was about to begin his 'doom-scrolling' when the thought of his father's nagging voice.

Get a job, snowflake!

"Ugh...". He groaned moving from one of his social media apps to the job board app.

In scrolling through the various job postings, he started to wonder which was the more depressing: trying to find a job or searching for dates. On the one hand, most of the job postings either paid too little or asked for too much experience. As for dating sites, most of the people on there weren't what he was looking for.

Then again, after Angela...what else was there?

How depressingly familiar, Ray mused thinking back to the first few months out of college and the difficulty of finding work. Each scroll upward on his phone made his mood sink further and further into the swamps of despair.

Then there was one posting that caught his attention.

HOLIDAY HELP WANTED

PAPER PLAYGROUND BOOKSTORE

Must be passionate about books and fiction.

Pay: $17.50 an hour

Hours: 40+ per week

Holiday period from Black Friday until January 15th

With a few taps he sent out the application as well as his resume for the listing and then he resumed scrolling through the job postings.

Within minutes a response came through.

Curious, Ray opened it.

To Ray Adler,

Thank you for responding to my ad. I am in desperate need of extra help, do you think you could come to the shop today, please? Thank you for your time.

Signed,

Maja

Owner of the Paper Playground

The was quick, Ray thought but then wondered if it was a scam. Getting out of bed he concluded one thing, *Scam or not, I need to get out of this house just to shut Dad up.*

To Maja,

Sure, I'll be on my way in a few minutes.

Signed,

Ray Adler

With his response sent, he got out of bed, showered, and got himself dressed in his job interview suit. He gave himself as good of a look in the mirror to make sure that he would make a good first impression at this job.

Ray often would describe himself as average or even below average with his light brown hair that he kept short and professional looking. Though, in the more recent months he let it grow a little too long but then again with all that had happened to him, his vanity, if he had any left, took a far backseat. His build had a thickness to it that he inherited from his father but gave the appearance that he wasn't one who was built for manual labor. That much was for certain given how soft his features were as well as how soft his hands were. He was a man built for the desk or at least he had been.

One of the few features that he liked about himself was his pale green eyes that he inherited from his mother. Everything else he couldn't help but wish it was different from his rounded face to his nose, his forehead, and his ears. But he tried to pull himself away from his self-hatred as there was a job interview to go to.

Here goes, he thought to himself and headed downstairs.

Coming to the main floor he went to where he set his coat while he heard the television playing at a loud volume for one of his father's football games. He hoped to make his way past him and out the front door without being noticed.

How wrong he was when he reached for the front doorknob.

"Where you going, liberal arts?" his father asked.

"I have a job interview at the mall, Dad," Ray answered trying to keep any sound, cadence, or inflection of annoyance out of his tone.

"Oh good. You'll fit right in with the other philosophy majors pouring coffee. Keep on being poor, son, while the businessmen get rich off you and the other lib-tards."

Hearing his father repeat everything he thought he knew about his son's life from Fox News made Ray grind his teeth and grip his hands so hard that he thought his fingernails would make his palms bleed.

Yet, he held his tongue.

He turned the doorknob and was about to head out.

"Don't cry too hard into your avocado toast!" his father cried out with an echoing laugh.

He stepped out and closed the door behind him.

"Ugh," Ray grunted to himself shoving his hands into his pockets and trekking through the snow and icy sidewalks towards the mall. "*Fuck you, Dad.*"

The anger and resentment that Ray had towards his father burned in him at such intensity that he was certain that each step he made would melt the snow and ice around him. Yet, by the time he made his way over the first cross-street to the mall, he was starting to feel frozen on the outside.

The kind of cold that made one think that if they just touched their own skin, it would flake off like shavings of ice from a windshield.

But he reminded himself that he was almost there.

Upon stepping inside the mall, Ray was given the pleasant assault of senses between the bright and bold colors of the Christmas decorations along with the sweet smells of the holiday treats. He could already discern what each scent was but the one that he always found loving at that time of the year was the candied almonds. The sweet smell of sugar and the pungent cinnamon was so thick that he imagined that not even the aromas from the local soap and body wash shop could push it away. Then there was the delicious warmth that melted the frozen sensation from his face and ears.

Moving past the doors of the mall, Ray located one of the kiosks that had the map layout of the mall. He zeroed in upon the store listing and found the name of "The Paper Playground" but what concerned him was the fact that the store sat across from the Barnes and Nobles.

Here's hoping for this job, Ray thought to himself before walking in that direction.

He thought over the right kind of answers for the job interview, in his experience, he often found that the jobs that required the most needed an interview. For jobs that required the least only needed the bare minimum of the applicant having a pulse. Still, he was prepared in his best suit, and he was certain that would give him points to his professionalism.

The trek through the mall was a lot more crowded than he remembered as a kid, but he had to remind himself that the town had grown over the years and, just like people, a town changes little by little. The same could be said of the Northfield mall and how so many stores had been lost and gained over the years.

It didn't take too long for him to find the Barnes and Noble and the Paper Playground across the way. He couldn't help but look back and forth between the giant chain store and the small shop.

Talk about competition, Ray thought as he made his way past one group of shoppers after the other until he reached his destination.

Stepping up to the Paper Playground, Ray couldn't help but think how old world the store was. There was a large store window display with a model town setup as if it were a craft shop. The model was a snow-covered model landscape with a toy train chugging its way along the tracks around a picturesque town. There were even tiny street signs saying, "Main Street" and "1st Ave" and so on with tiny cars that looked like they came out of the 1950s. As if it were a time capsule of how small towns in America were before Wal-Mart would stake its claim in it. The crowning cherry on the visual cake of it all was at the back where there were paper cutouts of mountains. Against them were books on vertical stands that loomed over the small town below like monoliths to words, thought and imagination.

"Wow," Ray remarked to himself.

Disengaging himself from staring at the window display, he headed inside. When he crossed the threshold, he couldn't help but take in the same familiar smell of paper as well as an undercurrent of leather and a hint of vanilla. Looking around he saw small bookshelves and tables stacked with books that had various signs from "This Month's Selection", "Holiday Favorites", "Independent Authors", and "Best Sellers".

Above him were Christmas ornaments that hung from the ceiling at different levels. At the edges of the ceiling were colored Christmas lights that ran the length of the store. Then there was the one thing that every store had to have: background Christmas music. The song that was playing was an orchestral arrangement of "Carol of the Bells". The store had a few people browsing the stacks with a small line at the register.

"Hello," a sweet voice called to him. "Welcome to the Paper Playground."

Bringing his attention to the voice's direction, Ray found a woman working the register. From his vantage point he guessed that she was a few inches shy of his five-foot eleven-inch height. As well as a few years younger than him. Her short bob style hair was a dark brown that became a silvery white at the tips that he guessed was the work of a masterful salon. She wore an ugly green Christmas sweater that had reindeer on it with a name tag that had a little reindeer frolicking in the corner with the name "Maja" written in elegant letters. Ray had to smile at the reindeer motif along with the pair of antlers sticking on out of the top of her head coupled with a pair of reindeer-like ears at the side of her head. Ray assumed that they were costume props, but they looked so real.

In front of her was a line of four people.

She really does need help, Ray remarked to himself.

That was when he approached the register.

"Excuse me," he called out. "Maja?"

The woman looked over and he even saw her reindeer-like ears twitch. Under normal circumstances, he would have been impressed at such prop work but there were other things that needed attention.

"How can I help?" Maja asked.

"My name is Ray Adler," Ray began while scratching an itch at the side of his face, "you emailed me earlier about the holiday job?"

"Oh, yes, Ray," Maja said resting a hand to her chest. "I am in desperate need of assistance, please, take one of the registers."

"Don't you need to interview me?" Ray asked feeling taken aback by the abrupt hiring.

"Well, you arrived and are willing to work, so, that's enough for me." Maja smiled. "Do you know how to use a register?"

"It's been a while, but I think I got it," he answered.

"It's fairly self-explanatory," Maja answered. "But if you need help with anything, just ask."

"Okay," Ray answered.

Taking a deep breath, he moved behind the counter, took off his winter coat, and looked at the touch screen register. He tried to remember his days of working at the coffee house and how the registers worked. Knowing that people were waiting he looked to the faces of the impatient customers and raised his hand. "I can help who's next."

The person who came up next was a short elderly lady dressed in thick brown faux fur coat and a faux fur hat. In her arms was a stack of books that she set down on the counter in front of him. Taking each book, he reached for the scanner and began scanning the barcode. One after the other he scanned each book but what he noticed was the titles. He saw books from Agatha Christie, Jonathan Kellerman, and Dick Francis.

Ray couldn't help but smile. "Excellent mystery choices."

"Thank you." The elderly woman smiled back.

With all of them scanned up, he brought up the total, and the elderly woman paid with a card. He was surprised at how much easier it was now. The readers did all the work.

"Thank you," Ray answered, "Have a nice day."

"You too, young man," the elderly woman answered, "and Merry Christmas to you."

"And you as well."

"You're a natural at this," Maja whispered.

Ray continued to smile as he helped with each customer one after the other. He wasn't sure how long he was at it since the line of customers seemed to stay consistent in its length. The last time that he looked at his phone it was a little past ten in the morning and when a small break came in the flurry of customers, he saw that it was already past three in the afternoon.

"Whew." Maja exhaled. "Finally a break. I'm sorry to have you jump into the fray like that, Ray, but I don't have that much help."

Ray turned to give Maja his full attention. "Was I the only one who responded to your post?"

"Well, you weren't the only one," Maja answered, "but you were the one that I felt was better suited for this place."

"What'd you mean?"

"Well, most people just want the job for monetary reasons, but I can tell that you know more about books than the average person," she said crossing her arms and leaning against the register. There was a slight smile that grew on her face while her eyes flicked up and down. "I have this sense about people. I can tell that you're a reader."

"Well, thanks. You got all that from my application?" he asked.

"Not only that but also your resume and your word choices," Maja answered.

Ray wasn't sure how to fully respond to Maja's assessment but was just thankful that he was working and out of the house and away from his father's berating.

"And you seem like you're dealing with a lot," Maja added with her voice switching to a sympathetic tone.

There was a moment of mortification at feeling so exposed by her statement, but he tried to keep himself shielded.

"A little," he answered, "I don't feel like going into it."

"It's quite alright," Maja stated holding up her hands. "There's no need to tell me anything that you're not comfortable in telling. But you're hired, Ray."

"Thank you," Ray said. "And I really like how you've decorated the store."

"Thanks," Maja smiled as she looked around the store. "Reminds me of home."

There wasn't much time to rest as another wave of customers came into the store and began browsing and buying up titles off the shelves. Time seemed to melt into water, and Ray was feeling the very familiar sensation from his days at working at the coffee house. It was the feeling of sore pain in his heels that traveled up to his knees and then into the middle of his back. He reached around and started to massage the muscles.

That was when Maja acted.

"Here," she said bringing out a high office chair for him to sit on.

"Thanks," he said sitting down and feeling the sweet pressure relieving relief of being off of his feet.

"It won't be long now," Maja assured. "It's just about closing time."

The number of customers began to die down little by little as the time for closing came about. It was by that time that the store was empty despite the still steady numbers of people out walking between the shops.

"There we are," Maja said closing her register and taking the money out of the till and slipping it into a blue zip-up bag. She came to Ray's side and made a gentle push to get to the till in front of him. He moved himself aside and got off the chair as she got the items. With the bags in hand, she turned to look at her new hire. "I hope I don't scare you off by telling you that this is actually a slow day for the store."

"It is?" Ray asked confused and then looked out the store window to the Barnes and Noble across the way. "How is it that you're able to compete with them?"

Maja shrugged, "It could be because of the store décor, or it could be because this store makes everyone think that they're in a Hallmark Christmas movie."

Ray had to laugh at that statement. "All we need is some blonde woman named Karen."

"And have it end with a wedding," Maja continued her ribbing.

Ray gave another laugh. The laugh gave him a small pause as Maja walked out from behind the register the store's front gate. The laugh was a true good laugh rather than a sad one or a sarcastic one. An honest genuine laugh at something funny in the darkness of the world that he had been plunged into.

How long has it been since I laughed like that? He wondered.

He was about to think back to that time but there was an interruption as Ray's eyes went over to Maja as she went to the front gate. He couldn't help but notice the way she moved. It could almost be said that her stride was as if she were skipping. Yet it was more like she was prancing like some four-legged creature that was asked to walk on two legs. There was also the inescapable aspect of how attractive she was with her lithe figure and the tight light brown pants that did little to hide the shape of her legs or her heart-shaped buttocks as she bent over when she pulled down the gate to its final inches.

At the moment he thought about her ass in those leggings. He imagined her out of them and that was when shame overtook him. When she turned around to come back to the register, Ray made the quick glance to one side to make himself seem like he was looking at something else.

"That's another day in the bank." Maja smiled picking up the bags of till money. "I certainly can't wait to see you tomorrow, Ray. I'll have a name tag ready for you as well."

"Will I also need the reindeer antlers and ears?" Ray asked smiling looking to that part of her.

"What?" she asked confused with an undercurrent of dread and panic.

"The antlers and ears your wearing," Ray explained. "They're excellent costume props, by the way. Will I be expected to wear those?"

Maja's face drained of color and her eyes went wider and more dumbfounded just like a deer facing the headlights of an oncoming vehicle.

"That's not possible..." she whispered.

"What?" Ray asked, feeling the iceberg tip of fear and panic coming into view.

Did I do something wrong? he asked himself as the wheels of anxiety and paranoia began to spin it's wheels. *Have I blown my chances with this job? Will I have to avoid this place for the rest of the time I'm living at home? WHAT?! What did I do?!*

"No human should be able to see through the glamour," Maja uttered bringing her hand over her face and looking Ray up and down like she was sizing him up. "Step into my office."

The moment that she said that Ray already felt like he was in trouble for something. Of course, the smart thing probably would have been just to step out of the store, leave, and never come back. Yet, there was something curious about what she had said to him.

No human should be able to see through the glamour? He repeated the statement in his mind and thought, *What does that even mean?*

It was that question that made Ray follow Maja to the back of the Paper Playground. Behind the registers, there was a small room with a door that opened outward, inside was a space that was a little bigger than an office cubicle. There was enough space for a desk, a small set of shelves, and another chair in front of the desk. Maja went to the chair behind the desk, sat down, and presented the chair in front of her.

Again, Ray felt like he had been called down to the principal's office or rather Human Resources.

"Alright, Ray," Maja began leaning forward on the desk, "I know we just met but what I'm about to tell you...you cannot...*ever, ever, ever*, tell anyone about. Do you understand?"

"Um...yeah...I won't tell anyone," Ray answered feeling himself shivering from the inside.

"These aren't props," Maja said bringing her hands to the reindeer-like ear. "They're very real."

She pulled back her hair at the side of her head to show that there were no human ears. There were only the reindeer-like ones.

"What the fuck..." Ray uttered at a low puff of a whisper but there was an odd sensation to his shock. He didn't feel fear. Instead, there was a sensation of curiosity. There was the want to reach out and touch her ears to feel them twitch in his fingers.

"Tell me, Ray, have you ever felt like that there's more to this world than what you're seeing, Ray?" Maja asked pulling her hand away from her hair letting it fall back towards her face. "Like there's something hidden out of the corner of your eye?"

Ray snapped himself out of his curious and locked daze and thought about the question.

Honesty was all he could give.

"I've felt that, but I thought that was just everyday paranoia or wishful thinking," he admitted.

When he was a young child, Ray wished for and wanted there to be more to the world than the boringness that all the adults told him about. He wanted there to be realms like what he read about in books, like Harry Potter, Neil Gaiman, and much more. But when one is a child there's the want and wish for the magical and sometimes, they create that in the mind's eye and the landscape of their imagination. Then time shatters the child into an adolescent and then the world further shatters the adolescent. And then comes the effort to piece themselves back into the mangled form of what is expected to be a successful grown-up.

"I'm aware that this is incredulous as it is unbelievable but it's true," Maja told. "All of it. Beings like fae exist. Fairies, trolls, goblins, elves, and so on. And I'm one of them. I'm a reindeer woman. If you still don't believe me, I can show you more."

"Okay," Ray said wondering what she was going to do.

She got up from the desk and stood off to the side and in a moment her body began to go up, up and up. Until the tops of her antlers were touching the ceiling. Ray looked down and saw how her feet were several inches off the floor. Looking back up she was smiling down at him.

"The look on your face is quite adorable, you know," she said lowering herself to the ground. "But there is one other thing I can show you that'll convince you."

"What's that?"

Maja turned around and lifted her sweater to further show the curvature of her ass thanks to her leggings. Yet there was something else that he didn't quite understand what he was seeing. Above the crevice of her ass there was a bulge in the material of her clothes. The answer as to what it was came when Maja hooked her thumbs into the waistband of her leggings and pulled them down just a little until it came down past the bulge. From the bulge burst a ball of soft fur. A tail. The thing was a small fluff of white and brown fur that began to wiggle.

"Oh my god..." Ray gasped, rising to his feet, and trying to reconcile what he was seeing and hearing with everything that his experience and broken pieces of his life would allow.

How is any of this possible? He wondered, *How can it be that all of this was happening?*

It was then that he thought back to his childhood and how much he wanted all of that to be real. To know that such magic exists and to have that innocence and optimism again.

"Are you alright, Ray?" Maja asked pulling up her leggings, coming forward and resting a hand on his shoulder.

"I...just...". Ray stumbled over trying to put any kind of cohesive thought together for Maja's question.

"I know it's an overwhelming amount to take in," she sympathized before stepping even closer in front of him. "Most humans can't accept this sort of thing. Then again, we must keep ourselves hidden for our own safety and survival given how we were once hunted and that's why we have a glamour."

Hearing this, Ray started to think up questions.

"Are there others like you that live in town?" Ray asked.

Maja smirked. "Yes, there are. If you can see through the glamour, then you should be able to see others."

Ray thought about it for a moment, and he hadn't seen anything like that since he moved back home. It was only when he came to the Paper Playground and worked with Maja that he was able to see through the glamour that she was talking about. Was his ability to see through it recent? Had he always been able to do it? He felt so confused by it all.

"But there's something else I want to talk to you about," Maja requested as she looked deep into his eyes. Her voice had taken on a less serious tone and took on a tone that Ray hadn't experienced before: seduction.

"What's that?" he asked as he began to lose himself in her gaze.

She smiled, tilting her head, and her eyes giving him an alluring glance.

Then there was something else that he could see in her cheeks. The growing pink bloom of blush.

"I think it's better if I show you," Maja said leaning in towards Ray, her hands gently holding the sides of his face before pressing her lips against his.

Ray's eyes went wide with shock as she kissed him. There was an impulse to pull back from her, but something made him want to keep kissing her. Maybe it was the feel of her body against him, or the smell of her that was a mixture of vanilla, paper, and leather.

Maja's hands moved from Ray's face and down his shoulders to his waist where she held him close. Ray responded in bringing his hands up to her waist and holding her. It was just like before with...with Angela. Yet, the memories of her began to fade and blow away like dandelion seeds in the wind.

In the sweet embrace of their lips, Ray could feel Maja's tongue begin its tentative push towards his mouth and he brought his to meet hers. At the threshold of their mouths their tongues began a feverish hungry dance and twirled against each other.

Ray could feel himself grow hard while his head felt dizzy as if he had stood up too fast. But then in a moment of stupidity, he pulled back and looked at Maja whose cheeks were still pink and eyes half open in a sweet lost and lustful daze.

"Is this too quick?" he asked her but knowing how stupid it sounded. "I just met you."

"Not at all," Maja whispered back. "I wanted you since you walked in. There's just something about you. There's this...*scent*...this...*aroma* to you. It's like you have the most delicious and inviting smell I've ever experienced, far more than anyone else I've ever smelt before. And I want it. I want *you*, Ray. It took so much self-control to not take you the moment you walked in. To have you take me then and there."

"But I..." Ray said still feeling like such an idiot.

"If you're worried about protection," she said leaning over to her desk. "There's no need to worry; part of being one of my kind is being able to control when we might get pregnant. Now, are we going to fuck?"

All sense, logic, and conscience had been lost to Ray. Especially when Maja kept her eye contact with him and leaned forward, giving him a tantalizing view down the inside of her sweater. His dick twitched at the sight of her firm cleavage and the lack of a bra.

"Yes," he said, pulling at his suit coat and tie.

With the tie and coat off, he went for unbuttoning his suit shirt while he watched Maja focus on his waist. Her hands bolted to his pants and pulled at his belt. He pulled off his shirt, then his undershirt, and that was when he found Maja had taken masterful dexterous motions to pull at his belt, open his pants, and pull down his underwear to which his cock sprung out to greet her like a flower greeting the sun after a long winter.

"Here, sit," she begged sounding so hungry and ravenous as she made Ray move over to the desk chair and sit down. As he sat down, Maja pulled down his underwear and pants to his ankles as she knelt and completed taking his clothes off.

On her knees, she came up to his lap and gazed at his cock as if it were the most delicious treat that she ever laid eyes upon. She leaned in, closed her eyes, and took a deep sniff. "Mmmmmm, such sweet *male* musk."

She placed one hand on his thigh, wrapped the other around his shaft, and opened her mouth before her antlered head dove downward to his groin with her antlers lightly scratching him and resting against his belly. Without much thought to it, he leaned back in the chair giving her more room so her antlers wouldn't scrape him.

"Fuuuuuuuuckkk...." Ray groaned out his pleasure, letting his head roll backwards as the intense wave of pleasure from Maja's mouth overtook him.

She pushed her mouth down as far as she could go. He could feel the back of her throat and that was when he heard her let out a puff of a gag before she pulled back.

"Watch me, Ray," she huffed before she cleared her throat. "Witness me in how I suck your cock. Keep your eyes on me."

Ray rolled his head forward and looked down. Maja was holding his cock to her face with a hungry and ravenous gaze locked with him. At the same time, her mouth was held open, and her tongue was out licking his shaft up and down then down to up before focusing on the tip to circle round and round the head. The tip of her tongue then came to the underside of Ray's cock, and he couldn't help but feel his eyes roll into the back of his head while his head flopped backward while a storm of shivers ran rampant through his body. There was a flash of a moment when he thought he was going to cum, but he didn't.

Collecting himself he brought his head back up to look down at Maja again.

"Mmm," she hummed before closing her eyes and kissing his cock. "Do you enjoy watching me do this?"

"Yes..." Ray shuddered. "It's been so long for me...I think...I'll...*cum*..."

"Well, don't cum yet," she said, shaking her head and standing back up again. "Because the real treat is between these legs."

As she rose from her kneeling position, she took the hem of her ugly Christmas sweater and pulled it up to her neck. His mouth dropped open as her beautiful breasts bounced free. The sight of them distracted him for a few moments before he noticed her visible struggle as she tried to get the garment off without it catching on her antlers.

"Here," Ray said getting up from the chair reaching out for her sweater and helping Maja pull the garment over her head and past her antlers.

"Thank you," she said when she was free of it. With the thing off, she crossed her arm over her breasts before leaning in and kissing him. "You're such a sweetheart. Now sit down and enjoy the show."

Ray sat back down and looked up at Maja who still had her arms crossed over her breasts. With a wink she wiggled and danced around as she showed off her figure and assets, giving him a slow teasing reveal. With her arms away from her body, she continued dancing for a moment in a slow sensuous motion of arms, hips, and legs as she watched the effect of her motions on her lover.

He was mesmerized as he appreciated her figure that was sculpted like an athletic, long-distance runner. Her arms had little fat on them but showed the definition of muscle, and the same could be said of the rest of her body such as the light definition of her abs and legs. But her breasts were the focus of his attention. They were firm, full and with a voluptuousness that could easily fill Ray's cupped hands. The thought of which Ray couldn't wait for.

Acting on their own, his hands were about to reach up to cup them, but Maja turned around and just like when she'd showed off her tail, she took hold of her waistband and pulled downward. The top of her pants came down past her tail then farther to reveal her sweet crevice, but then continued even farther. After a few more inches, she presented her mouth-watering, toned, bare ass to him.

Dear sweet god, Ray thought, *months since I've been with a woman and now this woman that I just met is throwing herself at me. What a Christmas season.*

Maja pushed her pants down further to her knees and then to her ankles where she pulled off her shoes and stepped out of her pants and panties. Kicking them aside, she straightened herself and turned back around to Ray, but she didn't display herself to him like she did with her breasts. Instead, she went over to the desk and sat on its edge facing him where she spread her legs to show herself off to her new lover. Her hand came down to her pussy to present the fact that she was clean shaven.

"How do you like what you see?" she asked.

"You are *goddamn beautiful*, Maja," Ray uttered feeling so overwhelmed that he wanted to praise whatever god was out there. "I feel so privileged."

Getting off the desk, she leaned forward and kissed Ray on the lips again before pulling away to whisper, "Get your cock inside me, you sweetheart of a human. Do you mind if we start from behind?"

She stood up, turned around and bent over her desk. Her head turned to look back over her shoulder at Ray as she wiggled her ass and licked her lips. Her cute little tail was wagging in excitement as well, and it didn't bother him in the slightest.

Without a single second of hesitation, Ray got up, and came up behind Maja. He watched how she moved and gyrated her buttocks to the open air giving a begging invitation of his cock.

"Put it in me, Ray, please," Maja begged. "Tease me no longer. Your musk is so strong. It's making me so *fucking horny. Give it to me!*"

Ray took hold of his cock and slipped it up against her slit feeling his way to her entrance. The moment he felt the head of it move into her he heard her cry out.

"AH!"

With that acknowledgement, he took hold of her hips and pushed into her.

"Nnnnnn...". Maja grunted. "*Fuuuuuuck...*"

"Too much?" Ray asked holding himself inside Maja.

"No," Maja answered shaking her antlered head while her hands held onto the edge of the desk. "Fuck me, Ray. *Fucking fuck this pussy!*"

Ray pulled himself back, held onto Maja's hips and thrust forward. Pulled back and thrust forward into her.

"Ah!" Maja yelped. "Harder! *Harder! Fuck* me *harder!*"

"Mmmmmm...". Ray pulled out, stopped, and thrust in and out of her. She felt so wonderful and tight. Losing himself to it, he pounded into her as quickly as he could, knowing he wouldn't be able to last long. He grunted as he felt himself at the point of no return. Pulling himself back and then he thrust forward, driving as deep into her as he could, and felt himself burst. The orgasm spurted deep in her, but he couldn't stop.

"Don't stop," Maja grunted, "I'm almost there."

Ray focused on her tight passageway as he kept thrusting, even with the feeling of his cock growing flaccid after his orgasm, but he wasn't about to stop. Here he was, fucking the most beautiful woman he had seen in such a long time.

"Ah! Ah! Ah!" Maja cried out in unison with his thrusts, "I'm…I'm…I'm gonna cum! Hnnnnn! I-I-…cumming! AAAAAHH!"

With that cry, Ray rested on her for a moment, hugging her body to him. After a few moments, he pulled back and sat back down on the chair, breathing out a sigh with how spent he felt. All the while, Maja continued to shake and quake in her aftermath while she lay on the desk.

"Uhhhh…". She uttered a satiated groan. Taking a deep breath, she pushed herself up, turned around and sat at the edge of the desk to look at Ray. "Mister Adler, that was the best orgasm I've had in a very long while."

"Same here," Ray added takin in a deep breath.

"How long was it for you?"

"Somewhere between months and I don't know. But…I-"

"You came first, huh?"

"How could you tell?" Ray asked starting to feel the mortification once again at his failure of intimacy.

"Don't feel bad." Maja smiled holding up a hand and shuddering as another tingle ran through her body. She cleared her throat, her ears flapped, and she shook her head a little before she continued. "My pussy can have that effect. Most men can't last as long as you have. They just cum once they're inside me. But you? You came and just kept going until I climaxed."

She pushed herself off the desk and came over to Ray, straddling his lap. Her arms wrapped around his neck and she leaned in and kissed him hard and overflowing with passion. Ray returned the kiss with just as much eagerness before they had to break it off to catch their breath. Pulling back, she kept her smile at him and tapped his chin.

"I think I'll keep you as my lover, Ray Adler," she said. "Now let's get dressed. And I expect you here tomorrow ready to work and ready to fuck."

"Shall I call you 'ma'am'?" Ray asked with a wheeze of a laugh.

Maja laughed in return. "No, but I do expect you to keep your promise. Don't tell anyone about me and my...antlers."

"Even if I did...who would believe me?"

Maja only answered with a wink.

Ray gathered his clothes and got himself dressed himself at a slow pace as he watched Maja do the same. Gazing at her body and the way she moved in such a mundane and simple task he had to remark one idea to himself.

And who'd believe I'm fucking my boss on the day I got hired?

Chapter 3: The Hushed Date

That Saturday was the busiest day that Ray had ever experienced. From the moment that the Paper Playground opened to when it closed for lunch had been non-stop. When the blessed break time came around, Maja had a look of exhaustion to her face.

"Aye me." She exhaled pulling down the gate. "I thought Black Friday was a Herculean challenge."

"And there's still some shopping days until Christmas."

"Please, hon, don't remind me," she groaned while giving a weak laugh.

As Maja was finishing up, Ray went for something that he had gotten after his first time with Maja. It was a black sketchbook. He hadn't felt like drawing or doing anything artistic since his life had fallen apart but since being with Maja, he felt energized, inspired, and able to draw again. Bringing the book along with his lunch out, he pulled out a small pen and went over to the section of the store where he and Maja would sit and read.

Ray couldn't help but look over at Maja and begin to sketch her in various poses. The book already had several pages filled with drawings of her and small doodles of various things such as practice sketches of hands.

The sketches of Maja always took up most of each page. He drew her as if she were a character in an anime or a manga complete with the large, luscious eyes with thick eyelashes. But he was sure not to over-exaggerate certain features one would expect of the style. Namely, her chest. He made sure to keep the art as close to his vision of her as possible.

After a few marks, he looked up and found Maja walking back from the register with her lunch along with the book that she was reading before she joined him.

As she sat down, he was half expecting her to make some kind of hint at sex. But then again with how worn out he felt after the rush he wondered if she felt the same way.

"I'm sorry if you're feeling horny for me right now," Maja apologized. "It's just been a long day and the day isn't half over."

"I understand." Ray nodded while closing his sketch book. He pulled out his sandwich and took the first couple of bites. "Plus, I figured with how much we've been going at it since you hired me, you probably want to give your body a little rest."

"Oh, sweet Christmas, yes," Maja sighed with her eyes rolling and her hand on her chest. "Even sitting down, I can still feel you inside me."

There was the certainty of her lust and desire for him when Maja spread open her legs towards Ray. Despite the dark of the dimmed lights, he could still see a visual cleft made by her legs in her tight leggings. She wasn't wearing underwear.

Ray couldn't help but smile at Maja and lick his lips.

"We will be doing more of that, hon," Maja promised.

"Actually," Ray interrupted, "there's something I wanted to ask you,

Maja."

"What's that?"

"Would you like to go out sometime when we're not working?"

Maja's ears twitched and then perked up when she heard that question while her face looked to him with a slight puzzlement. Seeing the expression, Ray started to feel a very familiar tornado of emotions. Fear, panic, and anxiety. They always happened when it came to asking women out. He had it since he was young all the way up to his ex-fiancé. His stomach twisted and he held his breath hoping that she would say yes.

"You're asking *me*, your boss, out on a *date*?" She rephrased the question, sounding both perplexed and flattered at the same time.

"Yes, I am," Ray answered still feeling the tornado gripping him and making him feel like he was in the first fall of a roller coaster stretching out over the seconds of the conversation.

Maja smiled and said, "I'd like that. But there is something you should know about me."

"What's that?"

"You know how I mentioned I have roommates, right?"

"Yeah..."

"Well, it's more than that. We're not just roommates, they're my lovers. You see, we're all lovers to each other and have a relationship with each other. And we each are allowed to play outside of the relationship. I hope that doesn't change your opinion of me."

"Nah." Ray shook his head. "I'm glad you told me all this. But are you still up for doing this date with me?"

"I would. And I have the perfect idea for a date."

Hearing her words brought on the sweet relief that expelled all the anxiety and fear that he had at that moment as if her words had exorcised the demon that always plagued him.

"What'd you have in mind?" he asked.

"Do you mind if I make it a surprise? I'll take care of the planning."

"Okay. This should be interesting. Are you sure you don't want to give me a hint?"

"You'll have to wait and see," she said licking her lips before she began eating and reading.

Ray kept his smile before he continued to eat his lunch and reading his current book on his phone.

***

Sunday always had a reputation of being a day of rest, and Ray wanted to take advantage of that as much as he could. He was lying in his bed looking at the ceiling and not wanting to move. The soreness in his body stretched down from the top of his neck, down through his back, through his legs, and into his feet. He could even feel his feet swell and throb with each beat of his heart.

There was also a soreness in his groin. By his count he had worked at the Paper Playground for less than a week and he and Maja fucked at every chance they got. From the time before opening, lunch break, and even a little after work.

So much sex.

Probably more in the past week than he had in the past year.

Yet, there was still the date with Maja.

You'll have to wait and see, she said.

Various scenarios played through Ray's mind.

Maybe we'll go to a hotel, he thought. *Or does she have something really sexy in mind?*

It was something that Ray had observed about Maja; she had the quiet air of a cultured and educated librarian but underneath all of it, she had such a beautiful vulgarity to her sexuality.

The thoughts of it rattled in his head to the point that he needed a distraction. The need made him pull himself out of bed, and he went to his desk. He pulled out the sketchbook and began to draw more of Maja. In previous pages there were simple portraits of her from the waist up doing various activities from working the register to reading to putting books away on the shelf. But the newest sketch was different.

He began to draw Maja naked.

The first was a simple nude of her posed in front of bookshelves but then he drew her in different positions one after the other. On all fours. On her back with her legs spread. And the one pose from their first time when she sat on the edge of the desk with her legs spread open for him.

Despite what he was doing he made sure to include his favorite features of her. The way her hair was, her ears, her antlers, and then there was her tail.

His hand was putting the final detail on her face when his phone chimed with a text message. The suddenness almost made him ruin the work by nearly dragging his pen across the page, but he had enough control to pull back.

Setting the pen down, he reached for the phone.

MAJA: Hey. What'd you say we do our date today?

Ray responded back without thinking.

RAY: Sure. What would you like to do?

The response was just as quick.

MAJA: Meet me at the public library.

RAY: See you there soon.

The library? Ray thought setting down his phone, *interesting place for a date.*

Despite the peculiarity of it, Ray didn't question it. It was, after all, the first date that he had in a very long time. He got up from his desk and went to get himself cleaned up. Thankfully, his parents weren't up so he didn't have to explain to either of his parents where he was going. But, just for his mom, he left a note.

Mom,

I'm meeting someone at the library. I have my phone with me if you need to reach me.

- *Ray*

Just like so many places in Northview Valley, the library was close enough to walk there but The Northview Public Library wasn't the most eye catching or glamourous building. Much like many of the government buildings in the historic downtown. It was the size that one would expect of a large town or small city in the middle of America. Just a simple wide brick building with two floors and a basement. The first floor, where one enters, had the "young readers" section off to the left of the main entrance with a few private study rooms and meeting rooms on the right.

The second floor, which was accessed by a wide spiral ramp, housed the reference section, fiction, and nonfiction sections along with the DVDs and CDs.

It had been years since Ray visited that building. As a child, he'd often go with his mother and grandmother who would pick up murder mysteries to read in the days long before digital readers became commonplace. He still expected the place to be quiet and almost deserted and that part didn't disappoint him. Passing the front entrance, the library was quieter than a tomb.

It's small-town America, he remembered, *most folks are still probably at church or maybe at the after-church brunch.*

Looking around the first floor, he didn't see Maja. Coming to the next conclusion about the place, he went to the wide ramp and went up towards the fiction sections. At the top of the ramp where there was the non-fiction to the left with the fiction sections to the right and directly ahead was a "study area" that had several large tables with chairs for people to do their research. Beyond the study area, there was a reading area with comfortable chairs and couches underneath a series of skylights that let in the luminous winter sunlight.

Ray found Maja sitting in one of the couches in the reading area. She was sitting back with her thick winter jacket set over one of the couch's arms. Her sweater was a simple white thick knitted garment while her leggings were tight and brown. Coming over to his boss and lover, Ray wanted to say hello, but the reindeer woman's ears twitched in his direction and her head tilted upward to see him.

She smiled holding up a finger to her lip and then pulled out her phone and began typing on it.

Ray's phone buzzed in his pocket to which he pulled it out and read the text message.

MAJA: Let's try to be quiet. We are in a library, hon. ;)

Ray smiled and decided to be equally cheeky to her.

RAY: Yes, Ma'am.

Looking up from his phone to her, Ray saw the look on Maja's face that hinted at the flirting arousal that she often did when she was showing her naughtier side.

MAJA: That comes later...promise.

Maja presented her hand to the couch and Ray sat beside her. He looked over at Maja who had brought the same book that she had at work, and she was continuing her reading. Ray gave a quick glance to the book and discovered its title: *Shadow* by Diesel Jester.

Taking the cue Ray did the same on his phone holding it in his left hand and resting the other on his knee. To which, Maja reached out and entwined her fingers with his. Feeling her touch, he looked over at her and saw the smile on her face and slight flap of her reindeer-like ears.

Ray couldn't help but smile at her gesture but then leaned in and placed his lips against hers. She kissed him back and pulled back before kissing his cheek and then leaned back against the couch to continue her reading.

It wasn't until a moment later when Ray shifted his position to leaning against the arm of the couch that Maja moved so that she was leaning with her back against his chest. Ray, in turn raised his arm around her shoulder and let it rest against her chest to which she reached out to hold it.

Sitting there with her, holding her hand and feeling her body against his and the two of them reading, it felt so nice and quiet as he read his own book. It then occurred to him how so many dates involved going places, doing things, and talking. All Maja wanted was to sit and read with him close by and enjoy the quiet of the library.

What a breath of fresh air, he thought.

He didn't know how much time had passed but then again it didn't matter because the time was with Maja. Although, he knew that he had started another chapter in the book he was reading and had finished it before he paused. He leaned over towards her, past her antlers, and kissed the side of her head. Her ears twitched at the show of affection. At the angle he was sitting he could see her set her book down before picking up her phone and texted him with one hand.

MAJA: You really are too damn sweet.

In the position he was in, Ray could only text back to her with one hand which made things trickier, took more time, and was a test of the dexterity of his thumb.

RAY: You bring it out of me.

She turned her head and leaned in to kiss his cheek before turning back to her phone to type her response.

MAJA: And you bring something else out of me, hon.

RAY: What's that?

MAJA: My naughtier side.

RAY: Is that so?

There was a pause in the silent textual conversation before Maja's fingers began to tap on her phone screen more.

MAJA: Are you familiar with remote controlled vibrators?

Ray didn't hesitate.

RAY: Yes, I am. Why'd you ask?

Maja pulled herself from the intimate embrace, sat up and turned to reach for one of the pockets of her jacket. Pulling her hand back, Ray saw that she held a small u-shaped object. One side of the u-shape was thicker than the other in its bulbous attribute. She turned her body towards the back of the couch to cover up what she was holding. The thing had a mat finish to its maroon-colored design.

Ray looked at it and then looked up at Maja who turned her head towards the librarian who was sitting at her station looking over various books. The reindeer woman turned back towards Ray with a smile and her cheeks developing the subtlest of pink hues.

She leaned in and whispered, "Wait right here."

Standing up, she slipped the hand that held the device into the sleeve of her sweater to conceal it. Walking away, Ray watched the way she sauntered and accentuated her ass in his direction with each step away from him. His head was spinning and swimming with so many scenarios upon scenarios fueled by porn and his own experiences. He could feel his heart going so fast that he thought he was going to explode at any moment and his cock went from soft to hard in a matter of seconds. There was a certainty to what Maja was going to do, which was confirmed as she was heading towards the bathroom.

Ray began to imagine Maja in one of the stalls of the bathroom and inserting the maroon-colored toy inside her.

Holy fuck, he thought watching Maja slipping into the bathroom.

Minutes passed and then a new message came through on Ray's phone.

It wasn't a text message. It was an image. Ray wasn't sure what kind of image it was, but he decided to turn himself so that, if anyone was around, they couldn't peer or spy what he was seeing on his tiny screen.

He opened the image and found that Maja had taken a picture of her bare pussy in the bathroom stall. Her pants and her panties were pulled down to her knees and her sweater was pulled up to her naval. Sitting against her pubic mound was the thinner part of the u-shaped toy.

MAJA: Sweet Christmas, I'm so wet, hon!

No sooner had Maja sent that message that a link had been sent for an app for the device. Ray clicked on it and downloaded it and as it did, he looked over to the bathroom and found Maja walking out towards him. His eyes kept looking towards her groin wondering if he would see the bulge of the toy. But the long length of Maja's sweater gave her a good cover.

When Maja arrived on the couch, she sat down next to Ray showing off a smirk that both belied her secret naughtiness and reveled in it. She then took out her phone and typed her message.

MAJA: Is your app ready?

Ray smiled and nodded at his lover. He switched over to the app and turned on the vibrator.

There was a very faint buzzing. He could feel it through his thighs, and it traveled into his groin thanks to the proximity of Maja. Her eyes closed tight, as she sucked in her lower lip. Her thighs came together and rubbed against one another. One of her hands went to the fabric of her leggings, and her fingers dug into the material, pulling it into a tight clenched fist that threatened to rip it.

Holding her thighs tight together, she wiggled her hips before the threat of the fabric ripping made her let go of the leggings. She picked up her phone. Her thumbs worked at a furious flurry while the device continued to make a low hum.

MAJA: Sweet fucking Christmas this is fucking hot. This vibrator inside me, and you controlling it while we're out public. Fuck...it makes me want to cum!

After she sent the message, she set her phone down and closed her eyes. Her hands made a slow creep up to the chest of her sweater and made the discrete caresses as she fondled her breast underneath.

Watching her made Ray feel the beginnings of a dominating side of himself. The power of her pleasure was in the palm of his hand. And she had given him that power. The thought of it made him turn down the intensity of the vibrator.

Maja's eyes snapped open and looked at Ray with surprise. Her hand stopped, and she looked down at her own crotch before taking on a pouty expression. It was one that she liked to do because of its comedic exaggeration with her lower lip jutting out.

She picked up her phone.

MAJA: Please, don't be cruel, hon.

Once Ray read that, he switched back over to the controller app and raised the vibrator's intensity up a little higher than before.

Maja let out a sharp gasp. Her face paled, her ears perked up again. One hand came up over her mouth and clamped down. To confirm her unspoken suspicion her eyes looked around the library to see if anyone heard her or was seeing them. The two lovers looked to the librarian once again sitting at the information desk. The librarian's head was turned down towards her desk, but they saw her eyes flick upward from her work in their direction. It was only a flash like she was looking to see what they were doing but not caring enough to divert her attention to them.

Maja looked back at Ray. Her hand came away from her face and she couldn't help but smirk before she leaned in to kiss him.

She whispered in his ear, "Let's find someplace...*semiprivate*, hon."

Ray kissed her back and whispered, "Lead the way."

The reindeer woman got up and grabbed her coat while Ray did the same.

Following her, she led the way down the spiral ramp from the second floor down to the first floor. From there they headed into the meeting room areas. Each step he made along with Maja was an effort to keep himself together with how his head was hot and spinning from his lust and the adrenaline. His brain still wrestled with the fact that Maja was wearing a remote-controlled vibrator and it was still buzzing inside her with each step she made.

This is like a porn movie, he thought.

Once they reached the bottom of the ramp, Maja took a few steps to the left and began to lean against a nearby wall.

"Are you alright?" Ray whispered his question while leaning towards her but couldn't help but notice how her legs were trembling to the point of buckling.

"I'm alright, hon," Maja whispered her answer with low huffs of breaths, "but I think...I think...I just came."

Maja took a deep breath, got herself to stand back up and made her way to one of the meeting rooms. It was a room with a door with a small window set at eye level in it and a set of windows that had the blinds drawn and closed. In the center of the room there was a large conference table with multiple chairs around it with a white board at the back.

She led the way into the meeting room and closed the door after Ray. There was a coat hook on the back of the door, and she hung up her coat, blocking the view into the room.

Ray didn't even have a chance to look at Maja before she took his hand and pulled him into her arms and kissed him hard. In response, he let his arms envelop her and his hands came down to her buttocks where he squeezed both cheeks. He felt her moan into his mouth while her tongue pushed past his lips into him.

Nothing could be held back.

Ray pushed Maja away, grabbed her by the shoulders, turned her towards the table and bent her over. Coming up behind her he reached around to the front of her pants and pulled them down over her ass and to her knees.

"Please," she begged but keeping her voice at a whisper. "I want you inside me."

Ray looked to the lips of her pussy and could see how the toy she had was still inside. He reached up to it and pulled it out of her, not caring about the lubricant or her womanly fluids on it. Tossing it onto the conference table, he reached for his coat to push it off his body.

It was a simple set of moves to unzip his pants, pull out his cock, and come up behind Maja. Spreading open her cheeks, he brought himself up and slipped himself inside her.

"....mmmmmm...." She moaned while her hand came up to cover her mouth and she took sharp and hard breaths through her nose. Pulling her hand away she sucked in a breath through her teeth and whispered, "Degrade me, Ray. Call me a slut. Call me a whore. *Please.*"

His head was flying with the adrenaline, desire, and fear. He kept making quick glances through the small window in the door wondering if anyone could see them. No one was looking in the direction of the door, he leaned forward and brought his lips towards her ears.

"You're such a fucking slut, Maja," Ray rasped making sure to sound as dominating as possible to his lover. "Such a whore letting me use this remote vibrator on you in such a public place. No shame from such a fucking slut like you."

"Yes," Maja moaned but tried her best not to raise her voice. "I'm such a filthy fucking whore. But I'm *your* filthy fucking whore."

"That's right," Ray continued his degradation of his lover as his hips thrust hard forward and held her close as he ground against her. "You're *my* filthy fucking whore. This *pussy* is *my* personal cum dumpster."

He wasn't sure where such dirty talk came from, but he loved doing it with Maja.

"When I cum," he said feeling a wonderful and arousing idea forming at his lips, "I wanna cum all over your face, and you will walk to the bathroom with it on your face."

"Oh fuck..." Maja moaned, "Fucking fuck, yes. I want your cum on my face. I want to be seen like the filthy fucking whore that I am. Fuck me. *Fuck me, Ray. Dominate my cunt.*"

Ray held onto her hips and thrust himself harder and harder against her so much so that her stance staggered. She made herself regain her footing with her feet inching closer to the table.

After another thrust from Ray, she pushed back against him before standing up.

Her lover took a step back while she stood back up, turned around and got down on her knees. She grabbed his cock, before she opened her mouth and took Ray's cock into her mouth.

It was a test of his will and endurance to take such pleasurable torture from Maja's mouth on his cock. He looked down and beheld the way her antlered head bobbed back and forth while one hand caressed his shaft and the other went down between her legs.

"Grab my antlers," Maja huffed.

Ray's hands came up to her antlers and curled his fingers around them but making sure not to hold on too tight.

"Take hold of them," she begged with her tongue licking all around his cock. "Hold them tight and fuck my face. Do it, lover. *Fuck my fucking throat.*"

Ray's fingers tightened on her antlers as if they were handles and thrust his cock into her mouth. Looking down, he found her mouth was wide open, and her tongue was out. His member was thrusting in and out while tiny puffing gags gurgled out of her throat.

He couldn't hold it in anymore. Letting go of her antlers, his hand came down to his cock, and pulled it from her mouth. The reindeer woman looked up at her lover and looked so hungry for him.

"Cum on my face," she implored of him opening her mouth and sticking out her tongue. "All over my face. In my mouth, on my cheeks, my lips, my hair. Give it to me, please, Ray. Spread your seed all over me. *Pretty please...*"

The words from his lover's mouth made Ray stroke his cock faster and faster with each word.

"Here I cum, you fucking filthy whore," he growled feeling his balls tighten and his insides contract while his cock began to leak, ooze and then spurt and shoot out his milky and pearly spunk across Maja's face. "Mmmmmmm...".

His knees began to weaken and buckle like it would at so many other times during his orgasm. The sensation of dizziness was similar to standing up too fast and there was the need to let the blood come back into his head. He took a deep breath and felt his senses come back to his control. Looking down, he saw the beautiful aftermath of his own climax.

The sticky translucent and white material had a thick glob of it on Maja's forehead that was making its snail-like journey down between her eyebrows and down her nose. Other globules of it were on her cheek and her chin and even a little on her lips. To which Maja's tongue flicked out and licked it all up.

"Mmmm," she cooed, "So delicious. Sweet Christmas this is *fucking* hot. But I think I should clean myself up."

She got up to her feet, pulled up her leggings as Ray stuffed his cock back into his pants. He watched Maja's face and saw how his cum still stuck to her skin while letting the forces of gravity work on pulling it down her cheeks and jaw like maple syrup down a stack of pancakes.

"Wait here," she said to Ray holding up a finger while she smiled. "I'm going to the bathroom and clean up. Oh, fuck, I hope someone sees me."

The reindeer woman took a deep breath and went to the door and stepped out.

Through the small window in the door, he watched Maja make the walk towards the bathroom, and he saw another library patron make her way to the bathroom with her. At the moment that he saw that other person Ray's mind began to fly with panicked wonders of if that other person saw what was on Maja's face and made the connection.

I can see why this is so exciting for her, Ray thought looking as the two ladies walked into the bathroom.

He then went over to the conference table and sat down. Looking down to the floor, he saw a few gobs of his cum. It was only with the purest of good fortune that someone had left a box of tissues in the room, so he used a handful of them to clean up. Looking around the room, he noticed that there wasn't a trash can. Feeling his own cum leaking through the tissues in his hand, he stepped out of the meeting room and went for the nearest trash can. Without one nearby, he dashed into the bathroom and threw the wadded-up tissues into the trash. Afterwards, he washed, pulled down some paper towels and wiped up his hands as best and as fast as he could.

Stepping out of the bathroom, he saw that Maja wasn't anywhere near-by. With more of his faculties coming back online when he realized something.

The toy! he thought feeling panic flash like lightning. *Someone could find it!*

He dashed back to the conference room. Hoping that no one was there or that no one had found the item. Otherwise, that would have been some embarrassing explanations as to what the toy was and why it was on the conference table.

Yet, no one was there, and the toy was on the conference table undisturbed.

Thank god. He sighed in his relief without saying it out loud. *No one else found it.*

He picked it up and stuffed it back into his pocket before heading out of the meeting room to wait for his lover. It wasn't clear if it was the rush of the adrenaline or his own impatience, but Ray started to wonder what was taking Maja so long. But he tried to remember the fact that everyone does things at their own rate.

Then his phone buzzed with a new message.

Pulling it out he saw that it wasn't text or an image. It was a video. The sight of it made Ray look left and right to see if anyone was nearby. With no one around, he walked back to the meeting room, closed the door, and played the video.

It started with a shot of Maja's face with the hem of her sweater being held in her teeth. As the video played it moved down her body past her bra enclosed breasts, her bare belly and to her exposed slit. Her hand was set in between her legs and rubbing away at the lips of her pussy.

"Mmm," she moaned in such a strained tone that he could tell she was trying to keep the volume of her ecstasy as low as possible.

She then let go of her sweater allowing it to fall down her belly while the shaking camera movements came back to her face. Her lips were parted open, her eyes rolling upward as the wave of pleasure came over her before she sucked in her lower lip and bit down on it.

Were it not for the fact that Ray had already climaxed onto Maja's face he was half tempted to whip out his half-hard cock and start pleasuring himself then and there.

"Mmmm..." Maja moaned in the video while her eyes stayed rolled in the back of her head and she toppled back against the stall's wall. Regaining control of herself she looked into the camera and whispered, "This is so fucking hot."

And that was when the video ended.

"Enjoyed the show?" a voice asked Ray.

The shock and fright sent a lightning flash of terror through Ray that made him leap several inches off the ground. He looked over to his left and found Maja standing next to him smirking. Ray closed his eyes and grabbed his chest while he felt himself lean against the nearby wall.

"Good god, Maja," he exhaled, taking one deep breath after the other.

"Oh, I am *terribly* sorry, hon," Maja apologized coming up and wrapping her arms around her lover and kissing him. "I've been told that I have softer feet than a cat."

Ray let out a weak laugh. "You certainly do."

"Come on," she encouraged and took his hand. "Let's go back and sit down and read some more."

After taking several deeper breaths to calm down from the scare that Maja had given him, he nodded to her request.

"But you have to admit, hon, this date of ours has been quite...*fucking*...arousing and exciting, wasn't it?"

"Oh, no doubt. Did anyone see you with my..."

"With your cum on my face?" she finished. "One person did. She caught a glimpse of me while I was in the bathroom. It was such an exhilarating moment. That's why I went into the stall and proceeded to give myself another orgasm. I *really* hope she heard me."

Hearing her talk like that brought the blood back down into Ray's cock as his heart calmed down.

"You really love putting on a show for folks, huh?"

"Oh yes. It's unclear to me as to why, but I just love the idea of showing off and people leering at me. Much in the same way that you ogle me while we're at work."

"I was wondering if you noticed."

"Oh, I notice. And it's the highest form of a complement that you give me, and I always notice the bulge in your pants."

"I just *love* how sexual you are. And sexually adventurous too."

"Is that all you love about me?" she asked with her ears turning downward, her lip jutting out, her face looking down while her eyes looked up at him.

"There's so much I love about you already," Ray affirmed coming closer to his lover, cupping her chin and bringing her face up to his for a sweet kiss.

"Thank you," she whispered in between his kisses.

"Now, let's continue our date."

"Yes, sir," she flirted while she turned around and bumped her bum against his groin.

The rest of the day passed in relative quiet with the two lovers holding each other while they read in the silence of the library. Though Ray couldn't be certain of it, he thought he saw a glint of approval in the eye of the elderly librarian when they passed her station to the reading area.

Did anyone see us? he wondered while his eyes darted around the library. *Did anyone notice what we were doing?*

He reasoned that if anyone did then someone would have said something or told them to leave. Then again with small town America maybe they wanted something scandalous to happen, so they have a story to tell.

Either way, Ray didn't mind, there was Maja. He leaned down towards her and kissed the side of her face.

She took out her phone again.

MAJA: You're so sweet, Ray.

Ray said nothing. He kissed her again before he continued to read and enjoy her company in the comfortable silence of the library.

Chapter 4: The Elf's Chocolates

Monday came so soon, but unlike most who dreaded and moaned about the day, Ray couldn't help but smile as he made his way to his job at the Paper Playground. There was a lightness in his step as he walked past the shoppers as if he had wings on his feet and his body was made of air. He also couldn't help but hum to the Christmas tunes that were playing from the mall's speakers. It had been a long time since everything seemed so good.

There was also the date he had with Maja the day before and it made him feel so much better than anything he had felt in a long time. There were even twinges of arousal in him knowing the activities that he was going to be involved in. Especially since he and Maja were going to fuck at lunch.

Maja is insatiable, he thought while continuing to smile. *And I love it.*

Coming to the front entrance of the Paper Playground, he saw Maja servicing the line at the register. Her eyes caught a glance of him, and she beamed her smile in his direction while she waved. Ray waved back while he went to set down his winter coat in the back along with a lunch he prepared and his black sketchbook.

When he came back out to greet Maja, he took a quick moment to take in the details of her for that day. She was wearing another ugly Christmas sweater. It was red but it was very different from the last one she wore. For one, the neck wasn't as tight, it was loose to the point that it had the appearance of a knitted dress with its wide neck. Her shoulders were exposed, and he was certain that she wasn't wearing a bra given the lack of straps at her shoulders along with what he knew about her exhibitionism.

Ray took to his task of servicing the line at the register but when there weren't any customers to serve, both he and Maja would open new boxes and stock more books on the shelves. He was kneeling while opening one of the boxes and Maja was in front of him doing the same thing, but she was leaning forward. The depth of her lean was so far forward that Ray could see down the front of her sweater. Her beautiful breasts of her bare bosom hung free, swaying with her movement, which confirmed that she wasn't wearing a bra. Her antlered head turned upward, and she caught sight of Ray's stare, and she couldn't help but smirk and wink at him while her lips mouthed the words 'Later, lover'.

As the day kept moving on, he kept looking at his phone to see the time. It wasn't just because of the hunger in his stomach, but the hunger in his crotch.

"Alright," Maja announced, "time for lunch."

She went the front of the store and brought down the gate, turned off the lights and put up the sign that read "Will open again at 1:45."

"Good thing I brought my own lunch," Ray said about to dip into the bag that had a small container with a turkey sandwich, but he was stopped when he heard Maja coming to the counter.

"I think there's something to do before lunch, Ray," she said reaching for his hand and bringing him to a section of the bookstore that was hidden behind a series of bookcases. "Feel like trying something daring?"

"What'd you have in mind?"

"Lie down," she said helping him down to the floor.

Ray felt a swirl of panic, arousal, and apprehension. He couldn't help but look around to make sure that no one could see inside the bookstore. There were the windows and the open-door area but with the gate down, no one would try to come towards the store. It was also thanks to the fact that the store was sandwiched in between two other stores that there were only the two front windows. Between those and the bookcases, they had visual cover but there was the sound.

"How are we going to do this?" he asked while he sat on his ass with his back against the wall. Maja got down on her knees and ran her hands over his body down to his groin.

"By being quiet and careful," she whispered the answer, "like we did at the library. Oh Sweet Christmas, Ray, thank you for doing that with me. It still arouses me and brings such heat to my cheeks and pussy to think about it. But I think I'd like you to do something for me first."

"What's that?" Ray asked.

Maja pulled at her sweater and with the wide and loose neck she was able to get it off and past her antlered head without much assistance. Her hands then came down to her shoes that slipped off of her feet with the ease of slippers before she went for her pants and pulled them off. When they came down to her knees, she sat back down on her buttocks and pulled them off.

"Switch places with me," she said.

Ray scrambled up and let Maja lean against the wall. Scooting her body down until only her head was against the wall, she brought her legs up and spread them open.

"I was going to ask to ride your face, but I think I'd rather try this position, you'll be able to start fucking me faster. Now, come here and eat my pussy, *please*," she begged bringing her hand down and spreading open the lips of herself.

Ray smiled and positioned himself so that he was lying on his stomach with his head inches away from her. Among the sweet aromas of paper and leather there was the sweet and salty musk that wafted from Maja. He often wondered what she was talking about when it came to his "musk" but in being reacquainted with the scent of a woman's pussy, he understood far more than ever before.

"Don't keep me waiting, Ray," she teased, "We don't have long. So, hurry up and eat your dessert first."

"Yes, ma'am," Ray teased in return before wrapping his arms around her thighs and shoved his face into her pussy and began to lick and lap at her. His nose rested against her mound while her tongue curled up against her clit.

"Mmmmm," Maja groaned at the volume of a whisper while her hands reached down to Ray's head and her fingers curled into his hair. "Oh, Ray...you are so *good* at eating pussy."

Ray pulled his face up from Maja's groin and looked up at her, "Just be sure to keep it down. We don't want the shoppers to know what we're doing."

"That makes it so much *hotter*," Maja answered.

"Such an exhibitionist" Ray teased.

"Oh god, yes. I love the idea of being watched or people looking at me and thinking dirty thoughts about me. That's why I love visually teasing you. It's so easy to see the dirty thoughts on your face."

"You're such a naughty girl. Maybe I should bring you close to orgasm and deny it."

"Oh, please don't. Pretty please?" she asked batting her eyes at an exaggerated pace to him. "I'll do anything you want, lover."

"I'll hold you do that, my little reindeer," Ray said bringing his mouth back to her pussy. He took his hand away from her thigh and brought up a single finger to slip inside to find her g-spot.

"Ah-" Maja yelped but her hand slapped over her face to muffle herself, and there were only sharp exhales through her nose.

Hearing her sounds drove him mad with ecstasy from pleasing her, and he pushed his face farther into her before he shook his face from side to side while he hummed against her.

"MMMMM!" Maja squealed under her hand while the other one clenched in Ray's hair. "MMMMMMMM!"

Her body went rigid with her hips pushing upward, and her thighs clenched at the side of Ray's head.

Pulling back Ray felt a small burst of liquid hit his face, and he let out a grunt of surprise.

"Oh, Ray..." Maja called out sitting up, "I am so sorry. That's never happened to me before."

Ray chuckled wiping away the liquid from his face.

"It's okay. I want you to completely lose control," Ray assured her before leaning in to kiss his lover. He pulled back. "But now…"

He reached into his pocket and pulled out the condom. Maja looked at him and smiled while that same adorable blush rose in her cheeks again.

"Get on your hands and knees," he ordered.

"Ooooh," Maja cooed, "yes, sir. I love it when you're dominating."

"Maybe I should put a collar on you as well," Ray said moving into position.

"Oh, no, sir." Maja shook her head. "Collars are not my thing. They just feel too constricting."

Ray made a small huff of a laugh. "Okay then."

"Now, I believe you were about to fuck me, sir?" Maja suggested wiggling her ass at Ray while her little fluff of a tail wagged.

"Oh yes," Ray said first pulling off his sweater and shirt underneath before his pants and underwear letting loose his hard cock to the open air. With haste he got into position and pushed himself into her.

"Hmmmm…" Maja grunted while lifting herself onto one hand and covering her mouth.

Ray leaned forward and whispered into her ear, knowing how much she loved it when he did such things to her. "Aww, I thought you like being an exhibitionist. Don't you want everyone to see what a sweet slutty whore of a woman you are? Fucking your own employee on the floor of your own shop."

"Yes…I'm such a slut, sir," Maja whispered back keeping in character of their roleplay.

"Oh, yes you are. You're such a sweet little exhibitionist of a slut," Ray grunted, pulling himself out of her and making a slow insertion back into her depths. "Just imagine everyone's eyes looking at you while you're being fucked by your employee. Thinking about how slutty you are and how shocked they'd be finding out what a slut you are. Just imagine how they would get themselves off to you, knowing what a slut you are and seeing how you like your body used. Or do you like the idea of just me getting off to you?"

"Hmmm, oh yes, sir. Ah! Ah! I love the idea of you jerking off to me," Maja grunted but made sure not to raise her voice. "I love the idea of you in your bed jerking off to thoughts of me. I'm such an egotistical slut. I admit it, sir. I want you to see how sexy I am. I'm *your...filthy...fucking...whore...*"

Ray responded by leaning forward and nibbling on her ear while his pacing became faster and faster until the skin of his thighs and balls slapped against the exquisite ass, toned thighs, and sweet pussy of Maja.

"Degrade me more," she begged of her lover. "Please, sir...*Ah*...like at the library...ah...call me sexy and awful things. Ah. Call me a slut. Ah! Call me a whore, Ray. Please...pretty please...ah..."

"Fuck this cock, you filthy whore of a boss," Ray ordered into her ear. "Cum on this cock that you hired, you exhibitionist cum hungry slut."

"I'm cumming, sir!" she uttered at a low squeal. "Let this *filthy...fucking...whore* of a boss cum on your magnificent dick. *Please.*"

"Cum, you fucking slut," Ray approved.

Maja allowed her torso to fall to the floor while both her hands clamped over her mouth. Her high-pitched squeal escaped from her covered mouth and nose. Within moments, her hand came away from her mouth and she was back on all fours. She rocked herself back against Ray, showing she was ready for more.

"Cum in me, please," Maja begged, "I know you haven't cum yet. Please...cum for me. *Please*...I'm such a filthy fucking whore. *Cum inside this filthy fucking whore that belongs to you.*"

Ray grabbed hold of her waist and pulled her onto his cock while he thrust harder into her. His control was already slipping, but hearing her words pushed him into overdrive. His pace grew faster and faster and faster as if her pussy had become a consenting toy for his cock.

"I'm gonna-" Ray grunted, and he burst inside her. They both shook as the waves of pleasure crashed over them, as they both slid to the floor with Ray on top of her. After he weathered his orgasm and had emptied himself into her, he took a deep breath and exhaled.

He pulled out and leaned himself back against the wall. "Oh, fucking Christ. That's so good. And I want to say sorry if I went too far there."

"Oh, Ray," Maya replied turning herself around and bringing herself over to curl up next to her lover. Her body at his left side while her head was resting on his shoulder, but she kept herself at such an angle that her antlers didn't scratch or annoy him. "If you went too far, I would tell you and we'd talk about it. But I so love it when you're dominating. I especially love it when you call me things like a slut or whore."

"Really?" Ray asked.

"Yeah, I don't know why," Maja shrugged. "It's the same of why I'm an exhibitionist. I just love the idea of people seeing me and seeing how much of a slut I am."

"And how much of a 'slut' are you?" Ray asked feeling his curiosity overruling his arousal. "And why haven't we done this at your place?"

"Well..." Maja began sounding sheepish and wishing that she could avoid the question. "You see...I have...roommates. I'd like to keep you all to myself for now."

"Ah," Ray said, understanding the situation, "and you don't want to put on a show for them? Thought you were an exhibitionist."

"I am, it's just...*different*...they tend to be nosy, and they'll definitely be interested" Maja answered. "But I promise on the nights that they're not home, we'll fuck there."

"Okay," Ray said. "I don't know about you, but I feel hungry and I'm craving some sweets."

"You mean besides the sweet nectar of ambrosia that is my *puss-say*?" Maja teased while her hand came down to cup Ray's balls while his cock still leaked onto his thigh and her hand.

"You do have a sweet *puss-say*, Maja," Ray teased back, "but I think I'll get us something sweet because you've been very sweet to me. You hired me and you-"

"Take you the heights of sexual ecstasy when I fuck your brains out at each opportunity?"

Ray smirked and shook his head. "That too. But I'll get dressed and get some sweets for us."

"Don't take too long, hon," Maja requested leaning in to kiss him, "I think I may want seconds."

"I think I can manage that."

From that moment, Ray got dressed in great care, so he wouldn't accidentally flash anyone passing by the front of the store. Once he had dressed and gotten his shoes and socks on, he stepped out behind the bookcases and headed to the front gate where he pulled it up just enough to get himself out.

With the air of the mall around him, he headed down from the Paper Playground towards a shop that he came across in the days since working there at the mall with Maja. As he walked, he wondered if anyone saw or heard him with Maja and he couldn't help but feel an exhilaration at having sex in such a public spot.

Such a rush, he thought, feeling his head spin, taking a deep breath, and still smelling Maja's pussy on his face.

In the walk to the sweets shop, he remembered Maja talking about how he was able to see through the glamour of fae people. Since knowing that he might, he had kept his eyes open for other fae people. He did spy a couple here and there, such as a woman that he passed that was short, green, with wide ears but a sweet, rounded face. Then there were a few others who were just like Maja with reindeer-like ears and horns. He wanted to approach them and say something, but he wondered if it was a good idea to advertise that he was a human that could see through the glamour. Then he wondered if it really would have mattered if anyone else knew.

Why bother asking or doing anything about it? Ray wondered. *Things are great. I got a job, and I'm fucking my boss who is the sexiest woman I've been with in... ever. So, best not fuck it up.*

The sweets shop that Ray found himself at was certainly not a chain like See's Candies or Godiva. It sat in a corner lot at the mall's crossroads of the walkways. Above it was a sign that read, 'Decadent Delights' in elegant curves.

Walking inside, it had a similar aesthetic to an ice cream parlor and See's candies. The color white was everywhere from the walls to the floor and the countertops. There was also a certain chill to the air. Feeling the slight shiver come over him, Ray started to think that it was probably a good idea to keep the chocolate from melting.

Around the store there were a few people looking at the boxes of chocolates and choosing various assortments. While up at the counter there was a great glass case where there were various types of candies on display to choose from. There were three people in line to buy the chocolates, but it was the person behind the counter at the front of the line that captured Ray's attention, to the point that he started to stare.

Behind the counter there was a woman, but not just any woman. She was an elf. Ray knew that there were two kinds of elves in the popular imagination. There were the ones of fantasy fiction who were demure, tall, and statuesque people. Then there were the short, fat, and cute ones that one expects in Christmas decorations around Santa's workshop. Yet, this elf, who was selling the chocolates was neither of those.

Her height was a few inches taller than Ray, at least as far as he could tell from the distance he was at from the counter, which would have put her at six foot two. She had round full cheeks with freckles across them as well as across her nose, a soft pointed chin, a full figure, wide hips, and thick thighs.

The elf's hair was long, red, and straight as it came down to the middle of her back. She glanced over at Ray with a pair of green eyes before returning to the customers she was serving. Much like Maja, she was dressed in a festive ugly red Christmas sweater with white snowflakes in its pattern that was partially hidden by a deep green apron. The tips of her pointed ears came out just a little bit from behind the red curtain of hair.

The one aspect of her that wasn't hidden was her buxom quality with how prominent her breasts were inside her sweater and apron. He couldn't guess how endowed she was, but he was certain it must have been a size that only a few women on earth have. She was the elvish personification of a big, beautiful woman.

Trying to make it seem like he wasn't staring, Ray turned his attention back to what he came to that store for, the chocolates. His eyes perused over the various flavors and that was when he realized something that took over all thoughts in his mind.

I didn't ask what flavors Maja likes, Ray thought as he panicked. *Shit...*

"Sir?" A voice called out.

Ray turned his attention and saw that the red-haired elf woman was beckoning him forward since he was next in line. Acting without thought, he moved to the front of the line.

"How can I help you today, sir?" she asked sounding like such a massive ray of sunshine in the depth of the dark winter.

"Um..." Ray uttered, trying to get his thoughts together from the tornado of his wandering lustful thoughts as well as trying to figure out what to bring Maja.

"Getting an eyeful?" the elf asked.

"What?" Ray asked, feeling hot in his face and cold in his body, while wondering what it was that the elf was asking about. He tried his hardest not to look at her chest, but he couldn't help but glance at her name tag that read, 'Tuva'.

"The chocolates." She smiled with a playful glint in her eye, expanding upon her question. "Having a hard time deciding?"

"Oh...um...yes, yes, I am," Ray answered feeling his body coming back to equilibrium, "I'm looking to get some chocolates for myself and my co-worker, I mean boss, but I didn't ask her what she liked."

"Is your boss named Maja?" The elf asked.

"How did you know?" Ray asked, feeling exposed.

"You're still wearing your name tag for the Paper Playground," Tuva said, pointing to his chest.

Ray looked down and saw how right she was.

"And besides, I know Maja, she's told me all about you,"

Once again, the mortification came over him.

"Don't worry, she told me all *very* good things. And I know what her favorites are," she said, reaching for a small open box, some tissues and began gathering up a few of the chocolates from various containers. She brought out a small box and wrapped it up. "How about for you?"

"Hmmm," Ray said trying to concentrate and ponder upon the flavors. "I'll have six pierces of the white chocolate peppermint truffle."

"Excellent choice," Tuva said, taking out a small paper bag and setting the chocolates into it. She brought the box and the bag up to the register.

"How much for all of these?" Ray asked.

"Hmmm," Tuva said, rubbing her chin. "I'll tell you what, since you work for Maja, how about I'll give you these, and you can just owe me a favor at a later time."

"What kind of favor?" Ray asked.

"Nothing bad, I assure you, but I can always use help in some way or another," Tuva explained, holding out the box and bag to Ray.

"Sure," Ray agreed, taking the items. "If you know Maja, then that's enough for me to trust you."

"Thank you." Tuva smiled. "Be sure to come by again, and I'll be seeing you and Maja soon."

Having a closer look at her, Ray couldn't help but admire the level of cuteness that she had with her round cheeks and her freckles. Despite how most wouldn't think much of it or dismiss it entirely, Ray always found freckles attractive on a woman from the light splattering to the full-blown pattern of the dark brown dots a woman could have. Holding onto the box and the bag, he gave her one last look before heading out.

"Have a nice day," Tuva called out.

"Thanks. You, too," Ray answered back before he made his way back to his work.

When he came back to the Paper Playground, he saw Maja behind the counter inside the darkened shop with a sign of 'Be back at 1:45 p.m.' hanging on the door. She looked up, her gaze connecting with him, and her face lit up as if he became the ray of sunshine in the depth of winter. After smiling and waving at him, she came out from behind the counter to open the gate.

"I see you've met Tuva," she said, lifting the gate and allowing him in.

"I did," Ray answered, ducking under the gate to come inside. "She picked out your favorites for you since my dumbass forgot to ask you what your favorites are."

"Oh, you sweet man," she said before leaning in and kissing his cheek.

Once she picked up the box and let Ray have his bag of chocolates, she looked at him with an alluring glance. "So, what's your opinion of Tuva? Did you enjoy the sight of her?"

"Um…" Ray uttered, wondering how he should respond to that question. One of the options he had was being completely honest, which never helped anyone *ever*. On the other hand, there was the option of an outright lie, which he was certain Maja would see through. Or another option was to deflect the question by asking her.

"I mean her voluptuousness, Ray," Maja continued, teasing him while bringing her hands to her chest to emphasize her meaning. "She is quite *endowed*. But don't worry, I'm not the jealous type, if you were looking at her like that. You are a guy, and she's quite comfortable with everyone looking. Even enjoys it."

"Is that so?" Ray asked taking one chocolate out and eating it.

He expected the confectionary to be as rich and delicious as See's Candies or Godiva in its expert creation, but what his tongue experienced was far different. The moment the chocolate made contact with his tongue and melted in his mouth, he felt as if all his physical aches and pain melted away and was replaced with a quiet euphoria. It was as if the chocolate had washed away all his troubles in one sweet bite.

"Wow…" Ray whispered, continuing to savor the delectable treat.

Maja giggled. "I probably should have warned you. Tuva's skills have that effect on people. That's one reason why her shop is so successful."

"All other chocolate companies can suck it!" Ray declared before reaching in for another piece of Tuva's creations.

"Oh, tread with caution, hon, don't eat them too quickly. Or you'll make yourself sick," Maja warned. "Just hope that Tuva didn't over charge you for this."

Ray came over to the counter and sat on the stool behind the register.

"No," he explained. "She gave me these chocolates for free. But she did say that I owe her a favor."

"Did she say what?" Maja asked, sounding curious and cautious at the same time.

"Nope," Ray answered. "She just said she'll come by and ask for the favor. But she said that she won't ask for anything horrible."

"Ah. Tuva will probably just ask for you to help her with something."

"Hmmm...okay then." Ray shrugged, paying the whole thing no mind while he continued to enjoy the confections and feeling more than a little regret that he had gotten so few chocolates.

Chapter 5: A Volunteer Request

It was close to closing time again at the Paper Playground. Maja had already taken out the tills from both registers. Ray was in the process of pulling down the gate when he saw someone coming towards him. He looked and saw it was Tuva. The way she moved was just like her chocolates: magical. It was as if she had become her own clip in a movie where her entrance was in slow motion, accentuating every step she made and every bounce her voluptuousness could perform.

"Hi, Ray," she called, out waving to him.

"Hey, Tuva," Ray answered back. "What brings you over this way?"

"Why you." Tuva smiled, coming closer to him.

With such proximity, Ray could smell the sugar and chocolate clinging to her as if it were her perfume. Then there was the idea of her breasts that he could see pushing from the inside of her ugly red Christmas sweater that stretched out the snowflakes on it. For a flash, he couldn't help but wonder what they were like and what it would be like to hold them, but he was quick to rein in his thoughts to keep control of himself.

"What can I do for you?" Ray asked.

"Well, I want to cash in that favor I mentioned earlier today?" she asked as she brought an overtly innocent finger to her lips.

"Sure, what'd you have in mind?"

"You see, I volunteer at the local soup kitchen," Tuva explained. "And I'm looking for extra help on Saturday."

"Hey now," Maja called out coming up behind Ray. "I said I'd help out. Isn't that enough?"

"Bare minimum, Maja-dear," Tuva explained. "But having extra help will make things that much better."

"Well, you gave me those excellent chocolates," Ray interjected, "so I'd be glad to help out."

"Oh, you liked my chocolates?" Tuva winked.

"I think that they were magical," Ray expanded while smiling and reminiscing.

"Now you have face to face testimony," Maja said, giving a light playful slap to Tuva's shoulder. "I always told you that you were magic when it comes to this."

"Oh stop," Tuva teased, waving a dismissing hand while her freckled cheeks blushed.

"She is quite a harsh critic of her own work," Maja explained.

"Maja!" Tuva pleaded, sounding both like she was teasing and serious at the same time.

"Alright, everyone," Ray interrupted. "I'll help you out at the shelter. When do you want me to show up?"

"If you want to help out with the cooking," Tuva explained, "please come by at noon. But if you want to help with the plating, then around 4 or 5 would be all right."

"I'd show up at 4," Maja added. "Tuva can get quite dominating in the kitchen."

"Oh, I am not!" Tuva protested, still sounding humorous in her exchange with the reindeer woman.

"Oh, I dare say that all you need is black leather and a whip," Maja giggled before flicking a fist as if she were using a whip and trying to make the sound of a whip crack.

Ray wanted to laugh at that, but he had to hold it in due to the social pressure of not wanting to embarrass the elf. Yet, beneath it all Ray wished to impress Tuva. She was a friend of Maja's after all, and he knew that if a woman's friends approved of a guy, then that would eliminate complications.

"I'll be there at noon," Ray promised.

"Goodie!" Tuva cried out. "The soup kitchen is over at the corner of Deacon and Chandler. And I'll see you both there."

She came over to Maja, hugged her, and kissed both her cheeks before coming over to Ray and doing the same thing to him. There was a moment of uncomfortableness at another woman showing affection in such a way, especially since he was already with Maja.

When Tuva broke the embrace, he looked over at Maja who was smiling at him. Ray held a hand to his face feeling himself grow hot from the moment of contact. When Tuva left, he couldn't help but watch how she moved as she left. Her motions accentuated her curves as if she wanted Ray and Maja to know how incredible her ass was.

"You're so adorable when you're embarrassed." Maja giggled.

"You're not jealous that she kissed me?" Ray asked.

"That's Tuva for you. She's very affectionate and motherly. Just be sure she doesn't smother you to death with those gargantuan breasts of hers."

Ray let out a puff of a laugh, but he thought that if he had a choice of his own end then being smothered by a beautiful woman's massive breasts wouldn't be a bad way to go.

***

Saturday came quicker than Ray had anticipated as did the paycheck that Maja had given him the night before. The check came to $1,119.23. Far more than what Ray had expected, but as Maja said, when she handed him the check, "It's a little extra for the holiday season, hon."

With the money in his account, his spirits were far higher than they had been in months. The realization occurred to him while on the way to the soup kitchen at the corner of Ray and Chandler.

Being around Maja and the bookstore, he thought, *I've been smiling and laughing. I had forgotten what that felt like.*

The soup kitchen was in an area of Northview called, 'Historic Downtown' where most of the buildings were brick construction and narrow in their layout. The place that Ray came up to was a drab gray building with grey walls, narrow windows, and industrial looking front doors. Its industrial and plain appearance was so off putting to Ray that he had to look at the address and the location once more.

"This is the place," he assured himself.

Assured that he was at the right place, he parked his car at the front of the building, got out, and tried the front door, but it was locked. Going to the next logical move, he tried knocking as he peeked through the window on the door. After only a moment, he saw Tuva coming towards him. She fiddled with the front door until it opened just a little.

"Ray, you came," she exclaimed with a smile. "Head around back, I'll let you in through there."

Following her instructions, he walked around to the back of the building where there was a commercial dumpster, a loading area, and a large back door. It was there that the back door opened, and Ray found Tuva emerging. She waved him to come inside. Ray couldn't help but notice how she still wore an ugly Christmas sweater, but this time it was green with snowmen on it and yet her buxom figure filled it out to the point of stretching the snowman wider than intended. Over the sweater was a red apron that had a dusting of white powder on it. Her red hair was done up in a tight ponytail that was held together in a simple hairnet.

"Thank you for coming, Ray," Tuva said, bringing him in for a hug, kissing both of his cheeks again.

"No problem," he said, trying to ignore the heat in his face at her kisses, but he then looked down and saw the white powder that got onto his clothes.

"Oh!" Tuva cried out her hand reaching up to her lips before she started scrambling for a towel. "I am so sorry. I'm so scatter-brained sometimes."

She came over with the towel and started wiping away the white powder from his clothes.

"It's alright," Ray said giving his assurance while she continued to wipe off the powder off him. "This sort of thing happens in the kitchen, right?"

"Unfortunately, yes." She smiled.

"So, what do you want me to help with?"

"Well, I'm making some special cookies. Think you can help me out in cutting them out and setting them on the trays?"

"Sure." Ray smiled.

"I'll get an apron."

The kitchen itself was massive as to be expected for something that was commercial grade. He could already smell items being cooked or being kept warm. Such as several large turkeys, stuffing, and potatoes. Yet, the items that Tuva needed help with were on the stainless-steel island counter where there was a bowl of dough, an open bag of all-purpose flour, some cookie cutters, a spatula, and several stacked baking trays.

"Here you go," Tuva said holding out a red apron for Ray along with a box of what looked like black spiderwebs. "And these are the hairnets."

"Thank you," he said putting it on but still thinking about Tuva and her endowments. Once again, his thoughts went down the road of imagining what it would be like to have her join Mmaja and him. He had to admit that his thoughts had traveled that road multiple times when he'd been with Maja. He'd wanted Tuva to join in just to smother them both in her breasts. The fantasy made him start to grow hard as he slipped the hairnet on over his hair, but the fantasy thinking was stopped by Tuva's voice.

"Alright," she began. "I'm going to roll out the dough. I just need you to cut out the dough, scoop them up, and put them on the baking trays."

Ray looked to the tools and nodded. "Right away."

"Wait!" Tuva shouted.

Ray froze.

"Wash your hands first," Tuva said, sounding like she was referring to him having something on his shirt.

"Right," Ray stated before heading over to the sink.

After he was done, he turned around and watched as Tuva was rolling out the cookie dough across the stainless-steel counter. She was bent forward over the flour covered countertop and getting the powder on her apron thanks to her breasts and thick belly squishing against it.

Man, Ray thought, *I can't stop thinking about it.*

It was strange, as Ray thought about it, despite being with Maja and getting laid almost every day since he started working, Tuva kept coming to his mind as well. Once again, shame came over his mind like an imposing judge staring down at him from on high.

How could I think about another woman when I have Maja? He asked himself. *Then again, what are Maja and I? Boyfriend and girlfriend? Co-workers with benefits.*

He wasn't sure but still that question made him think about his ex-fiancé.

At least I'm not cheating on an agreed commitment like she did, he thought.

Even without having made a spoken commitment to Maja, he knew there was an unspoken one forged through their mutual pleasure. He wanted to be true to his commitments and knew he needed to control his thoughts better. They brought about the familiar feeling of melancholy as he came around the island. He took random cookie cutters and began to cut out the shapes in the flattened cookie dough. After he scooped up the cookies and set them into the baking trays, he went onto the next roll out from Tuva.

"Are you alright?" she asked.

"I'm alright," Ray answered trying his best to sound fine while looking up to the elf who showed such worry in her green eyes for him. But he kept his smile on and tried to sound as if there was nowhere else in the world that he wanted to be.

It was a trick that the depressed often learn out of necessity; how to fake being okay.

"You're not fine." Tuva smiled shaking her head.

"What makes you say that?"

"I've often been told that I'm quite empathic," Tuva answered. "I can often tell when someone is sad, happy, or anything else. In your case...there's a terrible air of sadness to you, like you're judging yourself that you're trying to hide. If you want to talk about it, you can, and I won't hold any judgement over you."

Ray *wanted* to say everything. He *needed* it. Just like when he told Nicholas, he wanted to share all the sordid details.

"My life...it...it didn't go as well as I had hoped," Ray began as he slipped each cookie onto the tray. He felt like he was repeating himself like what happened when he told his story to Nicholas, but it had to be told to her. "And for a while I thought that everything was going great. I had a great job in the city. I had a great place. And a fiancé who loved me...or so I thought."

"What happened?" Tuva asked continuing to roll out the cookies.

"It was actually about five months ago, and around my birthday," Ray began. "I came back home after traveling abroad for my job and found my fiancé in bed with my boss. She said that she was 'trading up'. In the aftermath of it all, she said that I wasn't enough for her. That I couldn't facilitate her dreams. She wanted *everything*. Marriage, house, kids, a life of luxury, travel, and not having to work. And being married to me wouldn't give her that."

"What a spoiled little girl." Tuva shook her head.

"Yeah," Ray agreed while his eyes sunk downward to the dough on the counter as the memories took hold. "And after that, not only did I lose her, but I was let go from my job due to a loss of a contract. She moved in with him, and I knew my boss just wanted to get rid of me, but I couldn't prove that. I told a few coworkers I trusted before I was walked out the door by security. So, I had to suffer the indignity of moving back home with my parents. 'Like every millennial in this goddamn country', as my father continuously reminds me."

Ray couldn't help but start sniffling and feeling the familiar sting in his eyes, while the water started to pool in his vision. That was when he heard the activity from Tuva stop, and he tried to stop himself. He knew one key fact of life about being a guy, especially in the culture he lived in: no one cares about a guy's problems. A man's worth was only connected to his usefulness. That was a fact that Ray had learned in the cruelest of ways.

Yet, something surprised him.

A pair of arms wrapped around his body and a soft, round, and voluptuous mass press into his side. He felt his body relax into Tuva's hug. Turning in her arms to face her, he was surprised at the sight of her smiling down at him in a way he had never seen before. Not even *his own* mother.

There was sympathy, empathy, kindness, and understanding in her look to him.

"It's okay, Ray," she whispered. Her voice was as warm as a cozy fire and inviting as a bed at the end of a long day. "None of it is your fault. And it's okay to not feel okay."

Ray couldn't help himself. He had needed something or someone to tell him that. He had needed someone to give him permission. The fact that such a beautiful elf woman like Tuva said those words to him unleashed something in him. Bringing his arms around her, he leaned in, rested his head against her shoulder, and began to cry.

"There, there. It'll be okay," Tuva whispered bringing up a hand to rub along his back and the back of his head. "There's no shame in what you're doing. You can let it all out as much as you want."

Her words made Ray cry even harder. Far more than he ever did as a young child trying to learn and control his emotions due to the expectations of society. Even more than the times he was drowning by himself in moments of his failures. It was as if everything he felt was a dammed-up reservoir that was ready to overflow, and the elf allowed the flood gates to be open.

Ray didn't know how long he cried, but finally he felt like he had done enough. With a deep breath, he pulled back, feeling his cheeks raw from the hot tears and his nose runny.

"Here," Tuva offered, stepping off to the side and bringing up a box of Kleenex.

Ray took it and began to dry his face and clear his nose.

"I'm sorry," he apologized amid him cleaning himself up.

"What do you have to apologize for?" Tuva asked, sounding confused by his statement.

"Self-pity can be obnoxious," he explained.

"Oh, Ray," Tuva said, placing her hands on his shoulders. "You men...so wound up with trying to look strong all the time that it exhausts you. Instead of trying to be a strong man, just be a good human being. Allow yourself to be imperfect and vulnerable."

"Thank you." Ray sniffled while continuing to dry his face.

Tuva brought her hand up his face and smiled before leaning in and hugging him once again. In her arms, Ray couldn't help but feel so warm and safe. It was the kind of safety and freedom to be himself.

Pulling back from the embrace, Tuva patted his cheek and said, "Now, come along, we've got cookies to make and hungry people to feed."

Ray cleared his throat. "Right."

He went back to the task of cutting out the cookies, scooping them up and setting them on the baking tray. The task was done in silence which made one thing that much worse for him. Silence was often the one thing the mind needed to think and thinking made him spin the wheels of his mind. He ruminated over the fact that he had cried in front of Tuva.

Did it change her opinion of me? He asked himself. *Does she think I'm some pathetic man? She said it was okay to be a human being. Was she just saying that to be nice? To be imperfect and vulnerable. But I still cried in front of her. Does that make it all right?*

Anxiety was such a monster to the mind that it made one's thoughts turn into a snake that eats its own tail. Ray tried his best to counter it by keeping himself busy with the task at hand. Yet he couldn't help but look up at Tuva who often looked back at him with a smile. But then there was a moment when she did the same thing and gave him a small wink.

He wasn't sure how to respond to that, and so he kept cutting out the cookies. Yet, there was still the attraction to the busty elf. Lustful ideas permeated his thoughts like the delicious smell of the cooking food all around them.

Hours passed as they worked, and they had managed to make nearly ten dozen sugar cookies of various Christmas shapes from trees to stars to bells and even reindeer. By the time that all of them were done, Ray looked up at the clock and saw that it was nearly four in the afternoon. Then there was a knock at the back door.

Tuva went to the door and opened it before crying out, "Maja!"

"I decided to close the store early and come by and make sure you weren't working my star employee too much," Maja explained coming into the kitchen and putting on an apron.

"Not at all, Maja-dear," Tuva said, waving one hand at the idea. "Ray has been marvelous. We just finished the cookies, and the food is almost ready for the dinner crowd."

"Marvelous," Maja said, tying the ties for her apron.

Maja's eyes locked with Ray, and she came over to him and wrapped her arms around his neck and started kissing him.

Ray pulled back and saw such a mischievous look in Maja's eyes and a slight flap in her reindeer-like ears.

"Shall we have a quick fuck?" Maja asked.

"Hey, you two," Tuva called out. "There's no time for that sort of thing."

"Oh, don't be such a killjoy, Tuva," Maja answered back over her shoulder.

"Under other circumstances, I'd let you two go at it, but we've got some food to serve."

"Oh, alright," Maja acquiesced, letting go of Ray, and moved onto helping in the kitchen.

By the time that five o'clock rolled around, several other staff members for the kitchen showed up, and the doors were opened. Time passed by in a blur after that with the influx of dinner guests of the small city. They came in and took one plate at a time of the turkey, mashed potatoes, stuffing, gravy, and a cookie.

It was coming close to ten o'clock at night when the last of the dinner guests had left and the doors finally closed. Many of the staff had left leaving just Tuva, Maja, and Ray.

"I shall head home, everyone" Maja said yawning and taking off her apron. She came over to Ray and gave him a passionate kiss good night. "I hope you have a *very fun* rest of the night."

Ray looked at her confused, but she just winked and blew him a kiss.

"That's quite alright, you've been a wonderful help." Tuva smiled and then looked over at Ray and winked at him. "Especially you, Ray, but I could use an extra set of hands with the clean-up, please?"

"Sure, I'll help out," Ray answered while stretching.

Before Maja left, Ray noticed something rather odd. He noticed a smirk and smile pass between the reindeer woman and the elf.

"Try not to wear him out too much," Maja requested, "I do require him at my shop after all."

"Can't make any promises, Maja-dear," Tuva answered sounding as if she were flirting with her.

Seeing the interaction between the two confused Ray. If it wasn't flirting that they were doing, then there was only one other thing that he would have likened it to. It was as if the two were betting each other on something involving Ray. He wasn't sure what that could have been, but he tried his best not to think about it and just focused on loading the trays for the dish washer.

Some of the other items required washing the dishes by hand.

Despite the effort to remain focused, his mind once again ruminated, and he kept thinking about Maja and Tuva. Thoughts of having them both stuck in his thoughts like a popcorn kernel in his gums.

It was when he was hand-washing a large baking tray that the night took a very different turn.

"Ray?" A voice called out to him.

The faucet was at full blast washing one of the baking trays. Without giving it any thought, he turned his head to see what was going on. His hand slipped and one end of the tray fell into the sink, redirecting the spray from the faucet. He didn't notice the water was spraying everywhere until it was too late. Water flew up and out onto Ray but also on Tuva who was standing not more than two feet from him. It splashed onto her ugly Christmas sweater drenching it into a dark damp version of its original color.

"OH!" Tuva yelped.

"Oh my god!" Ray cried out reaching out for the faucet to turn it off. "I am *so* sorry!"

His instinct was to try to find a towel to help her dry off, but he was stopped.

"It's okay. At least it was warm." Tuva smiled wiping away some of the water that had gotten onto her face and her hair. "I was planning on taking this off soon anyway."

Ray wanted to ask why, but the answer came quicker than he thought when Tuva reached down and pulled the ugly Christmas sweater off her body. The sight made Ray's heart seize in chest but at the same time his face grew hotter than the inside of an oven.

Tuva's breasts were far larger than he imagined, and they were held within the tight confines of a purple silken bra. The cloth of it was just as damp as the sweater and Tuva reached around her back and with the dexterous motions of one hand unclasped her bra and let it fall away from her chest.

"Oh, sweet gods," she sighed. "It feels so good to get out of that thing."

She pulled off her bra and tossed it aside leaving her bare breasts in full view of Ray who felt his jaw fall as far from his face as possible. His mind struggled to process the sight: the massive curvature of them, the hardness of her nipples, and how wide her areolas were in addition to the continued scattering of the dark freckles across her shoulders and chest. Her hand then came up to pull off the hairnet that held her hair captive, freeing her ponytail. She then reached behind, pulled at the ponytail tie, and let loose her hair in a move that bordered upon picturesque.

With her hair free, she shook her head, tossing her hair back and forth. Tuva's hands came up and began to play with and massage her breasts in front of Ray as if it were a private show just for him.

"I know you've wanted to see these since we first met, Ray," she teased. "Many people, both men and women want to see them just to see if they're as big as they seem. One of the troubles of being a busty woman is that most just stare at you for these."

"Um...Tuva..." Ray uttered feeling the fear twisting his gut and heart. "I'm with Maja..."

"Oh, don't worry your adorable little head about that," she said coming over and patting his cheek. "I spoke with Maja, and she's okay with you being with me."

"What? And...why?"

Ray already felt more like an idiot than before because this beautiful elf of a woman was in front of him, topless, and ready to do more with him and yet he had to ask a stupid question.

Tuva giggled. "Maja told me about you and how you can see past the glamour. So, you must already know that I'm an elf. And we elves are very empathic to the emotions of others. I can feel the lust of many who want me, but you, Ray? Your lust for me was louder than everyone else's, but you also have something else underneath it all."

"What's that?" Ray asked.

Tuva came closer to him, pressing her breasts up against him and bringing her lips to his. The sensation was so warm and sweet. The sweetness was not just a poetic form or description that Ray would think about later, but there was an actual sweetness to her lips as if she had sugar on them. He couldn't help but bring his arms up to wrap around her waist, pull her closer to him, he knew then that she felt how hard he was.

The elf woman pulled away to look Ray in the eye and said, "Underneath your lust, there is your sadness. And yet there is still kindness in you despite all that you've suffered. I want you, Ray. I want to feel all of it from you. Please."

"Yes," Ray answered before leaning in, pressing his lips against Tuva's, and letting his primal lust take over.

Two women in one month, he wondered. *Dear god, please don't let this be a dream.*

Tuva's hands came to Ray's chest, and she pushed him away.

"Here," she said before climbing up onto the stainless-steel counter, "hand me those towels."

Ray reached over for a set of dry towels. After handing them to her she began to lay them on top of the stainless-steel counter. With them laid out like a picnic blanket, Tuva began to work with the waistband of her pants and wiggle herself out of them.

Unable to help himself, Ray moved himself around to watch how much Tuva was wiggling her ass out of her pants. She angled her hips from side to side as if she were teasing him with her body.

"You like what you see?" She asked pulling down the material of her pants over her buttocks to reveal how extra round she was. A true big, beautiful woman.

"Fucking yes," Ray uttered.

"Then get up on this counter and get your cock inside me," Tuva begged. "You don't need to worry about protection. You can bareback me. I'm very well protected."

"Okay," Ray said pulling off his shoes and yanking off his sweater and shirt before pulling off his pants. He left them on the floor and was only in his underwear when he climbed onto the countertop.

The chill of the countertop almost made him lose his erection but the sight of Tuva in her bare form with her extra round buttocks and her massive breasts more than made up for the chill.

"Here," she invited. "Lie down on the towels."

Ray followed her instructions and lay down on his back. He looked up at her and watched as she got onto the counter, moved on her knees, and straddled his waist. As she leaned over him, he was captivated by the magnificent sight of the way her long red hair overflowed to form a silky curtain over Ray's face. Her beauty entranced him from her eyes, down her freckled spattered face and shoulders to the massive breasts that hung inches from his face. Reaching down for his cock he wanted to help get himself inside her, but she moved his hand out of the way.

"Before the main course, sweetie," she cooed. "Let's have an *amuse bouche*. Since you're very much a breast man, come, play with them, squeeze them, pinch them, and suckle on them."

Ray couldn't help himself. He did just as Tuva had invited him to do. At first, his hands came up to cup her breasts and marveled at how the warm flesh of her chest was filling his hands and overflowing from them. Cupping them, he leaned up and brought his mouth to her nipple and began to suck on it.

"Mmmm," Tuva moaned reaching down to run her hand through Ray's hair as she pulled his head into her bosom. "It's like you're a baby suckling the milk from me. Don't be afraid to do so. I give you permission to play with my tits at any moment you like. Oh! Ah!"

Ray pulled back. "Your tits are amazing."

"Better than Maja's?" she teased.

"Oh, that's not fair." Ray chuckled. "You're both beautiful in your own ways."

The elf cupped his face and leaned in to kiss his lips before letting go.

"Such a sweet man."

She reached down for his cock and slipping it inside herself.

"Sweet gods," Tuva moaned. "Maja was *right*...you are...*thick*...ah!"

"Am I hurting you?" Ray asked, pushing himself up a little.

"No," Tuva grunted, shaking her head. "I've just never had a man inside me who was as thick as you. Oh, fuck, I think I'm going to climax before I get to ride you."

"Then ride me," Ray commanded, reaching out to grab her thick hips as he thrust upwards.

"Yes!" Tuva cried out while she rolled her hips, gyrated, and ground herself into him.

Her pussy and tight channel felt wonderful as she squeezed him tight in response to each of his thrusts. Ray could already start to feel himself rushing to climax. It wasn't even a few moments later when the elf leaned forward, changing the angle of her body before she plunged back down on him. He went deeper than he had as a wave of pleasure washed over him. It was pure heaven and when he opened his eyes, her magnificent breasts dangled in front of his face. Her hard, long nipples beckoned him to latch on. He wanted them so badly, but a sensual squeeze enveloped his cock, pushing him over the edge.

"Tuva!" Ray grunted digging his fingers into her. "I'm gonna cum!"

And he did, letting go and giving in to the pleasure as he erupted into her. All too soon, the bliss started to fade, and the moment brought back a very unpleasant memory in his mind. Riding bareback allowed for such sensitivity, but the cost was just like that moment, when he overwhelmed him too quickly and he had climaxed within a few thrusts.

And he did and all too soon. The moment brought back a very unpleasant memory in his mind. He thought that he could bareback and not be so sensitive as he was that one time, but he remembered how she had begged him to bareback her and he did but he had climaxed within a few thrusts.

"I'm sorry," Ray uttered. "I came before you."

"Oh, sweetie," Tuva uttered, leaning forward and kissing him. "Don't apologize. I consider it a complement that I made you cum so soon. But I can still feel that you're hard. So, you can make it up to me now."

Ray smiled and said nothing, happy that she was such a considerate lover. He continued to thrust up into Tuva as she rode him while he enjoyed catching her nipples in his mouth. She made use of his hard cock, crying out as she maneuvered to have him hit the right spot. His hips bounced with such hungry fervency, and she huffed each moan and groan as her passion kept building. He knew she was getting close when she leaned back, arching her posture, and brought her hands to her breasts. She mashed them, and her fingers pinched her nipples as she rode him.

"AAAHHHH!" she cried out as she climaxed and went rigid, trembling and shaking with each wave of her orgasm.

As her orgasm started to face, Tuva fell forward onto Ray, her breasts squishing against her face. He made gentle kisses against her wonderful titties until she rolled over onto her side, taking one deep breath another. Her face was pink from the exertion and ecstasy, but Ray was filled with guilt.

What'd I just do? he asked himself.

Chapter 6: A Cooking Date

R ay came to work at the Paper Playground feeling a frightening mixture of different feelings. He could already feel himself rocking, teetering, and swinging between the conflicting sensations between his stomach, his head, and his cock.

On the one hand, he was swirling in a cloud of guilt and paranoia.

Did she really mean it? he thought. *I have to believe she meant what she said. But will this change my relationship with Maja? Will she be obsessed about what I did with Tuva?*

On the other hand, Ray tried to reassure himself.

Think, Ray, he told himself tapping the side of his head. *Think back to what Maja and Tuva said. She said she spoke with Maja and said it was okay. If she's a friend of Maja's why would she lie about that? Maja even said to have fun, and if they talked about it, she must be good with what happened. I just need to figure out the context and boundaries for our relationship.*

In the fractions of a moment in the reassurance of that thought, he wanted to go over to Tuva's shop and ask her to fuck again. He couldn't get the images of her massive breasts, sweet face, and long red hair out of his mind. Ray wanted more but the guilt, paranoia, and reassurance kept gnawing at him like an infection that refused to go away. The questions kept moving from one side to the other and it gave him a sickening sensation similar to being on a bad roller coaster.

Finally, he arrived at work and came up to the front register. He made eye contact with Maja who was smiling at him.

"So?" she asked with an anticipatory smile of glee, "How was sex with Tuva? And those titties?" Her eyes went wide as she waited in excited anticipation for his answer.

Hearing that, Ray froze, not just in movement but he felt as cold as the outside in the deepest part of winter and the night itself. The chill was such that he thought that his skin had taken on a sheen of frost and that any other movement or touch would make him crack and shatter.

The mortification of it was all too familiar to a time when he was a young boy and discovering the joys of masturbating and having his mother catch him on his bed at the exact moment of orgasm. When the sensation of ecstasy and joy had washed over him and all he was left with was shame when he saw the look of disgust in his mother's eyes.

Talk about memories I don't need now, he thought as the memory bubbled up in his mind. *She wants to know...so...that means she knew it was happening. But how am I supposed to talk about how good another woman was?*

Yet, the moment with Maja had become very different when he looked and saw that she was still smiling at him.

"Well?" she asked letting her voice show how much she wanted to know. "How did you enjoy sex with Tuva?"

"Um…" Ray uttered and realized how much of an idiot he sounded especially when it came to the ladies that entered his life in the past month.

Maja giggled. "She must have really blown your mind, if thinking back to it has all the blood going in your lower extremities, if that's the only answer you have."

Ray shook his head trying to get his head back into the moment and trying to figure out the peculiarity of the odd situation.

"So, you knew that Tuva and I had sex?" Ray asked, reiterating what he had already concluded.

"Of course," Maja answered, "She's one of my roommates. I told her all about you and she was very intrigued by you. Including how you can see through the glamour and especially when I told her about how excellent you are when it comes to our amorous activities."

The chill had left Ray when he started to imagine what that must have been like. He pictured such a banal moment of Maja and Tuva just sitting around a coffee table casually talking about the things he did with her sexually. Such a thing seemed so odd to Ray that people could talk about sharing a man like that.

"You seem confused now, hon," Maja observed.

"I just-" Ray tried to answer but struggled to put the words together as if words and syntax had become pieces of a puzzle where the pieces had no picture to guide him.

"I'm aware that this must seem unusual and even bizarre, hon," Maja shrugged. "But that's how Tuva and I are, we're very open and sexual beings. It might come as a shock to you as a guy, but most women discuss their sexual activities in detail with their close friends. But you are a first for us in one respect."

"How?"

"You're the first man that we've been with together and want to have some...". Maja trailed off while her finger came to her lips and her eyes flicked up and down over Ray's body before she continued, "repeat performances."

"Holy shit..." Ray uttered.

His mind swirled, twisted, and spun trying to come to terms with the situation. Not only had he managed to snag himself one beautiful woman but two at the same time and they've both agreed to share him. There was a twinge of a moment when he thought about bragging but then again, he learned his lesson. It's not wise to brag when one has more than others. So, taking a more humbling frame of mind, he took a moment for gratitude at his good fortune. Not only had he found a job but two women who wanted him and were wonderful to him. The sex was wonderful but the bigger aspect of how they treated him took on a much greater aspect in his mind and heart.

The thought of his treatment by them made him feel so fortunate that he wanted to shower Tuva and Maja with kisses and promise them both that he would do his best for them.

"Are you alright?" Maja asked coming out from behind the counter and placing a gentle hand on his shoulder. The worry in her face for him was as clear as a mark of ink on a sheet of paper.

"I'm okay," Ray answered. "It's just...so *unbelievable* that I'm in this situation."

"I know, hon," Maja acknowledged before leaning in to kiss his cheek and then his lips. "But you have two girlfriends now, but that also means you're going to need to satisfy two women as well."

Hearing her say that he could feel the stirrings in his groin as if his cock wanted to pop out of his pants and say to Maja, "I'll certainly try my best."

"Good. Now, come along, hon," she encouraged. "We've got a store to run today."

And so, the workday passed by at a fever pitch with the Christmas holiday getting closer and closer. There were a few patrons who came in and bought a couple of books that were Ray's favorites. Such as Coraline by Neil Gaiman and the Thief of Always by Clive Barker. As much as he wanted to talk with the customers about these books, there were other customers to attend to. Yet, he noticed how much Maja was teasing him again with her bending over and giving her ass a jiggle in his visual direction when no one was looking.

Off and on through the day his mind kept thinking about what Maja said. He had two girlfriends. On one hand there was relief as far as what to call what he and Maja had but on the other hand? He often heard about people in similar pairings that he was in. *Throuples* they were called. Of course, for someone like him he often thought that having one woman made him feel lucky but having two? And having women like Maja and Tuva, he felt like the luckiest man in the world. The thoughts and the questions about the situation kept whirling round and round in his head like a piece of debris in a tornado. The most noticeable of those was something that kept taking root while the others kept spinning around it.

It was something he needed to address with Maja.

When lunch time arrived, Maja was up front turning off the lights and pulling down the gate before coming to the register to pick up her book and her lunch. Before she moved away, she looked at Ray concerned.

"You seem rather lost in your thoughts," she stated her concern.

"Well, I was thinking about Tuva again," Ray answered giving the best honesty that he could about his thoughts. There were many aspects he wanted to say but that was the simplest way he could put to the cacophony of thoughts that were buzzing in the disturbed beehive of his mind.

"Would you like to go see her?" She asked sounding not jealous but supportive as if she wanted him to achieve what he wanted.

"Yes and no...ummmm.... it's something that I wanted to discuss with you first."

"Let's sit and talk then," Maja encouraged gesturing over to the reading area.

Ray took out his lunch and his sketchbook and before going over to sit beside her. It surprised him that having such a discussion with Maja didn't bring about any anxiety or fear in him. He felt safe being able to talk to her. It was also refreshing to know that Maja wasn't just interested in sex with him, but she also cared what he thought and how he felt, just like Tuva.

"What was it that you wanted to discuss with me?" Maja asked before opening up her lunch.

"Well," Ray began, "I'm with you and we've had sex and had that wonderful date at the library."

"Quite possibly the hottest thing I've ever done in my life," Maja agreed while she fanned herself but then stopped to add, "and it's wonderful and relaxing to be able to sit and read beside you, Ray."

"Well...I'm thinking of doing something like that with Tuva," Ray added. "I mean we've been having sex and had our date. So, it just seems fair that Tuva should have a date from me as well, right?"

"I agree." Maja nodded, opening her container and digging into her lunch. "So you're basically asking me for permission to ask her out?"

"I suppose I am," Ray admitted. "I have experience of being deceived and I don't want to do that with you or Tuva. I want to be open and honest with you both."

Maja got up from her chair and leaned over to Ray to kiss him.

"You have my permission. Though I do think now you should discuss it with Tuva as well."

"Everything feels so new to me in the past couple of weeks," Ray admitted.

"It's quite alright," Maja said while she took her seat. "As I said before, Tuva and I are very open and honest beings. If there's anything amiss, we'll be sure to tell you up front."

"It's refreshing to hear that."

"Thank you." Maja smiled.

***

After the workday was done, Maja was closing the gate and Ray was gathering his jacket. As he passed by the gate, Maja wrapped her arms around his neck and kissed him.

"I shall see you tomorrow, hon." She winked. "And good luck with Tuva."

"Thanks Maja," Ray said kissing her back.

Turning away and heading towards Tuva's store, Ray still felt that nervousness in the pit of his stomach. Yes, he kept reminding himself that he had both women but there was still that pesky insecurity that dug its weed-like roots deep into his psyche. It had been like that since he first developed feelings for the opposite sex and dealt with the first pains of rejection. Sure, someone on the outside would probably look in and say "Get over it" but his insecurities weren't so easily banished in the presence of something good. They're like shadows, sometimes they shrank in the light but then they'd grow when doubt set in. And it was the doubt that was making the shadow of his insecurities grow larger and larger.

He took a deep breath, and coming closer to "Decadent Delights", he saw the lights of the store being shut off and Tuva reaching out to close the gates. He watched as her voluptuous figure moved trying to pull the gate closed. For a moment, it looked as though the gate was caught and she was trying to pull it loose.

"Need a hand?" he called out to Tuva.

The elf turned around and beamed a wide and happy smile in Ray's direction.

"Yes, please," she answered.

Ray came over and helped pull the metal gate over the entrance of the store until the lock was in place and Tuva took out her keys to lock it.

"What brings you by this way, sweetie?" Tuva asked, turning around.

Ray cleared his throat and made his statement, "I want to ask you out."

Hearing himself say the sentence out loud made him feel like an idiot in the way he blurted it out. The shadows of insecurities grew larger and larger ready to envelop his world into the darkness of anxiety; all the while

Ray wished that he could for once be cool and suave with women.

He held his breath, waiting for Tuva to answer.

Tuva continued to smile and leaned in to kiss his lips. Ray's first instinct was to pull back but after everything that he and Maja talked about he let go of the instinct. The part that helped the most was Tuva's lips. They were so sweet that he wanted to stay there and savor her deliciousness. He wanted more of her but when he reached out to wrap his arms around her, he could feel her body pull away.

She smiled at him and said, "I was waiting for you to ask that, you know."

"You were?" Ray asked confused.

"Yes, Maja told me all about your escapades and how much of a sweetheart you are. I was hoping that you'd ask me out after our moment of passion at the soup kitchen. If you didn't, after a bit, I was going to ask you myself."

"But isn't it for the guy to ask first?"

Tuva laughed. "Oh you human men with your rules. So adorable."

She leaned in and gave his lips a quick peck.

"Well...um..." Ray began before clearing his throat, "I didn't know if you were going to say yes or no, or if you'd be available tonight, so I didn't have any plants for the date yet."

"Don't worry," Tuva said, waving her hand. "I have an idea for that."

"What's that?"

"Do you know of the store, *Sur La Table*?" she asked.

Ray thought for a moment and answered, "The cooking supply place?"

"That's the one. They offer cooking classes, and there is one that they'll be doing this Friday specifically for couples. A friend of mine is the manager of that store, so I'll see about getting us in."

"A cooking class huh?" Ray asked as he thought about it. He had often done the cooking when he was with his ex, but he also knew how much Tuva preferred to have control in the kitchen.

"We don't have to if that's not something you'd be interested in," Tuva replied, sounding concerned.

"Nah, let's do that."

"Wonderful," she said leaning in to kiss him. "This Friday at five."

"Five?" Ray asked, "I think I'll still be working at that time."

"I think Maja would let you out," she winked.

"I'll be sure to ask."

***

Friday came just as quickly as the people that had come into the Paper Playground. Ray was worried that he wouldn't be able to leave work in time for the date. Thankfully Maja was an understanding person and told him that she'd handle things, shooing him out to make it to his date.

On that day, Ray noticed how much Maja was smirking at him during the whole workday. He wanted to ask why she was doing that, but with the Friday rush crowd, so close to Christmas, they had been swamped in waves throughout the day. It wasn't until the five o'clock hour was approaching did Maja say anything.

"So, today's the big date?" Maja smiled giving Ray a playful shove.

"It is," Ray said, smiling as he continued to work.

As odd as it was to think about in the moment, but he had to admit the occurrence to himself. That for the past few weeks since meeting the women, he had thought about his ex-fiancé less and less. Then again, he didn't even want to because these ladies had treated him far better than she had. Ray admitted to himself at that moment that perhaps it was, what most would call, a "rebound" but he wasn't sure. After all, he wasn't one who had a lot of success with women which is probably why losing his ex-fiancé had been so painful.

Yet, the thought couldn't be held onto as Maja encouraged him.

"Ray," Maja said out with a hand giving a gentle push on his shoulder. "You better get going, or you'll miss your date."

"Oh shit..." he whispered before finishing up with one customer and dashing to get his coat along with his sketchbook. The moment he came out, he leaned in and kissed Maja on the cheek before leaving.

"Let me know how the date goes, hon," Maja called out.

Ray maneuvered his way out of the Paper Playground and took on a brisk walking speed through the mall towards *Sur La Table*. In the days leading up to the date, he had stopped by one of the map kiosks of the mall and located the shop so that he could plan out the path. He knew that this date wasn't like the one with Maja where it was a quiet impromptu meeting at the library. With Tuva it was more of a meet up. And meet ups to him always seemed so stressful because of the possibility of missing each other or something coming up or one person being delayed.

"Relax, damn it," he told himself. "This is not like those times with her."

Ray remembered how his ex would plan things. She would plan every single minute detail down to the minute and seconds of departure and if it didn't go that way she often grew angry and sour to the point of cancelling everything. One such event was a concert that Ray bought tickets for as a Christmas present to her. They both got well dressed for it but were having trouble finding the restaurant before the concert and that was when she took off her high heels, called for a taxi, and went home leaving Ray there.

Tuva isn't like her. He tried to remind himself while the flashes of the memory came back to him.

He looked at his phone again and it read 4:58. Seeing that he only had minutes he tried to make himself go faster to the point of breaking into a dash. He could already feel his lungs start to sting and ache from the exertion before he saw *Sur La Table*. The sight of the place made him begin to dash despite the pain in his legs and his lungs and within moments he was at the threshold of the shop, and he started looking for Tuva.

Making quick and panicked glances over the aisles and islands of high-end culinary merchandise he found the red headed elf in one corner of the store perusing baking trays, cake molds and cookie cutters. He smiled but then there was the sharp painful tickle in his lungs that made him cough. On instinct, he coughed into the sleeve of his coat. Once he was done coughing, he saw Tuva had stopped her browsing and was walking towards him.

Tuva had dressed up in a way that he didn't expect. She wore a tight red dress that dipped down her chest in a v-neck with small straps at her shoulders while the hem came down to her ankles with a cut up one side along her thigh. The tightness of the dress did very little to hide her curves, but she walked in it with such grace and confidence.

"Ray!" She cried out coming up to him and wrapping her arms around his neck, "You made it!"

It was then she began to kiss his cheek and then his lips despite how chapped they were from his running.

"Come this way." She guided him to a section at the back of the store where there was a wide set of open doors.

Beyond that was a small commercial kitchen area with two large tables. One wooden topped and the other stainless steel with a gas stovetop connected to it. Behind that along the wall was a commercial kitchen sink with a refrigerator off to the right. Off to one side of the room there was a table set against the wall with a large glass container filled with water, ice and lemon slices.

Without giving it any thought or pause, Ray went over to the container and poured himself a glass of water and drank it down in one gulp.

Then then poured himself another and began to sip at it.

"Someone's thirsty," Tuva teased, coming up behind him.

"You could say that." Ray chuckled, catching his breath.

With his thirst sated, he looked around and found three couples standing around the kitchen while there was one woman wearing a chef's jacket. While the couples were human, Ray noticed that the woman in the chef's jacket was an elf much like Tuva. But she was much shorter than Tuva, but she was just as curvy as she was. The elf chef looked over at Tuva and Ray and smiled.

"Alright, everyone," the elf chef called out. "The final couple has arrived. So, let's begin."

At the chef's statement, the four couples, including himself and Tuva, took their places around the wooden table.

"Good evening, everyone," the elf chef began. "My name is Cellica, and I will be your instructing chef this evening. For tonight's menu we have a reverse sear ribeye steak, truffle oil mashed potatoes and oven roasted broccoli. Paired with that is a Cabernet Sauvignon. Please, take your aprons, and we shall begin."

Ray saw everyone moving towards a small rack at one side of the room and saw aprons on hooks. He went over, set his coat on the rack, set down his sketchbook, and grabbed an apron and had tied its straps. Upon finishing it, he looked and saw that Tuva was already trying to tie the ties of her apron.

Coming over to her, he took hold of the ties and began to work it herself.

"Hey," she whispered turning her head and smiling at her lover.

"I got you," he whispered.

Tuva didn't say a word. She leaned in and gave his lips a short and sweet peck.

"I see love is in the air," Cellica called out.

There were a few chuckles to which Ray felt no embarrassment since it was true. With the aprons on, they began the class. During the class, Ray noticed something about Tuva. He noticed how she had taken a step back from the way she was from the last time they were in the kitchen together.

Each person in the class had been given one ribeye, a set of potatoes, and a single floret of broccoli. Ray had a moment when he thought that Tuva would take over as far as the peeling of the potatoes, the cutting of the broccoli or the seasoning of the steak. Instead, she concentrated upon what she was given to her.

Yet, while Ray had finished peeling the potatoes, he looked over at Tuva and noticed that she was already done. She had already cut up the broccoli, peeled the potatoes, and seasoned the steak. Seeing how ready she was for the next step, he glanced up at her and found her smiling and giving him a cute wink.

On and on the class went. Ray wasn't sure how much time had passed but he didn't care for he kept looking towards Tuva who was as much in her element as Maja had been when she was at the library.

Each time he glanced at her, she smiled back, and they shared a short moment. There was an instance when the elf saw him look in her direction and gave a sideways smile before her eyes and face turned downward. Ray looked down Tuva's side to the slit up the side of the dress. Her hand came to her side, and she pulled it up her leg past her knee and almost halfway up her thigh showing off her long, tantalizing leg. She held her long skirt up for a few moments to give Ray time to appreciate the view before she dropped it.

The sight of it made Ray's heart race, and he felt himself grow hard against the wooden table.

Tuva leaned in and whispered, "After dinner, sweetie. I've got a surprise to show you...and it's under this skirt."

The moment that she whispered her promise, Cellica called out, "Alright, everyone. Let's put the steaks in the oven, let them cook, and we will take a ten-minute break."

Some of the couples took off their aprons but others kept them on while stepping out of the kitchen to browse the shop or even step out into the rest of the mall. Ray looked over at Tuva and he wanted to ask her what the surprise was but on the other hand he knew that he should let her reveal it in her own time. Yet it was the fact of not knowing what it could be that made Ray's mind race. Was she wearing some kind of special underwear? Was she wearing underwear at all?

These thoughts went through his mind in the minuscule instances between the seconds that it took to hang up his apron. His lust was already starting to boil to the point of eruption despite all the attention that Maja had given him. He couldn't wait to have Tuva again and the anticipation was twisting his stomach and his heart race.

It was then that Tuva came up behind him and wrapped her arms around his waist, pressing herself into his back. He then felt Tuva's head resting against the back of his shoulders.

"I can feel how much you want me," she whispered. "Don't worry; I promise you that you will have all of me tonight. I think you'll love my surprise and the other surprises I have in store."

Ray turned around to face the elf who kept her arms around his body. He looked into her sweet eyes with one question.

"Surprises?" he asked. "Plural?"

Tuva smiled and brought a finger to her mouth, where she set it in between her teeth while she kept her eyes locked onto his. She gave no answer, but none was needed.

"So, this is the one you were talking about?" the voice of Cellica called out to Tuva as she stepped over to them.

"Why yes, he is," Tuva answered turning around.

The chef came up to Ray and shook his hand. He could feel how strong and sure her grip was when her fingers curled around his hand. So much so that he thought if she'd wanted to, she could have gripped him hard enough to have broken his hand.

"He must be quite something to get you dressed up like this," Cellica remarked looking her over and then back at Ray.

"This is actually our first date," Ray mentioned.

"With this one, I'd say it's quite an honor to come to a cooking class," Cellica observed. "If you've tasted her chocolates then you know that she doesn't even need a class in cooking anything."

"Oh, stop," Tuva blushed waving a dismissive hand at Cellica.

Ray smiled, seeing the modesty that Tuva had when it came to her skills in the kitchen.

"Well, I won't stop you two from your date," Cellica said, bowing her head and stepping away.

"She is right," Ray added.

Tuva only gave a small shrug, while making her way towards the store. "Well, how does that old adage go? Never stop learning?"

"I think it goes something like that." Ray nodded following her lead.

"I do so love coming to this store," Tuva remarked. "It makes me feel like a child in a toy shop. I especially love the baking section. Come."

She brought him over and showed off all the various baking trays in the multitude of shapes and designs that they came in.

Seeing how she gushed over each of them, Ray couldn't help but smile. "I think I know what to get you for Christmas."

"And here I thought my Christmas gift was all of you, sweetie," she flirted, while coming up to him and kissing him.

After enjoying her kiss for a few moments, Ray pulled back, glancing at his phone, and saw it was time for the class to continue.

Tuva saw him looking and said, "Oh yes, best head back."

Coming back, they saw that the other couples had come back to the class and the elf chef was waiting for them.

"Now it's time to cook the steak, everyone," the chef announced.

Each member of the class was given a burner and a cast iron skillet for cooking the steak. In addition to the steak, they were given butter, garlic, and sprigs of thyme and rosemary to season the steak as it cooked.

"Very good," the chef complemented Ray in the way he basted the steak by turning the pan to one side to pool the butter. He took his spoon and ladled the butter on top of the steak.

"Excellent skill," Tuva remarked.

"Thank you," Ray said not taking his eyes off the steak or the task he was doing. He couldn't be sure if it was the heat, but he thought his face felt warmer than normal.

"Alright everyone," the chef called out. "Let's feel the steak for doneness and then it'll be time to plate."

The chef came around to each couple to help them test the level of doneness of each steak. Some wanted it rare, while some wanted it medium rare. When it came to Ray, he preferred his medium well, so his steak was left in the pan the longest. As soon as it was ready, he pulled it out and set it on the plate. He filled the rest of the plate by spooning out the mashed potatoes and oven roasted broccoli.

Around the island, the chef came by to take away the cast iron pans and burners and helped lay out glasses for the wine along with chairs.

Upon sitting down, Tuva had taken the bottle of wine and began pouring it for her date. Ray had to take note upon how she was doing it, holding the top of the bottle's neck in one hand while her thumb was hooked into the bottom of the bottle and her fingers set along the body. Once the bottle was tipped over and pouring into the glass, she held it but the bottom in such delicate and deft fashion.

"Thank you." He smiled then sat down next to the elf, but when he watched her cut up the steak and eat it with dainty glee a question came to him.

"You look like you have something on your mind," Tuva observed.

Ray leaned in and whispered, "I thought elves didn't eat meat."

Tuva giggled before taking a sip of her wine. She leaned in and whispered, "It depends on the elf. Some like meat. Some don't. We're just like humans that way. But for me, I like all forms of taste and deliciousness."

She pulled back and kissed the side of his neck.

As she pulled back Ray saw the way she licked her lips before she went back to drinking her wine and eating dinner.

He admitted to himself that it felt good to eat such a rich and fine meal as what was in front of him. Then again, in his past, he was often the one who did the cooking, and there were some skills that weren't as easily forgotten.

Continuing to eat his meal, he looked over at Tuva as she continued her meal.

It was often told to Ray that you can tell how good the meal is when everyone eats quietly. This was especially true when it came to the wine that paired with the meal. He wasn't much of a wine drinker but the sensation and taste of the wine with the steak was sublime.

Now I understand why red wine goes with red meat, Ray thought to himself.

For a while, he had lost himself to the deliciousness of the meal and forgot that Tuva was next to him and that there was to be a surprise after the meal. When the detail came back to his mind, he couldn't help but want to rush through the meal. He found he was already nearly finished with the ribeye, and he peeked over at Tuva who had pulled up her skirt up her leg even more. Her hand even ran over the exposed skin of her thigh.

Ray looked up from her thigh towards the elf's face and saw how she had given the slightest turn of her head. Her eyes were locked on his while her mouth was open with the fork near her lips with her tongue licking the prongs of the utensil.

The elf once again leaned to him and whispered, "Save room for dessert, sweetie."

At the moment that her utterance was made, Ray felt her hand on his thigh. He almost let out a groan as she inched it closer to his crotch where after a slight hesitation, she cupped him. Her fingers curled around the section where his balls were, while his cock stirred with the feeling of her palm against him.

Feeling his lust stir and awaken once more he made quick glances around to see if anyone had caught a peek of what was happening. To his relief, all the other couples were so entranced by what was made and being with each other that no one even bothered to glance in their direction.

Without any eyes in their direction and emboldened by Tuva's hand, he reached out and placed his hand on top of her bare thick thigh. Her skin was warm, soft, and silken but his hand hungered for more.

While he continued to eat slowly with one hand, his focus was on his other hand as it moved up her thigh towards her honeypot. He teased her just as she was teasing him, slowly caressing her skin as his hand moved higher. It didn't take long for him to feel the material of her dress stopping him, but after a moment, the material fell away from his fingers. He glanced over at Tuva and saw the smirk on her face. She finished adjusting her skirt with her one hand and went back to eating after giving him a wink.

She was giving him passage to her pussy. The slit for her skirt had been perfectly designed and allowed much more access than could be perceived.

With such sweet permission, he moved his hand in between her thighs, he made a shocking and arousing discovery.

Tuva wasn't wearing panties. His fingers gave a gentle brush to her hot, wet pussy, causing her to exhale a soft moan.

The discovery made his eyes shoot to the elf's face, and he saw her looking at him with such lustful eyes a smirk of glee was the only other sign she gave that she knew that he'd found out one of her surprises.

"Surprise," she whispered before leaning in and adding, "and there's more to come."

"I can't wait anymore," Ray whispered back. His voice was thick with the hunger that was raging within him from wanting Tuva.

"You've waited long enough, sweetie," Tuva answered back. She pulled her hand away from his groin and pushed his hand away from her pussy. Getting up, she took off her apron and hung it up on the row of hooks around the makeshift dining area. While she slipped on her coat, she winked over at Ray who followed suit.

"Thank you for coming tonight," the chef called to the departing couples.

"And thank you for a very stimulating dinner," Tuva complemented and bowed her head.

Chapter 7: Sketches in the Suite

Ray followed his elvish lover out of Sur La Table and into the rest of the mall that was beginning to close.

"Where are we going?" Ray asked catching up trying to keep hold of his sketchbook.

"I have a hotel room reserved for us," she answered. "You know of the one next door to here, right?"

Ray thought for a moment while his legs kept trying to catch up and he dodged the various shoppers while trying to keep up with Tuva.

"Yes, I know the place," he answered which was half true. He knew that there was a hotel, but he forgot what it was called.

Upon stepping out one of the many covered entrances and into the cold night air, he looked across the parking lot and the street ahead and saw that it was an upscale hotel. Or at least as upscale one could get in a small city like his but certainly far above a cheap hotel. The lobby with how expansive and sheik it was in its holiday decorations as well as its interior design confirmed his impression. Yet, his eyes snapped away when he noticed something about the hotel clerk.

The clerk was a young woman who seemed human for the most part but seeing through the glamour he discovered that she was a fairy. She stood at the same height as him, with long flowing red hair that seemed to have a dusting of sparkles in each strand while her green eyes held a welcoming warmth along with her smile. At her back were a pair of wings that had the shape of dragonfly wings but had the color and vibrancy of butterfly wings. They fluttered and gave off shimmers of colors in blue, green, and purple with twinges of pink.

The two breezed past the reception desk and straight for the elevators. Waiting for the elevator felt like it was taking too long but Ray tried to exercise his patience. It proved difficult knowing that he and Tuva were about to fuck again.

DING!

When the elevator door opened, the two lovers dashed inside, eager and anticipating the doors closing. With the doors closed and seeing that the compartment was closed off, Ray unleashed himself onto his elf lover. He pushed her up against the elevator wall while he felt the dull pull upward. His hand went underneath her skirt and he found her bare pussy ready for his hand. Spreading open her lips with two fingers and using one to find her clit he began to rub it while his lips found hers.

"Mmmmm," he moaned.

"Mmmm!" Tuva moaned back into his mouth, but she pushed him away and turned around. She lifted her skirt over her ass to show her bare behind to him to which she spread open her cheeks to show herself off to him and that was when he made another discovery.

Nestled in between Tuva's thick cheeks was a blue jeweled anal plug that sat sparkling in the shine of the elevator's lights.

"Do you like it?" she asked.

"Oh my god…" Ray uttered. "You were wearing this all through dinner?"

"Oh no…I've been wearing this all day and wanted to show it off for you, sweetie," she explained letting her dress down. Turning around she faced Ray, "It's one of my kinks. I love anal play. Toys…plugs…beads…*cocks*…I love things in my asshole as much as my pussy. And you're going to have it all tonight and more."

DING!

The elevator stopped and the doors opened. Tuva took Ray's hand and dashed from the elevator down the hall and to room 314. Once there she pulled the card out as if it were something that was going to save her life and tapped it over the door handle to which it whirred, and a light turned green. She opened the door and pulled Ray inside.

"Let's get you out of these clothes," he huffed, pulling at her dress while the door closed behind them. They were too focused on kissing and feeling each other's body for the clothes to come off. Her dress was bunched just below her breasts.

"Mmmm," Tuva cooed. "You can be so hot when you're dominating."

"I can't wait to dominate your ass with my cock." Ray smirked, leaning in and sucking on her ears.

"Oh gods…I think I just got wetter," she uttered while her hands came up to his shoulders and she held him close to her body.

Ray leaned in and began to suck on Tuva's ear lobe before running his tongue along its long length.

"I want to be inside you," he whispered while his hand came up to her bare breast, cupped and massaged them.

"Come here, sweetie," Tuva said, taking his hand and brining him over to the bed. She paused at the bed before saying, "Before you get to be inside me, there's something else I want."

"What's that?" Ray asked as he set his sketchbook on the nightstand before he began to pull off his clothes piece by piece.

"Go the refrigerator."

Ray looked around the room and saw next to the desk was a small refrigerator. He opened it and found a can of whipped cream. The dots connected in his head as he took it out and opened it when he came back over to the bed.

"You've done this before, haven't you?" she asked, seeing the smile on his face.

"No," Ray said shaking his head. "But I've always wanted to."

"Then do what you want with that and me, sweetie," she said getting onto her knees and pulling the tight red dress over her head and letting all of her curvaceous glory bounce and captivate with the movement. With not a stitch of clothing left on her body, she lay back down on the bed and spread her legs for Ray.

He came over shaking the can of whipped cream and feeling how freezing cold it was against the palms of his hands. Before he was going to do what he planned to do, he smirked and brought the cold container to Tuva's breasts and had the edge of it touch her nipple.

"AH!" she yelped but cooed as her thighs came together and rubbed one another. Bringing them apart once again, her hand came down between her legs to touch herself. "Don't tease me, sweetie."

"You're gonna be teased and like it," Ray answered back still keeping his dominating tone in his voice while he brought the cold can over to her other breast and let the cold metal touch her rising nipple.

"Oh!" she cried out again.

Ray saw how her nipples were starting to rise and harden. The sight made him lick his lips, and he couldn't hold back any longer. He lowered his head, opened his mouth, and began to suck on them.

"Mmmm," Tuva moaned. "I know you've missed my titties, haven't you, sweetie?"

Ray pulled back with her nipple only an inch away from his mouth. "I can't stop thinking about them...your tits are amazing, Tuva."

"Then take your fill of them," she said, pulling his head back to her chest while his mouth opened and suckled upon her once again. The sensation had put Tuva into such a frenzy that she began running her fingers through his hair and pressing his head to her breast. "Ah..."

Ray pulled himself back and brought the can of whipped cream to her chest and began to spurt the white topping over her nipples. First one and then the other.

"I told you to save room, sweetie," Tuva said holding up her breasts to him. "Dessert is served."

And once again, Ray dove headfirst into her breasts. Licking. Sucking. And even giving each nipple a small bite and not caring if the whipped cream was smearing across his face.

So good, he thought to himself while losing himself to the sensation and taste. Yet, he still had enough self-control that he took himself away from her breasts, took the can and began to spread the topping to other spots he wanted to lick. First, her thighs, then her belly, and a small dollop on her mound. Tuva lay back spreading herself as Ray made the slow licks of her body. Her moans and shivers encouraged him to continue enjoying her. Leaning down, he licked the cream off her thighs, then his tongue made it's travels around her belly before inching downward toward her pussy.

With the sweet musk of her sex in his nostrils, Ray pushed aside her thighs even farther and pushed his face into her pussy. Using his lips, he pushed aside her vaginal lips to find the crown jewel of womanhood. He began to lick at it with his tongue in up and down motions then in great circles in one direction and then the other before opening his mouth and sucking on it like her nipples. With her tiny pearl in his mouth, he let his tongue dance and swirl around it.

"YES!" Tuva cried out not holding back any further, "Eat me out, sweetie! Eat my pussy! AH! Oh, sweet gods! AH! AH! AH! I'm *fucking* in *love* with your tongue! Don't stop! *Please*, don't stop...mmmm..."

Her body thrashed upward against his face, her thick thighs held his face in place while her hands came down into his hair and gripped it while she took in one breath and let out a very strained cry of pleasure.

"AAAAAHHHHHHHHH...MMMMMMM..."

Her body shook and jerked in her climax, as her thighs came away from him. He could feel them shiver and shake like they wanted to move but didn't know how to move. He enjoyed watching her body weather the pleasure she received while her face turned away, her eyes rolled upward, and her lips formed a large smile.

"Are you okay?" Ray asked, sitting back on his legs, and looking down at her.

Her eyes looked downward, and she laughed.

"I'm fine, sweetie," she said. "That's just how I have one of my more powerful orgasms. I tend to just...I guess space out while the pleasure washes over me. I've met very few people that can do that to me. And you, sweet Ray, really know how to do it."

Ray smiled especially how she punctuated her point by tapping him on the nose.

"Thanks," he said before getting up onto his knees. "But there are a few more courses in this night of sex."

"If you keep me cumming like I did just now, I think you'll put me into a coma." Tuva laughed, sitting up and kissing him.

"Mmm, does my pussy taste like honey to you?"

"Mmmm, sweeter," Ray answered licking his lips. "Now, get on your hands and knees."

"Yes, sir," Tuva said as she complied showing her ass to him and spreading her cheeks as she did. "I have another surprise for you. Go over to the closet and you'll find a case."

At the elf's behest, Ray got up from the bed and headed over to the closet. At first, he pulled at the door that slid sideways, expecting it to be somewhere at eye level, but then he looked down and found a pristine-looking suitcase. He reached down, picked it up and took it over to the bed where Tuva had moved to sit up against the headboard with a smile on her face. The look the elf had, if Ray could liken it to anything, was akin to that of someone who had bought a gift for a loved one and couldn't wait to see the look on their face when they opened it.

Ray set the bag on the edge of the bed and unzipped it. Upon opening it, he couldn't help but marvel at the various toys that were in it. There were plugs, dildos, dongs, and vibrators of various kinds and sizes.

"Surprise," Tuva said, sounding extra sultry in the display of her collection. "Which one would you like to use on me first?"

Ray perused over the assortment of metal, polyethylene, and latex before his eyes settled upon one in the corner. It was bright purple with a set of spheres along a string starting with a small nub at one end before coming to the biggest at the other end where there was a ring that looked big enough to hook the index finger through. Reaching down, Ray hooked his finger through it and brought it out to show to the elf who held her hand to her lips in a mock expression of shock.

"Oh, so naughty," she said, sounding over dramatic before taking on her normal tone that spoke deafening volumes of her desire. "And I love it."

She got up onto her knees, turned around and got onto all fours with her head facing the headboard. Tuva wiggled her ass in Ray's direction making the jeweled plug sparkle with the motion.

"Go ahead, sweetie," she huffed. "Pull it out of me."

Ray got onto the bed to get in closer to the elf before reaching out for the toy. He slipped his thumb and index finger around the base of the toy and began to pull. Her tight ass fought the motion of extraction. Her tight anus puckered around the base of the metal implement and wouldn't let go. At least until Ray kept a constant pull on the toy. Her sphincter muscles gave the slow release of their grip with widening dilations and obvious waves of pleasure.

"AH!" Tuva cried, pushing herself against the headboard while her hand came up to her mouth and she bit down on her finger. "MMMMMM!"

Outward and backward Ray pulled the jeweled plug out of the elf until it widened to a crescendo, and the toy was released from her asshole.

"Ahhhhh..." Tuva moaned while her buns and thighs shivered. "I came a few times during that..."

"A taste of many more to come," Ray promised setting aside Tuva's jeweled plug.

"Yes, please," she begged. "Put the beads inside me. I beg of you...my asshole begs of you...but please, don't forget the lube."

Hearing her request, Ray went back to the bag and found several bottles of lubricants. He knew enough about toys to know that certain types go with certain toys. Reaching in he pulled out a water-based lubricant. The first instinct was to pour it onto the toy, but he had an idea that was far more fun.

"Spread open your cheeks for me," he said sounding dominant as ever.

"Yes, sir." Tuva giggled, reaching behind and spreading her back crevice for him.

He came over and squeezed the lube into the crack of her ass. Using the anal beads, he smeared the lube all over her crack while lubing the beads up and down before bringing the small end up to her puckered rosebud.

"Ooooh, that lube always feels so good," Tuva moaned, "so cool...ah-hhh..."

Ray didn't say a word, as he brought the tiniest part of the beads to her rosebud and began to push it inward. The first part slipped in without much trouble, but the sweet sexual resistance of it began at the third or maybe fourth bead that made it widen.

"Unnnnnnnngggghh..." Tuva groaned while her buttocks shivered and squirmed from side to side. "Oh, gods, it feels *so fucking* good."

"How about this?" Ray asked holding the beads in one hand and reaching his other free hand underneath Tuva to rub her clit.

"AHHHH!" she cried. Her back arched backward and then upward, and her hips thrust against the anal toy and his fingers. "Inside me! Get it all inside me now! I want it all! Your cock! The beads. Fuck both my holes with them, Ray! I can't wait anymore!"

Without any other teasing, Ray began to push and shove the remaining beads into Tuva's anus until the ring was resting against her puckered sphincter. With the toy inside her anal cavity, he came up behind her and brought his hard and waiting cock to her pussy and shoved himself inside.

"OOOOOH! Fuck...*yes!*" Tuva moaned while her body began to pull forward and push back against Ray.

He reached out and grabbed onto her thick sides and pulled her up against his groin as he thrust in and out of her.

"Ah!" she cried out.

"Oh god..." Ray grunted.

He could feel how wonderfully warm, inviting, and dripping wet her insides were. They hugged and squeezed his cock. The sensation of her insides tickled his cock to the point that it was about to burst with his cum. He slowed his thrusts, savoring each movement in slow inches, as he confused on his control. His cock screamed how good it was feeling and how much it wanted to cum, but he didn't want to finish too soon.

"Oh, Ray..." Tuva moaned. "Pull one of the beads out. Please. Pull it out but not all the way."

Ray reached up and began to pull at the beads making her anus pull back and fighting the pull until it began to dilate and release it.

Tuva moaned while her back hunched, and the cheeks of her buttocks clenched and shivered.

Ray had pulled out a bit to allow better access to the beads. He could feel the base of his cock becoming exposed to the open air with Tuva's juices coating and chilling him. The head of the member was still inside her, but he wanted to get back to thrusting inside her as much as his cock did. In the midst of his lustful hunger, he had an idea. He decided to use that last bead to fuck her ass in sync with when he thrust into her. He gripped onto the last bead and pushed it back into her while he slammed his cock back in.

"Fuuuuccccckkk..." Tuva squirmed. "Keep that up, and I'm gonna cum."

"Then cum, my sweet elf. Explode for me," Ray answered back, giving himself over to fucking her pussy with his cock and her ass with the bead. He steadied himself during the thrusts with one hand on her hip while he thrust into her, making the flesh of her buns produce rapid slapping sounds against him.

"AH! AH! AH!" Tuva uttered with each thrust that Ray made. "Ray, I'm...I'm gonna cum! AHHHHHH! Pull the beads out of me! Pull them hard out of me you *wonderful fucker* of a man! PLEAAAAASE!"

Ray could feel his own orgasm coming, and it took every ounce of control that he had to keep thrusting as he began to pull at them. At first there was resistance from her asshole, but she'd told him to pull hard. He wrapped his whole hand around the ring and yanked hard, pulling it away from her. The first bead came out with a soft wet pop before the others, but that was nothing to the scream Tuva released.

"AHHHHHHH!" she screamed with her hands gripping the pillows.

It was too much for Ray and his control vanished.

"HHNNNNNNN!" Ray grunted feeling the rest of his orgasm burst within the elf. In pulling the beads out, he had turned and pulled himself backward. His cock was still firing when it slipped out, spurting the rest of his cum and onto the bed and part of Tuva's thick thighs.

The power of the release was such that it made Ray dizzy, and he tipped forward onto Tuva's back. They slipped to lay on the bed before he rolled off her and over onto his side.

"Oh my god..." he huffed, taking deep breaths and licking his chapped lips.

"No fucking kidding," Tuva agreed while she let herself lie face down on the bed. "You really pulled hard on that."

"I'm sorry," Ray said wondering if he had gone a step too far.

"Don't apologize, sweetie," Tuva assured him, reaching out to his shoulder and patting him. "I did ask you to pull hard on it. And wow, no one has pulled that hard while I had an orgasm that powerful. I'm still trembling."

Looking over to the elf's body from her back to her round buttocks and thick thighs, he could see that she was right. There were a series of tremors running through her body from her lower back to her ass and to her thighs that made her flesh jiggle like cheesecake that hadn't been fully baked.

Seeing it, Ray gave a huff of a laugh. With his senses coming back to him, he looked to his right hand and saw that he was still holding onto the anal beads. He set them aside on the bed before rolling over to the elf. In the closeness that they had he wrapped his arms around her bringing his face close to hers and kissed her.

Tuva responded in kind with one arm wrapping around his body. At first her hand ran over the skin over his back before it traveled down to his ass where she squeezed one cheek.

"Mmmm," Ray responded pulling back and smiling at his lover. He saw the redness in her cheeks, the haze of her desire, and the raggedness of her breath that begged for more. "I want you again."

"I know, sweetie," she said, reaching up from his ass cheek to the cheek of his face. "But you human men need time before you're ready again."

After her hand caressed his cheek, it flitted down to his cock when her eyes went wide with surprise to find that he was still hard.

"Oh, my," she uttered. "You really have some stamina in you."

"And you? Think you're up for another round?"

"Give my insides some time to calm down, sweetie." She laughed before rolling onto her back.

Seeing her laugh and the way her breasts jiggled and wobbled, resting against her body, made him want to lean in and suckle them again.

"Oh my, how did you get so fantastic at this?" Tuva asked. "Tell me. How many women have enjoyed your expertise?"

"Three," he said. "My ex...she was the first I was with...and the *only* one I was with."

"Oh, sweetie," she uttered before bringing up both arms and pulled him against her breasts while her hand rubbed against the back of his head. The hot and cold sensation melted away to be replaced with simple warmth.

She let go of him and said, "Let us not spoil this evening with talk of her."

"Okay."

"But there is something I wanted to talk to you about," she added.

"What's that?"

"That black book you have," she said, raising an eyebrow. "What's in it?"

"Oh, my sketchbook," Ray answered. "Before I moved back to Northview, I was a graphic designer. But truth is I went into art because I wanted to be a comic book artist. I only chose graphic design as a career because I figured it was the best way I could make money off of my skill. But after everything that happened, I haven't set pen to paper in a long time. Until recently."

"May I see what you have in there?"

"Promise not to tell Maja?"

"Why?"

"It's just a little embarrassing, and I don't want to embarrass her."

"Ah, you've been drawing her, haven't you?"

"Yes,"

"Well, I won't tell her, but you should show her. I can tell you that I know she'd be flattered."

Ray didn't say anything. His eyebrows raised, his eyes moved over to the side as he wondered if she was right or if Maja would be appalled.

"I'd love to see what you have.".

"Okay," Ray said, getting up from the bed and heading over to the nightstand where he had set the sketchbook.

Bringing it over, he handed it to Tuva who was sitting up with her back against the headboard. She took it, opened it up, and began to flip through it.

"Ah, I see you have an eye for the Japanese style," Tuva observed after the first couple of pages of sketches showing Maja in various tasks.

"Always have," Ray admitted, sitting down next to his elvish lover. "Ever since I saw my first anime, I wanted to create art like that."

He saw that Tuva was only a couple pages away from the more explicit parts and she had turned the final page to when he began drawing Maja naked and in various sexual positions.

"Oh my..." Tuva uttered, while her eyes went wide, and a single finger came to her lips.

"I know," Ray answered back, sounding ashamed of what he did. "I'm a perverted fuck and I know it."

"It's beautiful...I can feel your desire for her in these. You're not a perverted fuck," Tuva said, using her free hand to shove his shoulder. "Don't be ashamed of your desire or your talent. Besides from what Maja told me of the things you do, I think this is very flattering. But...do you think you'd be willing to draw me the way you draw her?"

"Do you want me to?" Ray asked.

"Oh, yes, please."

She leaned in and kissed him, already starting to feel flashbacks of a certain movie.

"Too bad we don't have a diamond necklace for you to pose with," Ray snorted before getting off the bed.

"You could always give me a pearl necklace," Tuva joked while giving him a wink.

"I would if I hadn't finished inside you." Ray laughed, continuing with the joke before heading over to where he dropped his jacket.

Finding it on the floor, he reached into one of the pockets for his pen. Or at least the pen that he always kept on him when he was doing sketches at work. At home, it was another issue. Since working at the Paper Playground, he had the money to get other art markers for his art. His work sketches were in black and white, but the work he did at home had more color to them.

Coming back with the pen, he came over to Tuva who held out the book to him. Taking it, he went over to sit down on one of the chairs the hotel suite provided. He sat there, still naked, and began to draw the elf.

He held the book vertically so that he could have more room to draw his enthusiastic subject. First, he made light marks of where the proportions of the body would be on the bed and then made the initial marks of the outline of the body. The sketch only took a couple minutes since it was all that he needed of the outline of the body.

Once he was done, he came over to the bed where he sat down next to Tuva and began to fill in the details of the elf. He drew her just as he saw her on the bed, sitting up against the headboard posing as naturally as anyone would with her face looking in his direction.

"You've drawn me to be so beautiful," Tuva remarked looking over his shoulder.

"Well, you are beautiful," Ray added.

He stopped sketching when Tuva's hand came to the front of his face, and she turned him towards her when she leaned in to kiss him.

Pulling back, she sighed, "Such a sweet man you are. Sweeter than any chocolate in my shop. But please, don't let me stop you."

Turning back to the sketch, it seemed like he was done, and he was, but he wanted to draw more of her. He turned the sketchbook in its original layout like an average book that one reads and began to draw Tuva's face up close. After a few marks he drew her face as if she were laughing.

"If you keep drawing both myself and Maja," Tuva observed, "you're gonna run out of pages in the book."

Ray smirked. "Well, that could be something for you to get me for Christmas."

Tuva leaned in to give him a peck on his cheek. "Noted, sweetie."

"But what about you?" Ray asked. "What could one get for you for Christmas?"

"Hmmm," Tuva pondered while holding a finger to her chin. "You may think it strange to hear but I love porn films."

"That so?"

"Oh yes, but for me, I like golden age smut. The stuff you humans made back in the 1970s. Back when you made more effort to the story rather than the sex."

Ray had an inkling of the kinds of movies that she was talking about. The ones where the picture had a grainy quality to it, and the music was a type of disco sleaze.

"I think I know the ones you mean," Ray said.

"Oh, you don't have to lie to me, sweetie." Tuva smirked while her hand came down to Ray's crotch and cupped his balls. "I know you watch those."

Ray couldn't lie.

"Yeah, I watch," he answered, "but not that particular genre. But which titles are your favorite?"

"Ever heard of 'The Devil in Miss Jones', 'Debbie Does Dallas', or 'Deep Throat'?"

"Heard of them but never saw them."

"Those are my favorites, but it's not just smut that I have a liking for, but I'm afraid you might find this a little weird."

"I won't judge," Ray assured as he capped his pen and set it aside along with his sketchbook.

"I love horror movies," she admitted. "Again, I know it's weird, but I love being scared as well as aroused. Not at the same time, though."

"What sort of horror movies?"

"Evil Dead," Tuva said beginning her list. "Tales from the Crypt. Vault of Horror. Creepshow. Movies like that before people started relying more on gore and jump scares."

Hearing her talk about that, he couldn't help but start to feel the wheels turning in his head.

"Hmmm," he said. "You know, I think I have an idea for a little art of you, Tuva. If you're okay with it."

"What is it?"

"What'd you say to an art piece of you but as if you're on a horror poster?"

"Oh, Ray!" she cried. "That would be perfect!"

She threw her arms around his shoulders and kissed him. While in her arms, she made the gentle pushes to get him onto his back and climbed onto him, straddling his lap. Pulling back from the embrace of their lips she leaned back, resting her arms behind her head as if she were posing and looked down at her lover.

"Do you think you've rested enough?" she asked. "Because I want seconds of you."

Ray smiled while looking down at himself rising to the occasion. He said nothing else but took Tuva into his arms. They fucked and fucked and fucked until sleep pulled them away from doing any more.

Chapter 8: The Cat's Introduction

Ray awoke feeling naked and sore. But the soreness was one that brought a smile to his face knowing how it came about. He looked over to his side and found the bed empty. For a moment he thought that Tuva was gone, but he sat up and looked across the room and found the elf sitting naked at the corner table eating breakfast.

"Good morning, sweetie," she greeted. "You were still asleep when I woke up. So, I hope you don't mind but I ordered breakfast for us."

Not caring to get into any kind of clothes, Ray got up from the bed and crossed the hotel suite to his elf lover. Looking down he found that she had ordered a hearty breakfast of eggs, sausage, bacon, and toast complete with coffee and orange juice.

"Wow," he uttered.

"Is it alright?" she asked sounding worried.

Ray turned to her, leaned in, and kissed her.

"It's wonderful," he whispered.

"Good," Tuva answered back giving him another kiss. When Ray stood up she reached out for his hand. Since he was standing bare in front of her, she leaned over and kissed the head of his cock. "Such an amazing night you gave me, Ray."

"No question," Ray answered. "Never had a date like that."

"A good thing, I hope?"

"Very much," Ray said before sitting down and digging into his breakfast. "What time is it?"

"Almost eight," she said. "But we best hurry since our work is waiting for us."

"Don't you have an assistant at your shop?" Ray asked.

"I do but..." She trailed off before shrugging. "You've seen how I am in the kitchen."

"True," Ray said, continuing to eat but he couldn't help but look across the table at the elf and stare at her breasts once again.

She caught his glances and shook her finger at him while she smiled. "Easy now, Ray. I think we both need to recharge. Besides we don't have time for that."

"You can't blame me for looking at such art worthy beauty," Ray flirted.

"Oh, stop."

"Nah, I don't think I will."

"Eat up, Ray."

Ray continued to do so but as soon as he was done and began to sip at his coffee, he thought about all the things that he and Tuva did the night before. The anal beads. The plugs. The dildos. He couldn't help but think how wonderfully pornographic his life was. Both Tuva and Maja were such gifts to him, but then seeds of a question began to germinate and push through the soil of his mind.

"I'm going to shower," Tuva announced before getting up.

Ray watched how she moved in getting up from the table and saw how there was a cinematic-like grace to her movements. It turned sensuous when she went over to the bed, where she bent over and began to wiggle her ass in his direction.

"I think I'll come with you," Ray said getting up and already feeling himself grow hard at the sight of her.

"I'm sure you will," Tuva teased as she stood up.

Coming up behind her, he rested his chest against her back while his hands came up to cup and massage her breasts. They felt so warm and soft in his hands that he wished to bury himself into them.

Tuva reached up and pulled Ray's hands away from her chest.

"Let's shower, Ray," she said, before leading him into the bathroom.

Turning on the shower, she got in and Ray came in behind her. In the cascade of the hot water, Ray couldn't help but pull her into his embrace and kiss her. Amid the kissing and the roaming of their hands, Tuva brought up some soap. She began to wash Ray from head to foot, and Ray did the same for her.

The rest of the morning passed by in a blur with getting dressed, packing up, and checking out. With nothing else Ray headed over to the mall and into work.

***

"How did the date go?" Maja asked, seeing Ray coming up to the Paper Playground.

"Oh, it was quite the night," Ray answered.

"Oh, I'll bet." Maja smiled at Ray. "You'll have to tell me all the details of it when lunch time rolls around."

Ray got busy as the influx of customers came into the shop. Just like the morning in getting out of the hotel, the morning work hours passed by in a small blur, but there was still a question that kept growing and growing in his mind. It was the question about having these two ladies in his life. He never felt so fortunate to have not just one but two women who actually liked him and had such amazing sex with him.

At the same time as the question was taking form in the soil of his mind, there was another one that was in full bloom. It was one that he had to remind himself about when the time drew closer.

Lunch time rolled around, and the store was about to close for the break. As the store was closing for the break, Ray started to think about gifts for Tuva and Maja. One had already given him some ideas of the kinds of gifts that he could get, but Maja was another deal entirely.

"So," Maja said, coming over to her lover and employee. "Give me all the details of this lovely date with Tuva."

She asked as she made her way over to the sitting area of the store and Ray came over with her.

"We did a cooking class together over at Sur La Table," Ray began as he took his seat while trying to keep the gift question in the back burner of his mind. "We had ribeye, truffle mashed potatoes, and oven roasted broccoli."

"That already sounds like something that she would make at home," Maja observed. "What happened after that?"

"We...um..." Ray stammered. Even though he knew that it was okay to be with Tuva and Maja, there was still a bit of anxiety in his stomach about talking with them about each other.

"If you don't want to tell me, hon," she said, reaching out for his thigh, "it's okay."

"Nah, I'd like to," Ray refuted. "Tuva took me to that hotel across the street from here and we..."

"Oh, don't stop, hon," Maja encouraged. "I do so love hearing these sorts of things."

"She showed me that she was wearing an anal plug," Ray blurted out, feeling the first flushes of head in his face but also the flash of head in his chest and cock that he was telling things that he wasn't quite sure if he should.

"Keep going," Maja said, her eyes showing a hungry glee like someone watching a romance and hoping for the moment to come to fruition on screen.

"And she had a few other sex toys at the hotel for us," he added. "Including some beads that I used on her."

"Damn, that's hot," Maja exclaimed.

"And we just kept going at it all night until we couldn't stay awake anymore," Ray concluded.

"So, I'm feeling a little sore."

"Kind of like how I was after our first time," Maja said, giving Ray a playful shove. "You and that thick dick of yours."

"Hey, Maja," Ray asked, changing the subject and not wanting to lose track of the question in his head.

"Yeah, hon?" She asked.

"I wanted to ask what your favorite books are," he stated.

"All this time working here, and you never asked me that," Maja observed with a laugh in the undercurrent of her voice.

"Well, I was distracted by the fact that I managed to get a job and then there was-"

"Me helping you ascend to the heights of heaven with my *puss-say*?" she asked.

"Yes, there's that," Ray agreed, loving how upfront Maja was when it came to sex as well as how she had an eloquent vulgarity. It was as if a Shakespearean actress had gotten a job as a phone sex operator.

"But what're my favorites?" she asked, leaning back in the comfortable chair. "That's a tough question. You should know a true reader has too many favorites to name. But as far as genres are concerned? Promise not to judge?"

"I would *never*," Ray promised raising his hand as if taking an oath.

"I love reading smut." Maja smirked.

"Really?"

"Yeah, but it has to be *good* smut," Maja expanded. "I can't stand these stories that are put out where the woman is treated so *abhorrently* without her giving *permission* in any way. I just find it selfish and distasteful. That's not to say everything might be fun it its proper place. I mean I like it when you verbally degrade me, but at least I gave you permission and you knew that first."

"True."

"But apart from hetero smut, I also like lesbian and sometimes trans smut."

"Quite the array of tastes," Ray complemented.

"So, if you're looking to shop for gifts for me then just look for high quality smut stories. In paper format. Not saying anything wrong about digital books, just love the feeling of paper."

"I can understand why," Ray agreed.

"But what about you?" she asked.

"Hmmm," Ray said cupping his chin. "Off the top of my head, Neil Gaiman and Clive Barker but as an artist I do love art books. Such as whenever a movie comes out, I look for art books from the movie to see what the conceptions sketches were like, just so I can see how it looked on paper verses how it looks on screen."

"An interesting notion," Maja stated while her eyebrows rose.

"There's also the fact that I do these sketches," he said holding up the black book that held several sketches of both Maja and Tuva.

"So, sketchbooks and art pens?" Maja asked.

"Yes, but very specific brands," he said holding up the pen that he was using for the sketches in the book.

"I'll be sure to make a note of that for myself," Maja said but then she got up and held out her hand to him. When he grasped it, she pulled him up, wrapped her arms around him and kissed him. Her lips moved from his lips to his cheek and then to his neck where she nibbled at the side. "If it weren't for the fact that Tuva must have drained those sweet balls of yours, I'd suggest a little fuck with our lunch."

"I agree," Ray said, leaning in and kissing Maja while imagining him fuck the reindeer woman while Tuva watched.

"Hey, you two!" a voice called out.

The shock snapped the two lovers out of their enveloping cloud of lust. They looked in the same direction and found the voice came from the front gate of the store where there was the red-headed elf, Tuva. She was standing outside smiling and waving with a small bag of take-out in her hand.

"Got room for one more?" she asked.

"Of course, hon," Maja answered, breaking away from her embrace with Ray.

She came up to the gate and opened it for Tuva. Ray came up behind Maja to greet the elf even though it had only been a few hours since their last intimate moment together. Coming in, the elf leaned in and kissed the reindeer woman on the lips before Maja broke away to close the gate again. Leaving Maja to her task, Tuva came over to Ray, set down her takeout bag, wrapped her arms around him and kissed him.

Pulling her lips from his, she whispered, "I missed you."

And she kissed him again.

"Hey now," Maja cried out, sounding both joking and objectionable.

Tuva pulled her lips from Ray and craned her head towards the reindeer woman, "Don't be so greedy. You've had him so many times. I've only had him a few times. Let me have some fun with him."

"Oh my," Ray said, bringing a clenched hand to his lips.

Both ladies snapped their attention to their shared lover.

"What is it, sweetie?" Tuva asked, still holding her arms around his neck while squishing her voluptuous breasts against him.

"Having two ladies arguing over me," Ray answered. "I never thought that such a thing would happen to me."

"Well, you better treat us well," Tuva warned. "And were you two talking about me?"

"Maybe," Maja said, sounding so comedically innocent in the way she had her hands behind her back, and her head tilted off to the side.

"Well, that's alright," Tuva said. "I was wondering if it was going to be Ray or me that would share the details of our date. But since we're on the subject, Ray, did you show Maja the sketches that you've done?"

"What sort of sketches?" Maja asked.

"Um…" Ray uttered feeling like he was being put on the spot for something that he shouldn't have done, but the drive to be honest with these ladies far outweighed his want to hide that part of him. He held up the book and began, "I mentioned how I sketch…and I like to sketch beautiful things…and people. So…I've drawn some sketches of both you and Tuva."

"May I see them?" Maja asked, not sounding suspicious, annoyed, or even angry. Her tone sounded eager and excited.

"Sure, I just hope that it won't offend," Ray said while handing the sketchbook to Maja.

She took the book and opened it up to the first page. Upon seeing it, her eyes went wide along with her mouth.

"Exquisite," she uttered.

"You like it?" he asked.

"I do," Maja said, holding the book in one hand and taking her other hand to run it over the pages in the book. "You made me look so beautiful."

"Just wait until you see the other pages, sweetie," Tuva encouraged.

Watching Maja turn the pages made Ray's heart freeze once again. He knew it was weird to feel such fear about judgement about his work, but at the same time the subject was his lover and his boss. What was she going to do when she saw those pages?

The answer came when she turned the page, and her eyes came upon the page that Ray knew was when he started drawing Maja nude. When she came upon that page, her eyes still kept wide and her mouth was still wide, but even in the low light of the shop, he could see a light blush in her face. Maja's hand even came up to her face.

"Oh my..." she uttered.

"Is it alright?" Ray asked, feeling the freezing fear coming over him.

"I love it," Maja said looking it over. "But I would love to do an actual pose for you."

A rush of relief hit him, and he almost wanted to weep in his thankfulness for the situation, but he held it.

"You should see what he did of me," Tuva interjected.

Maja continued turning the pages until she reached the pages that Ray had sketched of Tuva. Studying the sketches, Maja smiled and then looked over at the elf and back to the book.

"He really captured your beauty, Tuva," Maja observed. "But I'm surprised that he didn't sketch you wearing a diamond necklace."

"HA!" Tuva guffawed at that statement. "I said the same thing to him last night."

"But, Maja?" Ray asked feeling the need to hear an answer to one thing on his mind.

"Yes, hon?" Maja asked.

"You're not upset or anything that Tuva posed for me first?"

"Oh, hon." Maja smiled shaking her head. "It matters not who posed first or asked to pose first. It's a silly thing to obsess over. I think the fact that you had one done in the first place is what matters most."

"I agree," Tuva added. "But Maja-dear, we really need to introduce him to Hedvig,"

"I agree as well." Maja nodded.

"So, there are three of you?" Ray asked.

"In our house, there are three of us, yes," Tuva answered.

"In that case, I'd like to meet the third lady."

"Since it's still our lunch break," Maja added. "Why don't you go over and meet Hedvig? She runs a gaming shop near the food court. It's called 'Gamers Loot'."

"Okay. I'll go meet her," Ray said before moving towards the gate.

***

Ray couldn't help but feel a certain elation in being around Maja and Tuva. Not just because of the sex but they made him feel good about himself.

The encouragement.

The caring.

All of it.

The last time that he felt anything similar was during the few year of being with his ex. They had been so kind, considerate, and passionate with each other. Ray redirected his thoughts to the mall before they ran off track.

He noticed the bold saturation of the colored Christmas lights and accompanying decorations. Then there were the sweet smells of the foods and candies being sold in the mall. This was especially true of the cinnamon and sugar of the candied almonds.

But his mind had an important thought that wanted to surface, so like so many times before the joy crashed when that question that had been germinating in the soil of his mind spourted and reached for the sky of his consciousness.

Am I in love? he wondered on his way to the food court. *But what if it isn't love?*

Under other circumstances, Ray would have thought more about the subject, and the thinking would have turned his mind into a car trying to free itself from loose sand. The wheels of anxiety and thoughts of what ifs would spin and spin and spin without getting the car anywhere. All that would be accomplished is throwing out more sand and wasting gas.

He reminded himself of that fact and shoved the question aside as he kept walking towards the shop. After all, if he was going to have Maja or Tuva in an actual bed at their home then he needed to meet this third roommate. His mind started to ponder upon another question as his eyes drifted over the people in the mall.

Ever since he had met with Maja and Tuva, he kept noticing other fae people.

Among the faces of the crowd, he found elf men, women, and even children. Then there were those who were like Maja with the reindeer-like antlers and ears. But there were also others that Ray would glance at but try his best not to stare. Such as a few who were short and had elf-like ears along with a few others that had other animal like ears such as wolves, rabbits, and foxes. All of this he observed but tried his hardest not to draw the attention to himself.

Probably best that if only Tuva and Maja know that I can see through the glamour, he thought. *But then again what reason would I have to tell anyone else?*

After making his way through the shopping crowds, Ray found himself near the food court where the sweet, savory, and pungent aromas danced in the air. It was five stores away from the food court that he found the sign for "Gamer's Loot". The logo was a bright red with a treasure chest underneath it with coins, game controllers, and dice spilling out of it.

Inside, the place looked a lot like any other gaming store with a library of video games for the current consoles along the wall, but it also had a little more. Such as there were items for tabletop gaming, books, dice, dice towers, miniatures and an island that featured board games and puzzles.

As much as he wanted to look the items over his attention was drawn to the registers.

On one register he saw a woman, but not a human woman. She was unusually short given the proportions of her arms, hands, and upper body. He guessed she must have been standing on some kind of stool to reach the height of the register. Added to that were her large wide ears that stuck straight out from her head that gave her an almost alien quality along with her green skin tone as well as her pink eyes and long, curly dark purple hair.

A goblin? Ray thought to himself but trying his hardest not to stare. Her nametag said, 'Hul', so he realized this wasn't Hedvig.

Keeping in mind why he was there, he walked farther into the store and tried to make himself look like he was browsing around. Glancing up from one of the video game shelves, Ray found the one he came to meet.

She was at the register next to the goblin and had large cat-like ears whose white fur blended itself into her extra-long, white hair that came down to her waist. Her skin tone was a deeper and darker tan than Maja's while her face was small and sweet with an unusual pair of eyes. They were cat-like in their vertical slits, but one eye was pale blue while the other was a bright gold. She wore a blue ugly Christmas sweater with silver bells knitted into its pattern. The sweater was several times her size in how the wide neckline hung off her shoulders like a dress while its sleeves hung around her wrists like the sleeves of a robe. It was on one side of the sweater where her name tag was pinned, and it read: Hedvig.

"Hi, welcome in!" a voice called out.

Ray looked and saw that it was the goblin woman who was smiling and waving at him. Not wanting to be rude, Ray waved back and looked to the line of customers that Hedvig was serving and decided to wait until the line was a little shorter. Despite that, he also had to remind himself that his lunch hour was only an hour long, so it was best to speak to her while there was still time.

He moved out from behind the shelves and got in line for Hedvig. It only took a couple of minutes before it was his turn to meet with the cat woman.

"How can I help you?" she asked sounding as if serving him was the one thing in her life that made her happy.

It was an attitude that perplexed Ray given his experiences of working in coffee houses before his actual job took over. He had found that when someone worked in a service job, they'd start by being cheery but dealing with entitled customer after entitled customer eventually wore down a person's desire to serve with any cheeriness. So it was because of Hedvig's enthusiastic cheerfulness that Ray was fascinated by her.

"Hedvig?" Ray asked.

"That's me." She smiled tapping her name tag.

"My name is Ray," he said. "I'm..."

He paused a moment because he wasn't sure how to address himself as far as his relationship with Maja and Tuva. Yes, Maja did say that Ray had two girlfriends but how does one explain that to anyone else?

"I work with Maja over at the bookstore," he began, "and I got to meet Tuva. They told me about you and suggested that I meet you face to face."

"Oh yeah! So, *you're* Ray," Hedvig cried out before coming out from behind the counter. Her movements were quicker than anything Ray had seen of another human being. By the time that he blinked he discovered that she threw her arms around his neck as she hugged him. It was such a surprise to such a point that he stumbled backward a step from the force of her.

"Easy there, Hedvig," a voice called out from the counter. Ray assumed it was from the goblin woman.

"Sorry," Hedvig apologized as she let go of Ray and turned to head back to the register.

As she did, Ray couldn't help but notice she had a long, thick, and white, furred tail that snaked out from under her sweater and swished from side to side as she walked.

"Sorry, Ray," she apologized again. "Let me help out these customers, and then we'll talk."

Ray looked over his shoulder and saw the others standing behind him. He stepped aside and let the cat woman continue with her job. It took only a few minutes before her attention was brought back to him.

"So..." Hedvig said, locking her dual-colored eyes to his. "Is it true?"

"Um..." Ray uttered, once again feeling like an absolute moron every time he made that verbal utterance. "Is what true?"

"That you can see through the glamour," Hedvig answered.

"He can what?" the goblin woman asked pointing to him.

Ray looked over to the goblin and made a point of reading her nametag, 'Hul'.

"From what Tuva and Maja told me," Hedvig said keeping her eyes locked on Ray while leaning over and telling the revelation to her goblin coworker, "this one can see us as we really are."

"He can?" she asked, looking him up and down. "What's so special about him that he can do that?"

"I don't know." Ray shrugged. "I just can."

"Well?" Hedvig asked presenting herself, "what'd you think?"

"I think you both are cute and beautiful." Ray smiled answering with honesty without fear of it.

"Thank you." Hedvig smiled while her tail rose and nearly hit the shelf behind her.

Hul began to blush which was odd to Ray's eyes to see the color of red blossom in her cheeks against the green pigmentation.

"Excuse me," a voice said from behind Ray.

He glanced over his shoulder seeing another small line of people forming. He turned back to Hedvig.

"Sorry to make our first meeting short, but I've got to get going," Ray said at a rapid pace showing how much of a hurry he was in. "Hope to see you around soon."

"Oh, don't worry about that, Ray," Hedvig said, waving good-bye by flexing her fingers towards him. "I'll be seeing you very soon."

Ray smiled and waved goodbye before leaving the store.

***

When he came back to the Paper Playground, Tuva had already left to go back to her store. The gate was pulled down and the lights were turned off and there was the sign that read "closed for lunch. Will open at 2 p.m.". Inside, he could see Maja in the back corner of the reading area eating lunch and reading her book. He reached down and pulled up the gate and ducked his way inside. Knowing how little time he had left until lunch was over, he went to the register and pulled out the lunch he had made for himself and came over to sit down with Maja.

In the quiet between them, she was the first to break the ice.

"Well, what's your opinion of Hedvig?" she asked, setting down her book and looking at her lover while sounding excited and anxious to hear his thoughts.

"I like her," Ray answered. "She's...rather cute."

"You can be honest about what you like," Maja encouraged placing a hand on his shoulder and rubbing it as if she were petting a dog. "I think it's been established that I'm not a jealous type. Neither is Tuva."

"Well, she's pretty *damn* cute and upbeat, then," Ray amended. "But she's a cat person?"

"Technically, she's what's called a yule cat-woman," Maja explained.

"What's a yule cat?" Ray asked.

"Well..." Maja began, "in the old days, the yule cat was a being who came around Christmas time making sure children wore clothes that their parents gave them."

"Is that so?" Ray asked.

"More or less. But they don't do much of that anymore."

"I have been seeing more people like you, Tuva, and Hedvig since I first came to work here. Do you all live here in the human world?"

"Some of us do, but others of us live in a realm called *Alfheimr* or 'fairy land', as some call it. Maybe one day, we can take you there and show you what it's like."

There was another moment of quiet while Ray at his lunch at a rapid pace, but there was something else going on in his mind. Another seed of a question that had bloomed in his mind and had been nurtured until its fruit was heavy and begging to be asked. After he swallowed, he cleared his throat and asked.

"But seeing all of you like this," he began, "an elf woman, a reindeer woman, and now a yule cat woman...does that mean that Santa is real?"

"Yes, but at the same time not in the way that you may think. It's a complicated thing and a little outside of my territory, but maybe one day we'll find someone who can explain that. But in the meantime," she added, pointing towards hers and Ray's food, "let's finish lunch quickly since it's almost time to open again."

Ray looked at the clock in his phone and saw that he had only five more minutes. He took to finishing his lunch with as much rapidity as his jaw, throat, and stomach would allow.

With the hour approaching, Maja went over to open the gate, Ray braced himself to face the next flooding wave of customers that were coming in for their Christmas shopping. It still boggled his mind that there were so many people buying physical copies of books while there were such things as Kindle, Nook, and so on. As far as he was concerned, he admitted that there was a certain gratification of holding paper between one's fingers while reading. The knowledge and sight with his own eyes that there were others who felt the same way warmed his heart.

Chapter 9: Closing Time

Closing time had come once again for The Paper Playground and the Christmas Holiday was drawing ever closer. But as Maja was pulling down the gate and came over to the registers to gather the tills, Ray couldn't help but look at her and think about both her and Tuva.

When Ray had come back home to his parents, he had known that he was a broken man. He hadn't even been sure how he was going to piece his life back together, if he even could. Then he met Maja and got the job at The Paper Playground. It'd be easy to think that she as well as Tuva helped him piece his life back together, but that wasn't the truth. The more Ray thought about it, he had already been piecing his life back together in the wake of the cataclysm of what happened, but Maja and Tuva helped him see the point and worth of putting the pieces back together.

Their help and the realization seemed like a far greater gift than anything that he could buy or give either one of them. Giving a man a purpose was beyond any kind of price.

Maja had taken the tills to the back room but as she came out, she called to him.

"Hey," she said, sounding very coy and seductive. "Would you be willing to try out something for me?"

"Sure," he answered, turning towards her as she stepped around the registers.

"Well, since you've drawn Tuva," she began, "and she posed for you. Could you do that with me?"

Ray smiled. "What'd you have in mind?"

Maja crossed one arm over her chest and tapped her chin. "Why not pose me here among the bookshelves? You've already done that in some of the sketches but now you have me posing how you like."

"Alright," Ray agreed taking out his pen and the sketchbook. "Let's pose you over there."

He pointed over to the spot of the bookstore that was the most well hidden from public eyes. The spot where he had fucked her. Ray couldn't help but often look over in that section of shelves and feel pride and arousal at the memory.

She walked over and gave an eager smile back at him. "Like this?" Maja asked leaning her back against the shelves. She tilted her hips and shoulders while lifting up one leg and resting her foot against one of the shelves. Bringing up her arms she held them above her head while tilting it off to the side.

"Perfect," Ray called out, grabbing a chair from the reading area and sitting it at the mouth of the section of shelves. Sitting down, he opened the sketchbook to a blank page and began to start the sketch. "Just one question," he began, while making the marks for the proportions. "Shall I sketch you clothed or naked?"

Maja laughed. "Naked. Always naked, Ray. I swear if it weren't for the fact of the cold temperatures and social conventions, I'd go naked all the time."

Upon saying that she began to undress herself, first her sweater, then her bra followed by her pants, shoes, socks and finally underwear. She set them onto a pile in the corner near the bookshelves and took to her pose once again. Taking the cue from Maja he began the sketch putting in the details of her bare form. Once the outline of it was done, he started making light marks of the bookshelves behind her.

He was drawing in the finer details of the sketch around her face and her antlers when there was a voice that called out from the gate.

"Maja-dear!' the familiar voice called out. "Aren't you heading home or is Ray with you?"

Ray looked over his shoulder towards the front entrance of the store and saw Tuva standing on the other side of the gate.

"I am here with Ray, Tuva," Maja called out breaking out of her pose and moving past Ray to poke her head around the bookshelf to see. "I was just having him make a sketch of me, like he did of you."

"Oooh, can I see it?"

"Come in and see," Maja said.

Ray hopped up and hurried over, raising the gate and letting in the elf.

He quickly went back to his chair while Maja returned to her pose. Tuva turned the corner to the small section where Ray was drawing the naked Maja.

"Oh...oh my..." Tuva said looking at Maja and laying a hand on her chest.

As Tuva enjoyed the view, Ray kept to his seat and continued adding in the finer details of the posed Maja. He had all he needed in his mind's eye, so he stopped glancing up to see Maja. As he kept drawing, his perception could already tell that Tuva had moved behind him to watch. He could feel her as she leaned in and her bosom pressed against his shoulders.

"You really do make all of us look so beautiful," Tuva remarked.

Ray leaned back, pressing into those wonderful titties before he looked around and found Maja had gathered up her clothes and was getting dressed again. When she finished, she came to his side and looked at what he had done.

"Oh my..." Maja breathed. "I look like a goddess."

"A goddess of books," Tuva amended for her.

"I'd be quite content with that." Maja laughed. "But there is something I wouldn't mind having right now."

Her hands came over to Ray's face and turned towards him where she kissed him.

"Let's not be greedy, Maja-dear," Tuva protested. "Let someone else have some of this sweet man."

Maja let go of Ray's face, and he turned towards Tuva who gave him the same sweet and loving treatment with her lips. With his eyes closed, he capped his pen and closed his sketchbook, setting one on top of the other in his lap. Upon releasing his hands from his sketchbook, they traveled up and cupped Tuva's breasts through her sweater. They felt wonderful, but then Ray wondered for a fraction of a moment at the peripheral of his thoughts about Maja before that was answered.

He felt another set of hands coming down to his lap where his sketchbook and pen were. The hands, he was sure belonged to Maja, took them away before they began to run over his thighs and cup his groin.

Tuva was the first to break the kiss with Ray and she turned her attention to Maja who was kneeling in front of him. The elf got down on one knee and cupped the reindeer woman's face and brought her close for a sweet kiss. Watching his two lovers giving each other gentle and passionate kisses. It was such a sweet and erotic moment in the way their lips touched, retreated, and touched again with Tuva's tongue poking outward, wanting to reach for Maja's.

The elf pulled back and whispered, "I think we should find a more private spot."

Maja protested, "Aww, but you know how much of an exhibitionist I am."

"Yes, Maja-dear, but we don't want to be arrested or give the security guards reason to come in," Tuva pointed out.

"Oh, very well," Maja said giving a comedic and over-the-top pout. "Follow me, my sweet lovers."

She got up from her knees and led the way to her office.

Tuva and Ray followed behind her.

Not a single moment was wasted. Tuva pushed herself up onto the desk, reached out for Ray and pulled him in by his sweater until he was pressed up against her. Her hand cupped his face until she brought her lips up to his once again.

With the elf's lips against his, Ray closed his eyes and let his hands travel over Tuva's body. He then felt Maja's hands caressing his chest until they snaked down to the front of his waist. There was no protest from him as he continued to kiss and fondle Tuva while Maja's hands worked with his belt and pants. He even wiggled a little after she had undone them, so that she could move them down to his ankles.

At first, Ray thought she was going to pull down his pants then his underwear, but the reindeer woman was far hungrier than he thought.

Maja gripped his waist band and yanked down both his pants and underwear all at once.

"I have an idea, Tuva," Maja said, pulling Ray from her embrace.

Ray opened his eyes and looked at her wondering what she had in mind.

"What is it, dear?" Tuva encouraged.

With his pants and underwear down around his ankles, Maja pulled him away from the desk and brought him over to one of the chairs to sit down. His bare butt made contact with the synthetic upholstery, but material's texture and temperature did nothing to stop his rock-hard cock from standing at full attention for its coming attention.

Maja then dropped on her knees, leaning over Ray's cock, and took it in her hand, kissing the head of it.

"Hey now," Tuva objected coming off the desk, and sitting down on the floor next to her lovers on the other side of Ray. She placed one hand over Maja's as it held Ray's cock and came in to kiss the side of his shaft.

"Oh, sweet fuck," Ray uttered, watching the two women kissing his cock.

"Isn't his cock more divine than any other you've ever gazed upon?" Maja asked holding the appendage for her elf lover while she kissed it and licked it like the most delectable hard candy she could find.

"Oh, Maja-dear, yes," Tuva breathed, drunk from her lust and desires.

"Such a perfect and beautiful cock. So thick and perfectly made. And the head is shaped just right. And it's delicious."

Without another word, Tuva opened her mouth and devoured Ray; her lips came down to the base. She held it there for a few moments before bobbing her head up and down. Inside her mouth, Ray could feel her tongue swirling around the head and the sides of his cock. The sensation made him flop his head back and let out a sweet groan of satisfaction. It was as if all the energy that he had left for the day would be released into her mouth, and he could fall into a deep sleep with a smile on his face.

Tuva's tongue stopped, her lips let go of his shaft and her mouth opened. Her head bobbed up and down on him rapidly, thrusting him farther into her mouth, and she emitted loud sounds of wet gagging as Ray felt his lower head hit the back of her throat. After a couple of moments, she couldn't take it anymore, and she pulled back her head, gagging and coughing.

Ray brought his head back up and leaned forward.

"Are you okay?" he asked, seeing some tears roll down her cheek from the gagging.

"Oh, I'm alright." Tuva smiled wiping away her tears and a little spit from her lips. "I just love to gag on your cock."

"That's not all she loves, is it, my voluptuous cocksucker?" Maja asked petting her red-haired head.

"Yes, my dear Maja," Tuva confirmed. While her finger came to her lips, her head downturned and her eyes looked up at Ray.

"Go on and tell our lover what you love," Maja encouraged. "Haven't you already told him *all* of your kinks and fetishes?"

"Well," Tuva began, getting to her feet and turning around, pushing her pants down until the waistband moved inch by teasing inch over her plump ass. "I love to be spanked."

The last of the material of her underwear and pants had moved over the climaxing curve of her buns until it came down to the top of her thigh.

Maja reached out a hand to squeeze her lover's cheek as if it were a plump fruit ready to be eaten. The sight and the softness of it made her lick her lips.

"Go ahead, Ray," Tuva begged. "Give your elf a good spank. Make my cheeks pink by your hand."

Ray extended a hand to her, cupped her buttocks, pulled it back and brought it down in a swift strike. The moment that the skin of his palm made contact sent out a crack that ricocheted throughout the small office. He pulled back his hand seeing the pink imprint of his hand on her milky and freckled skin.

"AH!" Tuva cried out. "Oh yes, Ray. *Harder!* Spank me *harder. Please.* Pretty *please.*"

Obliging the elf, Ray spanked her again, this time harder until it stung his palm and fingers and made the imprint grow to a darker red.

"AH!" Tuva cried out again as she climaxed but then sucked in her breath and let out a long exhale. "Oooooooh..."

Ray noticed the subtle move in her flesh just like the night at the hotel. The way her pale buttocks jiggled in the small storms of trembling.

Maja brought her hand underneath Tuva, cupped her pussy, and shoved a finger inside her.

"Maja...". Tuva uttered as her cheeks tightened.

"Mmmm," Maja hummed pulling out her finger from the elf and bringing it to her lips. "Someone's extra wet today."

"Maja!" Tuva squealed at a low volume showing how embarrassed she was with her whole body flushing in a light pink. "I wanted to say that!"

"Well, tell Ray more about what you love, hon," Maja goaded her lover, while her eyes glanced over at Ray, showing how much she wanted them both in her half-lidded glance along with her tongue licking her still wet finger.

"Hmmm, well," the elf began, placing a finger on her chin in an over-the-top expression of thinking, "I love...*food play*...not just the whipped cream we used, Ray."

Tuva turned around, and finished pushing off her pants, underwear, socks, and shoes off until she was bottomless.

"I want to bathe you," Tuva continued, reaching for the hem of her sweater she pulled it up and off her body, showing her majestic breasts barely contained by the bra that she was wearing. "After we shower, I want to bathe you in milk, drink the milk and dunk cookies in it. I want to lick the milk off your sweet body and perfect cock."

"What else?" Ray asked, feeling so close to his climax that he felt that one utterance from them would make his cock explode in a firework shower of sticky white cum.

"I also love having my ears played with," Tuva answered. "Like we did before. When I asked you to suck on them, nibble on the lobes, and breath into them. Oh gods, I *love* that."

Tuva went to unfasten her bra, but Ray said, "Here," and stood up with his hard cock, he took great care to keep his balance because of the constrictiveness the pants and underwear around his ankles. "Turn around."

Tuva obliged, and Ray's hands came up and without any effort he unhooked Tuva's bra. But as his hands worked the hooks of the under-garment, he leaned forward and brought his mouth to her ear. He began licking and sucking the length of her ear while his cock slid against her crevice.

"Mmmm," she moaned and then complemented, "It's rare thing that a man knows how to unhook a bra quickly in one deft motion."

She turned around displaying her endowments to her lovers.

"Thank you," Ray said, backing away and sitting down again, "But what else are you into?"

"I love dressing up for sex," Tuva said, walking over to straddle Ray's lap after helping Maja back up to her feet. "I especially love dressing up in catholic school uniforms and cheerleader uniforms. Oh, gods, that movie, *Debbie Does Dallas,* makes me so *fucking wet.*"

She was about to sit in his lap but Ray smirked and stopped her. He grabbed her hips and guided her closer.

The elf inched one leg closer on one side of Ray while she brought the other one forward on his other side.

"Would you happen to have such a uniform?" he asked.

"Maybe," Tuva answered bringing a coy finger to her lips.

Ray didn't respond as her belly and breasts were close enough for him to enjoy. He leaned forward and kissed her belly before his hands were drawn to her fantastic breasts. His fingers began to rub and pinch her nipples that were at the level of his eyes. They captured his attention for a few moments before he couldn't help but look up at her.

Tuva giggled, "Mmmm, it's like you're kissing my pregnant belly, Ray. It's so sweet and sexy at the same time. And I think I'm wet enough for you now."

Leaning back give the elf room to move, he smiled. "Bring that pussy down to this cock."

"Sweet Christmas," Maja whispered.

Ray looked over to Maja and found she was leaning against her desk with her legs open and rubbing herself.

"Dominate her, Ray," she begged. "Dominate her like you do to me. I want to see that elf pussy fucked by you."

Ray looked up at Tuva and smirked. Grabbing the base of his cock, he reached out for Tuva's hip with his other hand and brought her down on his lap. At first his cock slipped upward along her slit, sliding against her with his underside rubbing against her clit.

"I think you need some assistance, sweetie." Tuva giggled, reaching down and brushing Ray's hand away from his cock, while she maneuvered it towards her opening. "Ahhhh..."

Both his hands grabbed her hips, gripping her thick waist tight, and he yanked her downward onto his lap.

"AHHH!" Tuva cried out with her eyes shut tight as her breasts bounced into Ray's face.

He leaned forward and buried himself into the soft warmth of her breasts while his hips thrust upward into her.

"Yes, Ray!" Tuva cried with her arms wrapped around his head and shoulders as she bounced off his lap using her legs. "Give it to me. Give me more. My pussy is starving for your perfect cock. Split me open with your girth!"

"Tuva!" Ray grunted, while he pulled her down on him and bucked his hips upwards into the elf. He could feel the way her insides squeezed and enveloped him. It wouldn't be long until he was ready to burst. As the chair that he and Tuva were sitting in creaked and scrapped across the floor, Ray bit into the flesh inside his cheek as well as his tongue in order to stave off the coming orgasm.

But it was feeling too good to ignore.

The sensation in his cock and the sights of Tuva's body bouncing up and down with her exquisite and voluptuous breasts so close to his face. Then there was the sight off to the side of Maja leaning back on her desk, her hand at her pussy and rubbing it while her head rolled back and forth from one side to the other.

"Oh, fuck..." Ray moaned before burying his face into Tuva's breasts. His hands let go of her hips and brought them up to guide her nipple to his mouth. Once inside, he suckled on them before biting down on it.

"Ray!" Tuva cried out with her hands on his shoulders. "NNNNNN-MMMM!"

Her arms wrapped around his head before resting on the back of the chair while her hips continued to bounce and grind against him.

"Fuck me *harder*!" she begged, "I'm gonna *cum*!"

Ray let go of her breasts, he brought his hands to her hips once again and held on while his hips thrust upward harder and harder to the point that his legs were the ones doing the heavier parts of the thrusting.

It only took a few good hard thrusts before Tuva to go over the edge.

"I'm cumming," she cried, "Ray!"

She leaned forward, held his head against her, and grunted into the side of his neck while her thighs clenched on both sides of his body.

After one more thrust, he felt the pressure, his orgasm was coming, regardless of anything else. His fingers dug into the flesh of Tuva's hips, and his cock erupted, launching his cup deep inside her.

"Aaaaah…" he groaned, feeling the orgasm twist and contract within his cock, his balls and groin, but he was still hard and wanting more.

As Tuva was riding the wave of her own internal ecstasy, Ray looked over at Maja and saw her lying on her desk with her legs draped over the edge. She was coming close to her own climax as her legs lifted and then her thighs came together. Her body clenched while she emitted that same cry she did when Ray brought her to those same heights. Within a moment, her thighs came away from each other, her body unclenched, and she relaxed against the desk's surface while her hands began to run over her body.

"Oh, dear sweet *fucking* gods…" Tuva huffed. "I think my legs are trembling and my pussy is singing."

"Mine too," Maja said sitting up. "Watching you two perform such acts of intimacy is such a wonderous sight to behold. Especially you, Tuva, with your exquisite buttocks."

"And here I thought my breasts were my most exquisite feature," Tuva teased while bringing up her breasts to display. "Don't you think so, Ray?"

"I think you're both beautiful," Ray answered taking deep huffing breaths while he licked his chapped lips. "From head…to toe…inside…and out…"

"So sweet," Tuva moaned, leaning in to kiss Ray's cheek before she got herself up off his lap and moved herself over to the second chair of the office taking deep breaths.

"Oh, I think I'll need...a few days in bed after that." Tuva laughed fanning herself while trying to catch her breath from her loving exertion.

"Perhaps." Ray exhaled as his breath caught up to him. "Perhaps...we could make this a regular thing at your place? I have met all of you, right?"

"It's true," Maja observed. "I don't see why that would be a problem anymore. Do you, Tuva?"

"Only the fact that you kept this marvelous man all to yourself, Maja," Tuva stated, sounding like she was scolding her lover but being overtly humorous and sarcastic about it. "You naught, naughty, *naughty* dear. So *greedy* you are. Hmph!"

She crossed her arms, made a fake and over-the-top pout, and flicked her head away from Maja's gaze.

"Oh, I'm sorry, Tuva," Maja said, coming over to her elf lover and kissing her.

At first Tuva looked annoyed, but then it melted into a smile at her lover.

"Awww...you know I can never stay mad at you, Maja-dear." Tuva laughed as she wrapped her arms around her lover. "But you know it wasn't fair of you to keep Ray to yourself like you did."

"I know," Maja said, giving Tuva another kiss, she broke her embrace and sat at the edge of her desk looking at Ray. "But I have a feeling that Hedvig may want to have Ray in bed as well."

"You think so?" Ray asked but then laughed. "Seems to be a pattern here. I meet one of you and then we have sex then there's a date afterwards."

Tuva shrugged.

"It may seem incredulous," Maja agreed, "but don't expect that you're going to have sex automatically with Hedvig. Let her make her own choice about that."

"Well, yeah." Ray nodded. "I would never force any of you to do anything you don't want."

"But there is something I do want, hon," Maja said, turning towards the desk and leaning against it with her ass facing Ray. "I want to see how good your stamina is."

Ray said nothing. He only smiled getting up from his chair and taking the rest of his clothes off.

Chapter 10: A Cat's Favor

The day was far quieter than the previous ones had been, and it gave Ray and Maja the opportunity to organize and stock the shelves. Ray was in a section of the store that he found the least interesting: biographies. He was putting away a copy of the Steve Jobs biography when he turned around to find Maja stocking shelves as well, but Ray saw someone coming to the store over her shoulder.

Maja's gaze came up to his face and the direction of his gaze made her turn and they found Hedvig. The yule cat-woman was sauntering in through the entry way, and Ray couldn't help but notice the way that she moved. Her hips gave subtle motions from side to side like her white tail that flicked in similar directions and motions. She came up to them and hugged Maja before giving her a quick peck on her lips.

"What brings you by my store, hon?" Maja asked.

"Him, actually." Hedvig grinned towards Ray.

"What'd you have in mind?" Ray asked having a small expectation of what was to be asked.

"My store had a toy and clothing drive for the local good will," she explained, "and we managed to get quite a lot this year. I'd like some help delivering it. If you're available and would like to help that is."

"Sounds good. I'd like to get to know you better. When do you need to do that?" Ray asked.

"After your work closes. I know Maja needs all the help she can get."

"Oh yes," Maja agreed. "Before Ray, I had been managing this store on my own. So, with him here, it has been a real breath of fresh air for me."

Ray nodded but then asked Hedvig, "Do you have your own car? We can use mine, but I'll need to walk home to get it."

"Nah." Hedvig shook her head. "My car will be okay."

"Alright. I'll see you after closing."

"Thank you," Hedvig said once again waving to Ray in that finger flexing way as opposed to waving one's whole arm from side to side. And with that, she sauntered away showing how her hips swayed in the same motions as her tail.

"Don't let her wear you out too much, Ray," Maja warned.

"Why? Is there something I should know?"

"I'll leave that as a surprise." She winked.

***

Closing time was drawing nearer as was the favor for Hedvig.

Ray kept thinking about what Maja had told him about her. The idea of that something being a surprise. He started to wonder if the encounter was going to be like his time with Tuva as well as Maja. The thought of the three of them wanting him sexually. He couldn't help but think one sentence:

Merry Christmas to me indeed.

He knew that most men would dream to have such a scenario but in all practicality, he started to wonder how he would be able to balance three relationships so that he was fair to all the ladies in the group. After all, he had been with Maja the longest and slept with her the most. Then Tuva joined in, and she took every opportunity to jump in and fuck him.

So, if things are going to go in the same direction with Hedvig, he thought, *what then?*

"You seem quite deep in thought," Maja observed while performing the closing duties.

"I've just been thinking about us," Ray answered, knowing he couldn't, or rather wouldn't, keep anything from her. "I've just never been in a situation like this before."

"You mean being with more than one woman?"

"Yeah..."

"If it makes you feel better, this is new for the three of us as well," Maja said while closing the gate before coming up to the register to take out the tills. "With how close the three of us are, there have been times when each of us have taken on a partner outside of our trio, but this is the first time when all three of us have wanted the same person."

Hearing Maja say that did make him feel a little better. There was always a sense of comfort in the solidarity of confusion. It was like being back in the classroom and knowing that no one else in class understood the material as opposed to being the odd person out.

"So, you needn't feel confused about how to handle such a situation," she added in her comforting tone as she came up to him. She wrapped her arms around him and kissed his lips and then his cheek before squeezing him tight.

"Thanks, Maja. I'll see you tomorrow," Ray said breaking the embrace, picking up his coat and sketchbook before heading out.

"Enjoy your time with Hedvig," Maja called out, sounding like she knew a secret that only she and the others knew, and he was about to discover himself.

He walked over to the Gamer's Loot and there he found the store being closed up by Hedvig and Hul. The yule cat woman looked up and started smiling and waving towards Ray but held up one finger towards him telling him that she would be one minute.

It was one of the few things that Ray didn't like to do: waiting. It reminded him too much of his time in the city where traffic was so horrible that the best way for anyone to get around was to use public transportation. And to use that was to stand on a street corner looking like an idiot. Standing outside and waiting for Hedvig, he couldn't help but feel like he looked like an idiot, but he tried to remind himself that she was coming and made himself exercise patience.

After a couple of minutes of closing up the register, he watched both Hedvig and the goblin woman, Hul, coming out with totes of Christmas wrapped boxes and bags. Hedvig had the most to carry but the goblin woman was trying her hardest to carry the most but was at the verge of toppling. Though he couldn't help but keep looking back at Hedvig who was still wearing a loose necked ugly Christmas sweater and baggy pants.

"Thanks for waiting." Hedvig strained while holding and balancing the boxes in her arms. "Sorry to make you wait so long. Getting everything together made us a bit late closing up. I know I hate waiting on people."

"It's alright," Ray fibbed while coming up to Hul and taking some of the totes off her hands and Hedvig's as well.

"Thank you." Hul smiled.

Hedvig set down her remaining totes and locked up the store before picking them up again.

"Alright, everyone, this way," she said leading the way.

The trip from the Gamer's Loot to the mall entrance seemed longer to Ray thanks to carrying so much. Then it seemed a little longer with the cold winter air hitting them once the sliding doors opened for the trio.

"Ugh," the goblin woman moaned. "Why'd you have to park so far away."

"I didn't know that we'd get so much from the drive," Hedvig contended. "But my car is over there."

Ray looked through the dark landscape of snow and slush covered asphalt. Thanks to the illumination of the mall's lights and streetlights, Ray could see more easily towards Hedvig's car. Several spaces up he saw a red SUV whose headlights flashed. For a moment he thought it was a car that was about to pull out of the parking space, but Hedvig maneuvered towards it with its backend opening. Coming up to the self-opening trunk, she set in the totes, boxes, and bags of items while the goblin woman came up and held hers so Hedvig could put them into the truck. At last, Ray came up to her and allowed her to organize the boxes into the trunk like a moving crew setting a person's house and life of boxes into a truck.

"Thanks for your help," Hedvig said to the goblin woman.

"No problem. See you tomorrow." The goblin woman said before heading off and muttering to herself. "*Fuck* it's cold...cold as *fuck*."

Hedvig chuckled to herself. "Not wrong, it is cold as fuck."

"But doesn't seem to bother you," Ray observed that she showed no signs of discomfort or chill despite her choice of wardrobe. If Ray were to call it anything he would say that she was comfortable with it.

"Course it doesn't bug me." Hedvig shrugged, closing up the back. "But let's get these dropped off. I'm getting pretty horny."

The sentence made Ray freeze for a moment. It made him wish that reality had its own rewind feature to make sure if his ears were deceiving him. She said it with the same matter-of-fact casualness as if she wanted to get home to catch her favorite show.

I'm getting pretty horny? Ray thought, repeating the sentence in his mind.

"You coming?" Hedvig called out, stepping up to the driver's side.

"I am," Ray said, snapping himself out of his confusion and coming up to the passenger side.

Getting in, he couldn't help but take in the smell of the car's interior. There was a pleasantness to it. It took a couple of moments, but he realized that the smell of the car's interior was just like a store inside the mall called *Lush*. It was a store that sold body washes, bath bombs, and lotions. The odor of the store and Hedvig's car had that same sweet dusty type of aroma but one that Ray didn't mind and kind of liked luxuriating in.

Upon driving out of the mall parking lot, which took nearly ten minutes with the combination of traffic and people trying to get out of the lot as well, Hedvig drove to a place that was near the soup kitchen that Ray volunteered at with Tuva. The place was a thrift shop where people were doing shopping as well but also donating their hand-me-downs. Hedvig drove around to the front where there was a worker taking in the donations.

Upon getting out of the car the worker called out, "Hey, Hedvig!"

"Heya Bert," Hedvig called out. "We've got quite a haul for the toy and clothing drives."

"Good, the kids are going to love it and I see you got a helping set of hands."

"Sure do." She smiled and opened the back.

Ray got out and went to picking up the totes, wrapped packages, and bags for the charitable event. It didn't take long to clear out the back of the SUV but once it was done there was an exchange of paperwork and signatures between Hedvig and the man named Bert. Maybe it was because of the dark but Ray could have sworn that he saw a tail hanging out of the back of the man's pants. But the sight was too quick for him to really hone upon and besides there was something else on his mind about Hedvig that he wanted to know.

Getting back into the SUV, Hedvig began to drive off.

"Thanks for helping," she said.

"Hey, it's no problem," Ray shrugged and that was when he had to ask the question, "What'd you mean...um...about what you said earlier?"

"How'd you mean?" Hedvig asked turning out of the parking lot of the good will.

"You said you were feeling...um..."

"Horny?" Hedvig finished and then laughed.

"Yeah?" Ray asked wondering what was going to happen next.

"Well, I still am," Hedvig said coming to a stop light and turning to look at Ray. "Do you wanna fuck?"

"Um..."

"Holy fuck, you're *soooo* cute!" Hedvig cried out while cupping her cheeks. "Tuva and Maja were right about you, and now I want to see what you're like when you fuck."

"Wow..." Ray uttered.

"Too much?" Hedvig asked turning her attention back to the wheel and driving along, "I've been told that I'm too *crude* and too *upfront*. I just don't believe in bullshitting, know what I mean?"

"Nah, I'm okay with it, I'm just not used to it."

"So, what'd you say? You want some yule cat pussy?" She winked at him while her hand came down to her lap and began rubbing over her thigh. "If you're worried, I asked Tuva and Maja. They said it was okay."

The situation had truly become unfathomable to Ray. Not only had he managed to snag and bed two women in less than a month, but there was definitely to be a third. Knowing what he knew and looking at Hedvig from head to toe, how could he resist?

"Um...hell, yes," Ray answered. "But where?"

"Well, the house that Tuva, Maja, and I share might not be a good place right now, but I do have an idea."

"What's that?"

"Ever heard of the Kissing Wood?"

Ray gave a snort of a laugh.

Growing up in a small town, Ray knew that everyone had heard of that spot. But for him, the place held a different kind of memory for him, but he had to answer Hedvig's question.

"I've heard of it," Ray answered.

"Then...let's...a-go..." she cooed while her cat-like ears perked up. She reached for the dashboard controls and turned up the volume of the most apt song for the situation: 'Doin' it' by LL Cool J.

As the song played, Hedvig began moving and gyrating in her seat, but Ray was nervous because of where they were going but couldn't object.

***

The official name of the Kissing Wood was "Jensen's Grove". It was, more or less, a park, where there was a manmade lake and wooded paths and trees. Off to one side of its parking lot was a gravel road that led a few hundred yards around a bend to a gravel parking lot in the forest that surrounded the town. The gravel parking lot wasn't visible from the parking lot, and the police didn't check it.

It was a good thing that Hedvig's vehicle could handle the thick snow that had fallen. Despite that, there were a few moments of fear that the vehicle would get stuck when it came to a patch of snow and its tires spun. But Hedvig managed to drive it out. The additional good fortune was the fact that there was no one there.

Driving to the spot, Ray wondered where it was when he was last there. The thought was halted as Hedvig parked the vehicle, turned off the lights and reached over the center console, wrapped her arms around Ray's neck and pulled him in for a deep kiss. Her lips felt a little cold but there was the radiating warmth that was coming from within her that brought heat back into his face.

Pulling back, she whispered, "This way, boy toy."

Climbing over the driver's seat, she went to the back where the seats were in their down position. Ray watched as she moved with the ease of an actual cat. The way she made her ass jiggle from side to side was all too human.

He expected her to lie down and wait for him but what she did made him wonder how much of the encounter she planned. She lifted one of the seats, reached underneath it, pulled out a couple pillows and blankets, and laid them down as if they were camping.

There was a sheer lustful excitement in Ray at the sight.

Three women this month, Jesus Christ, I'm turning into a playboy, he thought at the same frantic pace as his heart.

But then he remembered where he was, and he started to wonder if history would repeat.

"You've been here before, huh?" Hedvig asked who was kneeling and waiting for her soon-to-be lover.

"How can-"

"I've seen that look in the mirror myself," Hedvig answered holding up her hand to stop him but then her hand beckoned him. "Come here, Ray, and tell me about it."

Ray unbuckled himself and climbed over his seat to join Hedvig in the back. Moving out of the way, she lay down and propped up her head on one hand. But Ray brought himself over to sit in a cross-legged position while his eyes adjusted to the dark of the Kissing Wood.

"If you don't want to talk about it, Ray, it okay," Hedvig encouraged while setting a hand on his knee. "And you don't have to feel pressured to fuck me."

"No, I-I-I...I *really* want to," Ray insisted.

"Your tent makes that point obvious," Hedvig added, bringing her hand from his knee and pointing to his groin.

Ray saw and felt how hard he was through his pants, and he decided to expose another vulnerable facet to his new lover.

"I came here when I was in high school," Ray began his tale. "It was actually my very first date, and it was the only time I've been to prom. Her name was...Sophia Merril..."

He still remembered the girl. At the time, he was a senior and she was a junior. The two of them had met in his graphic design class and connected over so many different subjects from art, music, movies, and anime. He saw how much they had similar tastes and it looked like there was the beginnings of a relationship between the two. To the point that it almost seemed like she was his first girlfriend.

The memory of her appearance was still fresh in her mind. She was much shorter than he was with dirty blonde hair that she often wore in a ponytail. Her pale green eyes were often behind a pair of black designer framed glasses. To his eyes, she was already pretty but it was the connection that he had with her that he had liked the most.

But then came prom.

"I had gone all out for that night, the tux, the dinner, and all of it," Ray continued, "but then she wanted to come here, and I was so damn nervous about it that I think it was a miracle that we didn't get into a car crash."

"What happened?" Hedvig asked coming closer to him and reaching out for his hand. "Rest assured I won't judge you, and I'll *still* want to fuck you."

"Okay," Ray nodded, and he took a breath and continued his story. "We came to this spot, and we mostly sat in the backseat with her keeping on inching her way to my side and...well...I was-"

"You were inexperienced?" Hedvig asked.

"Yeah," Ray answered, "I knew how to do it; I just didn't know how to start. And I didn't want to force her. When I didn't make the first move without her agreement, she still wouldn't say anything or start undressing. She got mad and asked me to take her home. We didn't speak to each other for a week after that. Even in class, she wouldn't look in my direction or even at me. It was a complete cold shoulder. I tried to talk to her, but she ignored me or walked away. And after that, this rumor started going around that I was gay or asexual. Not sure if she started that rumor, but I don't care. Thank God it was my last year of high school, and I would never have to face any of it again."

"*Fuck*, that sucks." Hedvig shook her head.

"I know," Ray said, hanging his head and looking at the floor feeling like history was going to repeat itself. "And I know discussing this must be a *real* mood killer."

"I think it's sweet," Hedvig countered.

"How?"

"Most men would have forced themselves on her, coerced her, guilted her, or something else. The fact that you did none of those things says a lot about your character."

"Even though I was a coward?"

"You're not a coward, Ray," Hedvig said, sitting up, and coming to him before she brought her lips to his. She pulled away just an inch and whispered, "You're very sweet and that...turns me on even more."

"It does?"

"Yeah...do you still wanna?"

For a moment, Ray felt like that teenager sitting in the car so scared for his first time but he wasn't that teenager anymore. He was a man. A man with experience.

"Yeah, I do," he whispered back to her.

"Then...*fuck me*, Ray," Hedvig pleaded. "Show me how you make Tuva and Maja smile."

He leaned in and started kissing her while his hand went underneath her loose sweater and came up to her breasts that were held within a cotton bra. Without any other indication, he slipped his hand underneath her bra and cupped her breast.

"Mmmm," she moaned against his mouth but pulled back. "If we're gonna get...*nekkid*...let's have a little heat."

She reached over to the front seat and the console beyond to turn on the heater. Coming back, she wrapped her arms around Ray and kissed him again.

Ray pulled back and whispered, "Take off your pants."

"Aww," Hedvig whispered. "I thought you were a titty-man given what Maja and Tuva told me."

"Well..." Ray smirked. "You want me to show you how I make them smile? Take off your pants, and I'll eat you out."

"Oooh, you wanna eat this pussy's pussy?" She teased while she moved onto her back and began to pull off her shoes and socks. Tossing them into the corner of the back, her hands came to the belt of her pants, and she began to pull it off. Ray reached up and helped them down to her knees, but he couldn't wait anymore. Once they were down to her ankles, he parted her thighs and brought his face to her pussy.

In the low light of the Kissing Wood and the car's console lights he could see that she had a small thatch of pubic hair which he could feel rub and brush against his face while his tongue made its way to her slit. He didn't mind how it brushed his face when the tip of his tongue made contact with the tiny pearl of sexual pleasure.

"Oh!" she yelped before her lips shut tight, and she began to moan.

Ray tried to readjust his position, but he couldn't get to a comfortable position where she would be sitting, and he would be lying on his stomach to eat her out.

"Here, let me," she said, pushing Ray away. "Lie on your back."

Ray followed her instruction and lay flat on his back and his head flush against the back of the front seats. His legs were butting up against the back door and so he lifted them up and laid his feet flat.

"And here I come," Hedvig said, laying one knee on one side of his head and lifting the other up and over his body until the other knee was on the other side of his head. With her legs in position, she straddled his face, and her slit was coming closer to his lips. "Go ahead, Ray. Show me how well you can eat pussy."

Ray said nothing. He wrapped his arms around Hedvig's thighs and shoved his lips against her labia lips while his nose buried itself in her small bed of pubic hair. Using his lips and tongue, he parted her lips and began to lap and lick at her until his lips wrapped around her clit. She began to press and rub her pussy harder against him. In between his lips, his tongue thrashed at her clit.

"Oh fuck!" Hedvig squealed, "AH! AH! AH!"

Her thighs squirmed in Ray's grip while her hips ground against his face. Looking up, he saw her curl her body forward with her hands gripping onto the front seats. There was a wish that there were more lights on so that he could see the look of orgasmic joy on her face. Yet he couldn't help but love the fact that she was bottomless while she still had her sweater on.

The moment he thought about her sweater she began to lean back... and back...and back until there was the threat that she would fall backward had it not been for the strong grip of Ray's arms around her thighs. In her supported laid-back position, she pulled off her sweater and tossed it aside and finally her bra. Yet she didn't take the time to unhook it; she gripped it and pulled it over her head before tossing it aside.

"OH fuck...fuck...fuck-fuck-fuck...fuck this feels so fucking good," Hedvig grunted while her hands came down to Ray's hair and her fingers locked into them and she pulled his head harder into her cunt. "Fuck, not even Tuva or Maja can eat pussy this good."

"Mmmmm," Ray hummed against her.

"YES!" she cried out. "Hum against my clit...*Please!...Oh fuck!*"

Ray hummed through his lips against her tiny pearl.

"RRRRROOOOOOOWWW!" Hedvig cried out while her thighs clenched at the side of Ray's head and a little liquid leaked over his face.

Inching his face away from her groin, Ray looked up at Hedvig and saw how labored her breaths were as she leaned forward holding onto the front seats while her breasts bounced with each gasp over his head.

"Oh…" she uttered through her parted panting lips, "fuck me…"

With that she leaned to one side and let herself go and made a soft collapse onto the laid out bed beside her new lover.

"Are you okay?" Ray asked wondering about what happened to her and concerned if it was too much.

"Oh…my god…" Hedvig uttered while licking her lips and taking long breaths in and out. "I have not cum like that in a long time. I think…I think…my pussy just fell in love with you."

"That good?"

"Oh, Jesus Fucking Christ, yeah," Hedvig proclaimed after taking another deep breath as she shivered and let out a long exhale.

Watching her as she lay on her back Ray could see how her tail twitched and her ears wagged before she made quick shakes of her head.

"Mmmmm," she moaned. "Now, I see why Maja and Tuva are so damn into you."

"I hope that's not the only reason."

"Well, yeah," Hedvig pointed out while she got up from her leaning position and leaned in to kiss his lips. She started giggling as she pulled back. "You smell like my pussy."

"Sorry," Ray giggled back while wiping his face of Hedvig's juices.

"Nah, I like it," she cooed coming closer. She first kissed his lips but then began to lick at the places where her juices were smeared. "If you didn't smell like my pussy, you'd have been doing something wrong."

"But you said you haven't climaxed like that in a long time, does Maja and Tuva....ummm..."

Hedvig smirked and shoved his shoulder. "Let's leave that for another time, lover. Right now, my pussy wants something hot and thick inside it. Here."

She made gentle shoves against Ray getting him sit up and move back so she could lie down and spread open her legs.

"Come inside," she said with a smirk and giggle.

Ray made quick work on his clothes as he eyed her wet pussy waiting for him. He fumbled with his pants, pushing them to his ankles, and pulled out his cock.

Hedvig moaned as she spread her lower ips and cupped her left breast. She looked at him with singular intent and shook her head. "No. I got undressed. You get undressed too, mister. It's only fair."

"Keep talking like that, kitten, and I'll have to spank you."

"Promise?" Hedvig asked teasing him while she licked her lips.

"Get on your hands and knees, and I'll show you."

"Oooh. They said you had a dominating streak in you."

She got up from her back and placed herself on her hands and knees with her buttocks and tail facing him. Her buttocks wiggled and her tail wagged while Ray made the awkward and concerted efforts to get his clothes off. First his jacket, then his sweater and shirt but his shoes and pants were the hardest. He didn't even mind the slight chilly nip that came over his skin. There was also the effort he made to look around to see if anyone was around to watch, but the windows were starting to steam from their breath.

"Ray," Hedvig moaned. "My pussy wants your cock."

His pants were around his ankles, his cock was at its most raging hardness, and he couldn't wait anymore. He had everything off and could only think about getting his cock in her pussy. He got behind her, grabbed her hip with one hand and pressed down on the middle of her back before thrust into her wet, waiting pussy.

"AHHHH!" she yelped while her body pushed forward between the two front until her shoulders caught on the seats. He hilted into her as she made a sharp and abrupt stop causing her to grown out, "Mmmnnnnngggggg! Fuuuuuuuckkk. Fuck me, your soooo......*thick*!"

"Am I hurting you?" Ray asked feeling petrified if he was.

"No!" Hedvig grunted. "I just need a moment to adjust. Mmmmmm. None of my toys are as thick as you."

Her hands held onto the seats padding while she pushed back, keeping her pussy flush against Ray's cock as he got her waist back in line with her knees.

She took a breath and let out a long low aroused exhale.

"I think my pussy is ready for more," she teased while she pulled herself forward and thrust herself back, slapping her ass against him to get him as deep as possible into her. "You like this pussy?"

"Mmmm," Ray moaned. "Your pussy feels incredible, Hedvig."

"Better than Tuva or Maja's?"

"Oh, now that's not fair," Ray said as he made one hard and forceful thrust forward.

"AHH!"

"All of you ladies have such wonderful pussies. But I think that deserves some spankings."

Ray reached up his hand and spanked Hedvig's buttocks, making her cheek jiggle as his hand left a pink outline.

"AI!" she screamed then sucked in air hard between her teeth, and her ears flattened against her head before letting out a loud moan while her body shivered and her tail twitched.

Ray reached his hand up and spanked her other cheek.

"AH!" she yelped again. "Fucking Christ...I think I'm in love..."

"Just you wait," Ray grinned while his hands gripped onto her waist and he began to make his hard repeating thrusts into her.

"AH! AH! AH!" Hedvig yelped out while her body rocked forward against the front seats and making the entire car rock back and forth. "Go ahead...and...ah...cum inside...cum in my pussy....AH! Fuck! Mmmmm m.....MEOOOOOWWWW!"

Her back arched as she screamed out her meowing orgasm and Ray in turn felt himself burst inside of her as he thrust deep into her. He held them locked together as they both spasmed, oblivious to everything else except the waves of pleasure. As the tsunami receded, he collapsed on her back, feeling her facing heartbeat and ragged breath as he made his slow recovery.

"Ahhhh..." he uttered his whisper of a moan while he pulled himself out and flopped onto the flat area next to Hedvig.

"Oh, Jesus...*ass-fucking*...*cum-shitting*...Christ..." Hedvig moaned while she pulled herself off her hands and knees and lay down next to her new lover. "I don't smoke but *fuck me* I could use a cigarette...or maybe a glass of wine."

"If that's the case," Ray said as he caught his breath and let out a weak laugh, "then I'll drive you home."

Hedvig let out a loud laugh while she rolled over onto her side and curled up next to Ray bringing one arm over his chest and one leg over his thigh. He wasn't entirely sure, but he thought he could feel something from her. A low vibrating. But then with the blood coming back into his head, he realized what she was doing. Hedvig was purring.

Moving his arm up, he brought it over to her head and began to scratch at her ears.

"Mmmm, that feels nice," Hedvig cooed, luxuriating in her lover's touch.

"You really think you fell in love with me just like that?" Ray asked wondering how serious she was a moment ago.

"Well, I know my pussy fell in love with your mouth and cock," she said bringing her hand down to his groin where he still had the condom on. "But as far as the rest of me, lover? That remains to be seen."

"And you're amazing as well, Hedvig," Ray uttered.

"Thank you. And I do want to do this again. But when we do, would you mind if I bring in a few things?"

"What'd you have in mind?"

"Hmmm," Hedvig mused, bringing a coy finger to her lips. "Are you familiar with shibari?"

"You mean with the rope? Yeah. But I don't know how to do it all."

"Don't worry, lover, I'll show you. Now how do you feel about collars and leashes?"

"I'm okay with those."

"Oh good. Now do you think you can help me with one thing?"

"Sure."

Hedvig rolled off onto her back and opened her legs.

"I wanna cum again," she pouted showing her eagerness, "but I want to feel your fingers in me to do it."

She reached out for his hand and brought it over to her wet womanhood. As his fingers brushed her pussy, so shivered as a wave of pleasure zapped through her.

"I'm loving your hands right now, Ray," she whispered. "Now...click my mouse."

Ray obliged, and he did it again...

and they fucked again...

and again, until neither one could anymore.

Chapter 11: A Gamer's Date

It had been a long time since Ray had stayed up that late at night. He wasn't sure what time he got home, but all he knew was the slight pain inside his balls, cock and deeper inside his male anatomy was thanks to Hedvig. Then there was additional soreness in his arms, legs, and a little in his lower back and buttocks.

But he didn't mind it at all, after all, he had felt the same soreness in the first few days of meeting Maja as well as with Tuva.

I'm surprised that I still have some stamina after all this, Ray remarked to himself.

Thinking about it more, it seemed like his own sexual stamina had risen several times since meeting the ladies. Before...with her...his own sex drive had shriveled in the months of living with her but with these ladies it's like it was a flower that had blossomed to greet the sun and warmth of spring.

Who'd have thought? he mused as he walked up to and into work at the Paper Playground.

Maja was the first to notice when he came up to the register.

"Oh hon," she said coming up to his side and brushing his check while her hand was one his shoulder. Her voice held such empathy and her eyes such concern. "You look like you didn't sleep an ounce last night. Did Hedvig wear you out?"

"She did actually," Ray answered with a weak smile and laugh before he yawned. "But I'm not complaining."

"Still, Hedvig should know better," Maja said shaking her head. "That girl just does not know how to hold back but please, details, Ray. I'd love to hear what you two got up to. Hedvig left early this morning, so I didn't get to hear the story from her."

"You're all alright with kissing and telling?" Ray asked feeling the fear freezing into his stomach and face.

"Oh yes," Maja assured him, "I'll probably pleasure myself thinking about it. As soon as there's a lull in shoppers, tell me everything."

Ray was thankful that there weren't very many customers, if any, or the fatigue he felt would have made him sluggish. A very familiar feeling of his earlier working days in college. But when there was a break and a calm in the midst of it all and no one in the store, he regaled Maja with the exploits that he and Hedvig got up to at the Kissing Wood. Though he left out the more embarrassing story that he told Hedvig. He didn't want to derail her enjoyment by sharing such an embarrassing detail of his life just yet.

"Oh my," Maja said with her eyebrows raised and a hand coming up to her reddening cheek. "It's no small wonder why you're so fatigued today, Ray. Sex in any vehicle is such a test of one's dexterity, flexibility, and focus."

"You're telling me."

But Maja then smiled and leaned close to whisper, "If it weren't for the fact of how tired you are, I'd pull you into the office to have you here and now."

The reindeer woman then gave Ray a small peck on his cheek while her hand made the surreptitious move below to cup his cock and balls through his pants.

"Hey now." Ray smiled in a whisper.

"I know," she whispered back while pulling away to attend to her station. "But now that you've been with Hedvig, are you planning on asking her out?"

"What?" Ray asked.

"Well, that's been the pattern I've noticed you've done with myself and Tuva. You meet us. We have *amazing* sex, and then we have a date and have even more amazing sex. Aren't you going to do the same for Hedvig? Because if you aren't, I think she'd be quite hurt."

"The thought did occur to me. And yes, I would like to ask Hedvig out, but it'll have to wait until I recover a little more plus I'm not sure what to do for our date."

"I would say that's a very wise move," Maja agreed.

"But you know there's something I wanted to ask you, Maja?" Ray began.

"What's that?" she asked leaning against the register while smiling at him.

"What made you open a bookstore here in the human world?" he asked but couldn't help but realize how stupid he sounded in referring to the world he had known all his life as 'the human world'.

Maja continued to smile and shrugged. "I suppose you could say that

I always admired this world and humans' capacity for imagination. Even when there's the attempt to write stories about my people. It's cute to see how it's done."

"Has anyone been accurate?"

Maja scrunched her nose and shook her head.

"Maybe someone should do something like that," Ray mentioned.

The moment the words came out of his mouth and hit his ears, the budding sprouts of an idea emerged.

"Ray?" Maja called to him, trying to bring his attention back to the conversation.

"Sorry," Ray said snapping himself out of his thought and took out his phone to write down the note. "I had an idea, and I don't want to lose it."

"What is it, hon?"

"Well," Ray began while typing out the idea into the phones note app. "I've always wanted to write my own graphic novel. Problem is that I never had an idea to work with. But I think I may have one."

Maja came over to him and placed an encouraging hand on his shoulder. "Do tell. What's the idea, hon?"

"When you mentioned how humans depict your people they never seem to do a good job of it," Ray explained. "What if I were to do such a book but make it seem like fiction?"

Maja took her hand away from Ray's shoulder and began to scratch her head near the base of one of her ears.

"I do believe, Mr. Adler," she said as she began to smile, "that you're onto something there."

"And I know I have plenty of inspiration." Ray smirked pulling out his sketchbook.

"Yes, you do. And I will let you use my bookstore to promote your book."

Ray smiled back and leaned in and kissed Maja on the lips. Once he did, a voice broke through to them.

"Awww," the voice called out.

The two lovers broke their kiss and looked to find Hedvig standing in front of the register. She was leaning forward and using both hands to cup her face while she smiled at the two of them. Her expression spoke of the pressurized sensations of cuteness overload in the yule cat woman.

Ray shook his head. "You really are a cat, Hedvig. I didn't even hear you."

"You sure it wasn't cause of Maja distracting you?" Hedvig teased.

Leaning into the teasing, Ray added, "Well, you *both* could *distract* me."

"And I thought you were recovering," Maja answered back as she leaned against him and kissed his neck.

"Hey now," Ray whispered with a smile.

"Hey!" Hedvig interrupted, "we can all do the orgy thing later. I wanna ask Ray something."

"Sure," Ray invited.

"Wanna go out?" Hedvig asked but then pointed to herself. "With me."

Ray couldn't help but raise his eyebrows and look at Maja before looking back at Hedvig whose expression had shifted from hopeful expectation to confusion.

"What?" she asked, her voice inching towards annoyance.

"I was just talking with Maja about that," Ray said shrugging. "She asked me if I was going to ask you out, since I did the same thing with her and Tuva."

"Hah!" Hedvig balked, throwing back her head. "Beat ya to it!."

"Now-now, Hedvig, this isn't a competition," Maja pointed out.

"I know. It's just too damn *funny*." Hedvig giggled before turning her attention back to Ray and asked, "What'd you say?"

"Sure," Ray smiled. "But I think it'll have to wait until this Saturday since I still need to recover."

The yule cat woman leaned forward letting the loose neck of her sweater hang low to the point that Ray, at a quick glance, could have a look down her shirt. His eyes naturally wandered that way, and it gave the confirmation that Hedvig wasn't wearing a bra. His gaze locked onto her swaying breasts as he stared and remembered the night before. Glancing up he caught the look in Hedvig's blue and gold eyes.

"The power of this kitty's pussy," she whispered, giving him a grin.

"There's no need to remind me, hon," Maja purred, leaning forward and giving Hedvig a sweet kiss on her lips. The reindeer woman pulled back and looked behind her roommate and lover. "Time to get to work."

"Okay, I'll let you two get to work." Hedvig smiled before she came around the register and wrapped her arms around Ray's neck. She kissed him before whispering, "And I'll see you this Saturday."

***

Saturday came around as quick as the other times that Ray had gone out with the other two ladies. Of course, after the first day of recovery, Tuva, and Hedvig couldn't help but come over to the Paper Playground and have lunch together. Though, what made Ray wonder was the fact that neither Maja nor Tuva mentioned wanting to have sex. The idea made him draw several conclusions. One of them was that they didn't want to hoard him to themselves before Hedvig's date. On the other hand, maybe they wanted him to recover enough for her.

As far as the time and place for the date, that came towards the end of his shift.

A buzz came over on his phone.

Ray looked.

HEDVIG: Hey, good looking. Hope you're ready for our date. It'll be at "The Mainframe". I'll meet you there after work.

"Is it Hedvig?" Maja asked.

"Yeah," Ray answered, relaying what he read on his text.

"Oh, she's taking you to one of her favorite spots," she said.

"What is the Mainframe?" Ray asked.

"Hmmm...how do I put this? The best way I can describe it is that it's an arcade, a bar, and a bowling alley in one building."

"Ah," Ray acknowledged. He had been to a few places like that when he was living in the city.

"Well then," Maja said leaning towards him and kissing his lips. "Have fun with her. I do hope that you have enough built up in you for her. That's why Tuva and I held back a lot this week. And I confess Ray...these past few days have been torture but Tuva and I promised Hedvig to not have you until your date."

Ray smiled but at the same time he couldn't help but feel like he was being freely passed around like a marijuana joint. Still, how could he complain when three women wanted him? After very little thought, he decided he really didn't mind at all. On the contrary, he thought he would enjoy this last a long time.

He grabbed his sketchbook and headed off for his date.

The Mainframe was a wide one-story building that made Ray think of a bowling alley. The only aspect of it that gave other indications to the contrary was the sign for the logo on the outside that spoke volumes of a cyberpunk theme. The font was blocky and the backlighting of it was green against the dark winter night and falling snow.

Parking his car, Ray looked around to try and see if Hedvig was parked anywhere nearby. Without any sign or clue to that, he decided to head inside and wait for her there. When he came inside, it was as if opening the door had transported him back to his adolescence. By stepping across the threshold, he had gone back to a time when schoolwork took a backseat to things like friends and fun. In Ray's case, it was the arcade.

The interior of "The Mainframe" was dark with highlights given by yellow and blue neon lights that ran around the edges of the ceiling. Populating the floor and the visible walls, were dozens of arcade machines that made various noises of game play. His eyes perused the various titles from the retro games like "Pac-Man" and "Mortal Kombat". There were even old school arcade games like ski-ball, pinball, and even a punching bag game and a basketball game.

Nothing like what he experienced in the city was like what he saw. The place was an oasis in a time when nobody would leave their own homes to play video games.

"Wow..." Ray uttered as his eyes marveled at the feast of a gamer's paradise.

"Amazing, isn't it?" a voice asked beside him.

"Yeah..." Ray uttered but then as his eyes went over to his right, he found someone standing to his immediate right. It was Hedvig.

The yule cat woman looked over at all the games before she looked back up at Ray with a great smile on her face as if the place was a surprise that she wanted to give to him. There was also the way that her tail shook and waved from one side to the other in a motion that Ray could only describe as excitement.

Just like all the other times before, she wore an ugly Christmas sweater, but the one that she wore spoke volumes of the level of geek and nerd culture that she was involved. It was green and several sizes too large for her and had writing in it that mimicked white knitted lettering that read: "Merry Christmas, you filthy hobbitses!" Beneath that she simply wore a pair of blue jeans, but she still didn't wear a coat like most would when it comes to winters in the town of Northview.

The sweater made Ray smile the most.

"You like?" Hedvig asked, pulling at the hem of the sweater showing off the writing more clearly.

"I'm thinking of getting one myself," Ray answered smiling.

"Good." Hedvig smiled, leaning in to kiss his cheek. Pulling back, she clapped her hands together and rubbed her palms before asking, "Alright, where would you like to start?"

"Since you picked the date," Ray began, "you have the first choice of game."

"Goodie!" Hedvig cried out before reaching for her pants pocket for her wallet. "But first, I'll need to reload my card."

"Ah, it's one of those places," Ray observed. He then realized that he didn't really see the latest and greatest of video games until he moved to the big city. In his youth, video game arcades took quarters or dollar bills, but then he was introduced to places where you loaded a game card and used that to play the games.

He watched Hedvig take hers out and load over fifty dollars onto it. Then Ray came up to the machine and loaded the same amount onto his. Just by loading the amount onto the card made him feel good that he had money again to spend on such fun. Not like before. Not like with...*her*.

Taking the gaming card, he followed Hedvig to a giant game display that had the bright red, sharp, battered, and sleek letters of a game he was familiar with: TEKKEN.

"Have you played?" Hedvig asked, coming up to one of the player controls.

"A long time ago," Ray admitted. "But I think I remember it."

He wanted to admit that he wasn't very good at it, but his embarrassment prevented him from admitting the truth.

"Alright." Hedvig smirked. "Let's get it on."

Ray chose his fighter and Hedvig was quick to choose hers. He saw them come onto the screen and the countdown had begun for the fight. There was a moment when he tried to remember the moves but the last time that he'd played the game was when he was a lot younger. It was against his brother, and his brother won...as always.

"ROUND 1! FIGHT!" the game proclaimed.

Without as much of a blink of an eye, Hedvig had moved her character in on Ray's and within a few taps of the buttons, his health bar had gone down by half, and he barely figured out which button was for punching or kicking. With no other recourse, he tried to get to a position where he could block his date's onslaughts. But even then, it was no use for she managed to cut in and get him down.

"K.O.!" the game proclaimed and round one went to Hedvig.

"It has been quite a while since you played this game, hasn't it?" she asked.

"Yeah, it has," Ray admitted, giving a flinch of a smile knowing that he knew nothing of the game.

And there was still one more round to play.

Guess I'll do button smash, Ray thought to himself as the next round was about to begin.

"ROUND 2! FIGHT!"

With that he began mashing the buttons making his character flail everywhere as if he were a man blindfolded in the dark swatting at whatever he thought was there. There were a couple blows that he landed against Hedvig's character, but she still managed to squeeze in her combo and within seconds his health bar went to zero.

"K.O.!" the game proclaimed.

"I take it that you didn't play this one very much?" Hedvig asked nudging her body against Ray's sounding playful and teasing him.

"Yeah," Ray confirmed. "This one wasn't really my thing. My brother always gave me a smack down. But if they have one particular game here, it might be more my speed."

"What's that?"

"Marvel vs Capcom 2," Ray answered.

"You're in luck!" Hedvig proclaimed, taking his hand and pulling him towards one section of the arcade until he began to hear some very familiar sound effects. And there it was, the cabinet for the game, Marvel vs. Capcom 2.

"Wow," Ray breathed looking at something that he thought was lost but had returned to him.

"I take it that you played this one a lot?"

"Yeah. When I was in college, we had this game in the student union building. I would often go down there to play it, when I was frustrated with studying...or anything else."

"I picked the last game," Hedvig offered. "Let's see what you can do with this one."

"You're on." Ray smiled.

Coming up to the game and placing his hands on the controls it had such a wonderful sensation of familiarity as if he had come back to a place that he was away from for far too long. He selected his heroes, Ryu, Hayato, and Jin.

"Interesting choices," Hedvig commented, while she made her choice of Storm, Sentinel, and Cable.

"ROUND 1! FIGHT!" the game proclaimed.

With the eerie familiarly of muscle memory, Ray went in for the attack and began to make one combo move after other until Hedvig's first character went down without so much as a scratch on his character.

"*Goddamn!*" Hedvig cried out, sounding shocked. "Where'd all that come from?"

"I spent a lot of time in the game rooms," Ray answered, still holding onto the controls and making his moves against Hedvig's characters.

"Let's make this game interesting," she said while she leaned towards him, and her hand came down to his thigh and inched its way towards his crotch.

"What'd you have in mind?"

"You're the Dom," Hedvig pointed out. "You set the terms...dominate me."

"If I win," Ray said, "we fuck."

"That's not a bet. I'm going to fuck you regardless. Come on, reach down, and pull out that Dom."

Her hand cupped his thickening cock and tightening balls through the exterior of his pants.

Ray wasn't sure where the idea came from, but he leaned in and whispered the idea into Hedvig's cat-like ear. He pulled back and watched as her ears twitched, her tail stiffened, and her mouth went open, but her eyes held an aroused astonishment. Her agape mouth then broke into a mischievous smile.

"You're on," Hedvig agreed. "But if you lose, I got something special in mind for you."

The moment she made the declaration she went to the controls and the next round was about to begin.

"ROUND 2! FIGHT!"

Ray made the same moves as before, but he noticed how much harder Hedvig was fighting against his combos.

"Come on, you sons of bitches," she growled at the screen while she leaned into the joystick and slammed down the buttons. "I'm gonna win, goddamnit!"

But it was no use, Ray had the opening, and he fought and took down her entire team.

"K.O.!" the game proclaimed as Ray won.

"HAH!" Hedvig laughed smiling and not showing any sign of hurt or defeat at her loss. She came up to Ray, wrapped her arms around his neck and brought herself up to his lips. Her kiss was as fast as it was hungry before she made a slow pull back of a small inch from his lips. "And now for your prize."

She broke away from him and walked away but not before turning to give him a wink and a smile before she made the playful move of sticking her tongue out at him and raising her middle finger at him. Following behind, Ray saw her heading towards the women's bathroom. He couldn't help but feel a wide crack of a smile breaking across his face while his heart was beating faster and faster knowing about the prize that was coming.

Unsure of how long Hedvig was going to take in the bathroom, he took a quick stroll through the arcade just to see what other games the place had. He saw that they had the arcade version of the Star Wars trilogy giving the player a chance to play through the original movies with shooting in various ships and battling with a lightsaber. Another game he hadn't seen for a long time.

He was about to sit down and play it when he heard Hedvig's voice.

"I have something else you'll wanna play with," she whispered.

Ray turned and saw the blushing smirk that she had like she had a secret that she wanted to tell but didn't want to tell at the same time. Her head was cocked to the side while her tail swished and flicked with her hands behind her back. Bringing her gaze back up to her lover, she brought her hands out from behind her back and placed them into his. From the held fingers of her fist, she released them as if she were letting go of some kind of precious cargo.

"Hope you like your prize." She smiled.

Ray looked down and saw a wadded bunch of red silky women's panties. He looked back to Hedvig who was still smiling at him.

"I don't normally wear stuff like that but for you, Ray. I wanted to wear something special."

"I think it'll make a nice memento of tonight," Ray said, while pocketing the prize.

"You're good at that game," Hedvig complemented. "Hope you're good at Dungeons and Dragons."

"I never played that," Ray said. "But I've always wanted to. I just never had found a group."

"I think I can help change that." She winked. "But hey, what'd you want to play next? Besides me."

"How about a few rounds of skeeball?" Ray asked.

"You're on," she agreed as she walked in front of him.

Ray couldn't help but let his own heart speed up in his chest as he thought about Hedvig not wearing any panties. The only barrier between her bare skin and the open air was the thin cloth of her pants and he knew that he was going to peel them off soon. Yet, the thought was shoved aside when they came up to the game and began to play. Round after round they played racking up points and laughing at each time that they won.

Then there was a moment when Ray was aiming for the 100-point hole. A prize that he often would aim for but never got. Yet, like so many others, he wanted to aim and try for it.

If we don't aim high then it is certain that we won't achieve it, he reasoned to himself and he pulled back his arm and let it fly.

He watched the ball roll down the lane, up the sharp hill, and it rose up into the air past 10-point hole, then the twenty, and then the thirty. The ball curved off to the left towards the 100-point hole. For a fraction of a fraction of the moment, Ray watched and couldn't help but think that it wasn't going to make it. But then the ball hit the lip of the ring and it fell in.

"Holy shit!" Hedvig cried out.

Ray was stunned that he made it, but he looked down at how many points that he racked up and knew that he was getting close to spending all the money that he put onto his game card. Turning himself around, he looked towards a corner of the arcade where there was a small section where one could get prizes from points.

"Thinking of a prize for yourself?" Hedvig asked breaking into Ray's concentration.

Ray turned to Hedvig and answered, "I was actually thinking of getting a prize for you."

"Awww, you don't have to."

"I was thinking maybe a plushie."

He wasn't sure why he chose that for a prize, but he saw one of the plushies hanging on the wall. It was a ball shaped thing that had ears on it like a cat and a face of a contented cat that looked like it was sleeping.

"Ray…" Hedvig said.

The tone that Ray heard from Hedvig made had sent tremors and waves of fear and anxiety all through his nervous system. Memories of all the times that a specific person had said his name in such a way went through his head, and how her saying that it was usually followed by disaster. Had he said something wrong? Was it the wrong choice? He turned and looked at Hedvig who was looking at him wide eyes and wide mouthed.

"You want to get *me* a plushie?"

"Um…yeah…" Ray uttered, still wondering if he made the right choice.

Hedvig's hands came up to her face, her eyes closed, her lips broke into a smile once again and her body began to sway from side to side like her tail. She then let out a small joyous squeal and then threw her arms around his neck before she kissed him.

"I think I just fell in love with you, Ray!" she cried, giving him quick rapid kisses all over his face, neck and then lips.

Ray wrapped her arms around Hedvig's waist and kissed her back. If asked he didn't know how long he held her but the moment it ended, he wanted it more.

He reached down for his gaming card and took Hedvig's hand, leading the way to the prize counter. There was the uncertainty that he didn't have enough points to get the prize that he wanted but as it turned out, he had accumulated just enough to get it. From among the rows and rows of plushies that were strung up on the wall, he pointed to the cat. He passed it on and out to Hedvig when the attendant got it down. The cat girl wrapped her arms tight around the plush creation and rubbed her face into it.

"Thank you," she cooed but then loosened her grip on it. "You know, I have a room that I got for us for tonight."

"Do you want to head there now?" Ray asked.

"After you gave me this," Hedvig said, resuming her tight embrace on the prize and rubbing her face into it. "I'm having thoughts of you taking me here on this counter."

Ray took her hand and laughed. "If that's all it took, good thing I didn't take you to a build-a-bear."

"You got that right." Hedvig giggled.

"Where's the room?"

"You know that hotel that Tuva took you to? It's there."

"Then let's go."

Chapter 12: The Claimed Prize

The two lovers were in the elevator and on their way to the room. The atmosphere was still and silent with only the hum of the elevator's machinery working in the background. Then there were the quick glances that the two exchanged before one of them had to break the silence.

"You're being awfully quiet," Hedvig teased.

"I guess I'm holding back," Ray admitted. "I mean, you're not...as much of an exhibitionist as Maja, are you?"

"Well, I'm not up for fucking in public...I mean except for when we were in my car, but that was different. But I'm not beyond you say...grabbing my ass in public. Just so you can say who this ass belongs to and..."

A small, strained laugh wheezed past Hedvig's lips as her hand came up to her face.

"What?" Ray asked.

"This is gonna sound very cheesy."

"Try me," Ray challenged crossing his arms and leaning against the elevator wall.

"This plushie isn't the only thing you won tonight, Ray...you won...oh gods...I can't believe I'm gonna say something like this."

Ray came up and wrapped one arm around her waist while his free hand came up to her face and turned her attention up towards him. Her blue and gold eyes locked with the vertical slits of pupils began to widen in her locked gaze.

"You can say it, Hedvig," he whispered. "There won't be any judgement on my part."

"You won my heart, Ray," she said before she brought the plushie up to her face to hide her expression. "Fuck...I never thought I'd say something so fuckin' cheesy in my life but it's true!"

"And is that such a bad thing?"

"Nah, I suppose not," Hedvig said, dropping her arms and the plushie away from her face. "But you don't think it's cheesy."

Underneath it all, Ray knew that she was going to say something along those lines when she mentioned how the plushie wasn't the only thing that he won that night. Yet, he wanted to hear Hedvig say it as opposed to guessing it. He leaned in close to the cat woman and kissed her again.

"I think it's the most beautiful thing I have heard this evening," he whispered to her.

Hedvig kissed him back, showing how much she wanted him in the aggressive hunger of her lips.

"Just wait, Ray," she whispered back.

DING!

The elevator stopped, and the doors opened.

Hedvig led the way down the hall to one of the many doors to which she pulled out the room key, opened it and invited Ray inside. Once he was inside, she went further into the room with her lover following behind. At the bed, he found Hedvig setting down the prize plushie on the table and she turned to Ray and beckoned him forward with a wave of her hand.

Ray obliged, and Hedvig wrapped her arms around his neck, but she didn't kiss him. Instead, her eyes locked with his and he got lost in the dual colors between one eye and the other.

"Ray," she begged. "Don't just fuck me or make love to me. I want you to be *rough*...I want you to be...*primal*...with me. *Tear* my clothes off, *scratch* your nails into my back, *bite* into my neck, shoulders, my tits, anywhere you want. Do what you want with me. But if it's too hard I'll say 'yellow', but I want you to keep going. If I want you to stop I'll say 'red'. Okay?"

"Yeah..." Ray uttered remembering the night in the back of her car.

"Now...fuck me you beautiful fucker..." she growled as if she was hungry and antsy in her sexual demand while her tail twitched and her ears fluttered.

Ray leaned in and kissed her again. He wanted to wrap his arms around her and fall onto the bed with his lover, but she wanted him in a different way. And he was very willing to oblige.

At first his hands caressed up the sleeves of her loose sweater up to her shoulders while his fingers danced across the skin of her neck. He then placed them on her shoulders and took a firm grip before he pulled back and turned her around with his palm against her back pushing her forward onto the bed.

Hedvig's torso landed on the bed with a bounce with her feet on the floor, and she let out a shivering from her lips.

"Yes!" she groaned wiggling her hips and tail at him. "Claim your prize."

Ray reached up under the hem of her sweater to find the waistband of her pants and he yanked them down past her ass in one hungry wrench. Once it was past her cheeks and in the light of the hotel suite he took notice of something he didn't see in the dark. Hedvig had tan lines. It was in a sharp v-shape across the cheeks of her buttocks from her sides down into her sweet crevice with her tanned skin was in contrast to milky white.

"Please," she begged, "be rough...mmmmm...*claim* this pussy!"

"Quiet, pussy. I'm unwrapping my fuck toy."

Ray took her by the shoulders and pulled her up and without further warning or any instruction, he pulled off the sweater over her head and tossed it aside. As for her bra, he didn't even try to unhook it, he pulled the undergarment up past her shoulders and over her head until her breasts and body were free of it before tossing it aside. With his prize bare to him, he pushed her against the mattress with her ass facing him.

He gazed at the tan lines and couldn't help but smirk knowing that he was going to leave such scratch marks across her. Reaching out, he brought his nails to the top of her back and made the long scratch downward towards her ass.

"Fuuuuuuuuuuuuucccck..." Hedvig moaned while her back arched, her ears went flat against her head while her tail shot upward and went rigid while the fur puffed outward. But then he saw something rather odd of her, her fists balled up the sheets and covers of the bed but then she relaxed and began to run her nails against the surface as if she were kneading them. Her head turned and she looked at Ray, "Don't stop. My pussy is wet already."

"I said, 'Quiet pussy'. Looks like my pussy didn't obey." He raised his hand and swatted her right ass cheek hard. "Bad pussy." He did the same to her left as she moaned and wiggled her buttocks.

He grabbed her tail with his left hand and pulled it taut as he gave her right cheek another swat.

"Fuck!" she cried out, arching her back more.

He slipped his right hand down her crack to her dripping pussy before shoving a couple of fingers into her as he pulled on her tail a little more.

"AHHHH!"

He felt her pussy clamp around his fingers as she gasped and jerked. Keeping his hand tight and firm on her tail, her spams continued causing her to arch farther back as she lifted her face to the ceiling.

"UHHH! FUCK!"

Ray released her tail. He unzipped his pants, pulling his rigid and leaking cock out. He didn't care about getting out of his pants as he kept playing with her pussy. Positioning himself behind Hedvig as he rubbed her clit hard, he had to lower himself just an inch because of her height. As soon as the head of his manhood found the lips of her womanhood, he slipped his hand out of the way and grabbed her hair so he could give it a tug as he thrust into her, slamming his hips against her ass.

"AHHH!" Hedvig cried out. While her upper body strained back towards him in a tighter arch, her waist was pushed against the edge of the bed, causing it to bump against the wall. As he got into a rhythm, he heard a low hum, and realized she was starting to purr as she caught her breath.

With her purring permission, Ray had an exquisite idea. He placed his fingernails up near the top of her back, pulled his cock back and thrust forward with his nails scratching down her back leaving behind parallel red lines against her skin.

"AH! Ah! Ah!" Hedvig cried out each time his cock made the deep contact within her pussy. He could tell she was building for another shattering climax, and he had an idea of how to tip her over the edge.

As he kept thrusting harder into her, he timed the release of her hair to grab her shoulders and bit her neck at the top of her back as he hilted into her.

She climaxed hard without a sound as she went rigid and her whole body clenched. He realized she was holding her breath as she struggled to keep thrusting. He had to move his hands to her hips to help thrust against her pressure.

After a few moments of spasming, she collapsed on the bed as her whole body relaxed, and he heard her loud exhale and gasp for air. He was still holding her hips, deep inside her, but stopped thrusting as she recovered.

Her face was buried into the mattress as she caught her ragged breath. She pulled back her head and grunted, "Sweet fucking *fuck*! I can't stop tingling, and my pussy is your cock's slave...I thought I was ready, but *damn*, you sent me into another dimension...still haven't gotten used to that shit..."

"Do you want to me to stop?" Ray asked.

Hedvig turned her head back towards him and locked eyes with him and smirked, "Did I say 'yellow' or 'red'?"

"No," Ray answered.

"Then it's green, fucking fuck me green! You better keep fucking me," she said as a couple of full body shivers shook her. "I don't care if I walk funny for days. I give you permission."

He grinned as he spread her legs farther apart and started thrusting again.

"MMMMMMMMMMMM!" she uttered while she let her body lay flat on the bed and she took a deep breath followed by another and another. "Fuck...I just keep climaxing..."

"Really?" Ray asked.

"Really, but don't stop fucking, I want you to fuck me until you cum too."

The way she said the letter r in the word Ray couldn't help but notice how the sound from her mouth gave the trill of the tongue rolling the letter.

Ray didn't say another word he pulled himself back and thrust forward, then again, and again, and again, in quick successive bursts of primal lust and passion with his fingers digging into the sides of her hips holding onto them.

Despite the quick thrusts again and again, Ray didn't feel like he was going to cum anytime soon and he was okay with that, he wanted Hedvig to have many more orgasms before either one of them would fall asleep. And he loved watching the way she writhed on the bed; the way her tail puffed, and her ears twitched while he rocked her body forward and backward and backward and forward.

But then came the sensation of being winded as if he were running a marathon while standing still. That was when Hedvig pushed back hard, pushing him away from the bed and freeing her legs. She pulled off him and turned around to sit on the edge of the bed. She sat up, clamped her hands around Ray's face and kissed him hard before pulling back and sinking her teeth into his neck.

"NNNN!" Ray winced feeling her teeth in him as he pulled farther away

Hedvig plopped back on the bed before crawling backwards to the head of the bed. She lay onto her back and spread open her legs.

"I've marked you as mine, and you've marked me. Your pussy needs more fucking," she begged while her hand went down between her legs, and she began to rub at her clitoris.

Ray threw off his jacket and pulled off his sweater and undershirts while his feet did the job of taking his shoes off. His eyes never left her as she kept playing with herself, causing more shivers to race through her. Then his hands came down to the waist-line of his pants and pulled them off along with his boxers. Stepping out, he brought his feet up to take his socks off before climbing up onto the bed and setting himself in front of Hedvig and smiling at her.

"Put it in me, *please*," she begged.

And Ray sunk his cock into her sweet depths. His hips went wild as his cock was reunited with Hedvig's pussy while his arms came up and wrapped underneath his lover and he gazed into her uniquely colored eyes.

"Bite...bite into...ah...my neck...*hard*," she huffed.

Ray craned his head downward and sunk his teeth into the side of her trying to be careful not to so much as to draw blood. Yet, he knew that he must have hit some sweet spot as he felt Hedvig's hand come up to the back of his head and gripped into his hair while the other one raked her nails across his back.

"FUUUUUUCK!" she yelled out and her fingers relaxed as she continued to huff. "Don't stop, Ray. I'm gonna cum. Please, for fucking fuck's sake, make me cum again, *please*. I'll be a good little pussy for you. You can do whatever you want to me! AHHHH!"

Her hands pressed hard against him, her thighs came up and squeezed the sides of his body while a tight exhale of air exited from her nostrils.

"Uggghhh..." she uttered while her body went limp, and Ray continued pumping in and out of her but taking slower strokes. The yule cat woman looked at her lover in disbelief "Oh my gods...you have some stamina."

Ray laughed. "And I'm almost there."

"When you're ready to cum..." she asked her expression turning sheepish and her eyes flicking off to one corner. "May I ask you do one thing?"

"Sure," Ray said keeping his stroking rhythm in place.

"Cum in my mouth," Hedvig begged. "Your pussy needs her special cream. I wanna taste it and swallow it."

Ray smiled. "Sure."

With that he began to speed up his rhythm.

"AH! AH! AH!" Hedvig yelped holding onto his shoulders. "Cum in my mouth! Please, Ray. Make me swallow your spunk! Feed your little pussy!"

Hearing her say that had triggered something in Ray's mind and his groin as he could feel the ticklish sensation inside him that said he was about to. He pulled himself out of Hedvig and rolled onto his back.

"I'm gonna cum!" he grunted, taking his cock in his hand and stroking up and down.

In an action that Ray could only call 'pouncing' she moved from lying on her back to crouching over his lower region with her mouth open just above his cock. When she saw she had a moment, she moved more, so she was able to keep eye contact with her lover.

"Go ahead and cum for me,," she said. "Cum for this pussy's pussy. Make her swallow your seed. Give me that sweet, salty, and creamy treat." She stuck out her tongue and gave the tip a light flick, licking up a bead of cum.

"Hnnnnnggg!" Ray grunted as he felt himself lose control and then he burst forth. Hedvig made the expert catch of his first shots into her mouth before she raised herself up to swallow while he kept shooting, unloading the spunk on his lower abdomen. As the peak of his orgasm washed past him, Ray looked down to see if he managed to fulfill Hedvig's request. Her face and mouth remained untouched by his milky essence, and she was smiling like she was savoring a delicious dessert, but then she did something unexpected.

Hedvig leaned down began to lick at the spilt semen as if it were milk. First her tongue and then her lips until her whole mouth made contact with his body and slurped it up into her mouth. Once it was all in, she leaned back onto her legs licking her lips and making an audible and gulping swallow.

"Mmmmm-mmmmm!" she uttered while her body shivered, and her tail waved. "So good. You have some very tasty spunk."

"Never thought I'd hear those words in my life." Ray laughed in disbelief.

"Mmmm, think you'd be up for kissing me again after I had your cum in my mouth?"

"Oh, come here," Ray said sitting up and bringing Hedvig up to his lips before kissing her. Unable to hold himself up, he leaned back and beckoned his lover to come to him. She lay on top of his chest and purring while her hand began to trace shapes into his skin. "I just hope that you don't mind that I got rough as well."

She sat up and looked at him. Her face turned from satiated to terror.

"What?" Ray asked.

"Oh, my gods, I didn't..." she began and came over to Ray's neck running her fingers across his neck. "I guess I bit into your real hard."

"It's okay," Ray reassured reaching out for her hand.

"No, it's not." She shook her head before she wagged her finger at him. "If I'm being too rough, you gotta tell me, okay?"

"Okay." Ray smiled, "Come here."

He took her hand and brought her back down to cuddle with him.

"Hey," Hedvig whispered while her hand traced her fingertips from his chest down his abdomen and to his groin where she teased his cock. "Think you'll have enough energy for some other play?"

"Sure," Ray answered.

Hedvig sat up and pulled herself off the bed. The moment that she stood up, her stance wobbled backward, and she reached out for the bed to steady herself.

"Fuck." She laughed. "You really fucked me good, Ray."

Ray sat up and said, "And you loved it?"

She turned around and winked at him. "Fuckin' right, you beautiful fuckin' fucker."

As she disappeared into another part of the suite, Ray sat up and readied himself for whatever Hedvig was going to bring to him. He wondered if it was going to be anything like what he and Tuva had experimented with. But if the ladies had taught him anything in the course of the weeks, he had been with all of them, it was not to have any expectations and allow them to surprise him.

Hedvig came back to the bed with a black bag that looked like a gym bag with its straps and zipper that ran along its length. Unzipping it, she reached in and pulled out what looked like a long set of light blue rope. Dipping back into the bag, Hedvig pulled out a collar that one would expect for a dog and a leash to go with it.

"Ah, rope for Shibari?" Ray asked.

"Like to try a rope tie on me?" Hedvig asked, sitting on the bed near her lover, "It's a pretty easy thing. I'll guide ya."

"How'd we start?"

"Here." Hedvig beckoned taking the rope off the bed and standing at the edge of the bed.

Ray got up from the bed and came to Hedvig who was unfurling the rope letting its length fall to her feet. It was unclear how much rope she had, and Ray didn't want to guess. He felt excited, but at the same time he couldn't get his eyes off Hedvig's body and the sharp tan lines she had. Especially the milky white triangles over her breasts with the rosy, pink nipples she had. He even took a little extra time to look down at the white tuft of well-trimmed pubic hair that she had.

"Before we begin," she said, holding the rope in one hand and going back into the bag and pulling a pair of medical style scissors. "For safety's sake just in case you need to cut the ropes. Here."

She set the scissors on the bed and her hands worked the rope again before she held it out to him.

"It's divided in half. Place that loop around my neck."

She gathered up her hair and lifted it up so that Ray had a clear area to work with. He followed her instruction and had the rope around her neck with the two leads coming down both shoulders to the piles at her feet.

"Now," she continued, "you're going to want to create a series of four knots down my front. First, here in the center of my chest."

She let go of her hair and pointed to a spot just below her collar bone.

"A good way to make the knot is to lay your hand against the rope before you make the knot," she explained. "Like this."

Taking his hand, she laid it so that his knuckles were against her, and she brought the rope up and wrapped it around his hand.

"Now make the knot."

Ray followed the instruction.

"Good. Next one is here right below my tits."

"God, I love it when you talk dirty." Ray smiled.

"So I've been told by the others." She winked. "Keep going."

Ray continued onto the next knot. Being so close to her chest, he couldn't help but stop when he finished the knot and gaze at her breasts. He leaned forward, opening his mouth and taking her nipple into his mouth before suckling on it.

"Ah..." Hedvig exhaled before bringing her hand up to cradle her lover's head. "I was told that you were a breast man."

Ray pulled back, stood up and smiled at the yule cat woman. "I am," he said unashamed of his preference.

"Most men are," Hedvig observed. "And some women. Me? I like the whole package. Like you. You're so fuckin' sexy from head to toe, inside and out."

Her hand came out and began to caress his face.

"Keep going," she encouraged.

Ray made the next two knots with the last one just below her navel.

"Very good," Hedvig complemented. "You're off to a good start. Now, take the rope lead it between my legs, up my back and into the loop at the back of my neck. Be sure to let my tail slip through the two ropes."

Hedvig spread open her legs so that Ray could slip the ropes past her vaginal lips and up the crevice up her buttocks. When it came to her tail at the top of her ass, he allowed the tail to sit in between the two ropes as he brought it up to the rope that ran across the back of her neck. He fed the leads through it and pulled it though.

"Good," Hedvig said. "Now you can pull it tight, but I'll let you know if it's too tight."

Ray followed the instructions and pulled on the ropes but still had the fear in him that he was doing it too hard. Yet, the moan that escaped from his lover's throat had given him the encouragement that he needed.

"Right there," she breathed almost sounding like she was extra horny and this was lighting her fire. "Mmmmm....so yummy..." she then cleared her throat and said, "Okay, here's what you do next. Separate the rope ends so that you have one lead on one side and one on the other. Bring them under my arms."

She held out her arms as Ray followed the instruction coming around to the front of her.

"Bring them above my...*itty-bitty-titties*," she emphasized as she wiggled her chest and giggled, "and fold them through the ropes in between the first two knots."

"Like this?" he asked, trying to push the ropes in between the twin ropes in between the knots. Once they were through, he looked at her sweet eyes of blue and gold.

"You're a natural at this, Ray," she whispered before leaning in and kissing his lips. She pulled back and said, "Now you pull on the ropes and you'll see a diamond form between the two knots."

"Wow," he uttered, seeing the knot work that he had done. "What's next?"

"Bring the ropes to the back and cross them and then bring them back around to the front under my tasty titties and make the same diamond that you did before."

Following the instruction, he came back around and did the same steps as before and saw how he had created another diamond of rope across the front of Hedvig's body. He couldn't help but marvel for a moment and grow aroused once again in the way the rope contrasted against the pale skin as well as the tanned skin.

He was at the last diamond just above her pubic mound and brought the leads to the small of her back above her tail that continued to swish, flick, and even tap against his working hands and arms.

"What'd I do with all this extra?" Ray asked seeing how there were several feet still remaining.

"Just tie them as if you're about to tie your shoe," Hedvig instructed. "That's called a tension knot. It's one that is comfortable but is still some-what secure. Then just loop the ropes up the center going up and then back down and when you have just a little bit left, tie it in a neat bow."

Ray followed the instructions and began to weave the rope along the middle vertical part of the rope ties as if his hand were part of a sewing machine making the stitches. Until at last the rope came back down just above her tail, and he tied it as if he were tying his shoe in a neat bow.

Once Ray was finished, he took a couple steps back to fully admire the first set of shibari rope work that he had done. The way the diamonds spread across her chest and belly. He especially loved the way that the diamond spread outward at the top of her belly in symmetrical precision on either side of her navel before coming back down to the knot above her pubic region.

"Wow," he uttered once again in disbelief that such a simple set of instructions would yield something so beautiful, intricate, and erotic.

"Let's see how it turned out," Hedvig said with excitement as she bounded off to the bathroom to look at herself.

Ray followed behind and waited to hear her verdict on his first attempt. He wasn't sure how much of an expert she was at the art, but he trusted her opinion over his own judgement.

"Hmmmm," Hedvig hummed with eyebrows raised and her head nodding. "You did quite well for a first timer. I think I'll teach you some more about the art. Maybe one day we'll do a suspension."

"And you look amazingly sexy in it," Ray said, looking her over It was hot and he took in the exquisite sight. As he appreciated the understating of the fetish, might be the start of it become one of his own.

Hedvig turned to face her lover. "And I got a couple more things for ya."

She made her way out of the bathroom and past Ray who followed behind to see her take up the collar and leash that she had laid out earlier. He watched as she unhooked the leash from the collar and brought it up in her hands and presented it to Ray as if it were and offering to an old-world god.

"Please," she asked, "could ya put this on me? Your pussy needs her collar."

Ray didn't say anything. He came over and took the simple piece from her hands. The moment that he did, she came down onto her knees, reached up for her long white hair and held it up for him once again. Bending down to her, he placed the collar around her neck and locked it in place for her.

With the collar on, Hedvig bowed her head, she then reached out for the leash and held it out for him.

"Please...sir..." she said almost sounding like she was whimpering and aroused at the same time. "Place this lead on me."

He took the leash and clasped it onto the ring just below Hedvig's chin. When he held the lead of the leash, he couldn't help but feel a sensation of power over her.

"What does sir want to do with me?" she asked sounding demure but still carrying an aroma of arousal to her tone.

"Get on your hands and knees," Ray said sounding dominating like how he was with Maja and Tuva. "And crawl for me, as I walk you around the suite."

"Yes, sir." Hedvig complied as she got on her hands and knees, and she began to crawl with Ray leading the way. He allowed her to get a little bit ahead so that he could watch the way her ass moved with each step and the motion of her tail. Tugging on the collar he made her stop, before he got down on one knee and cupped her buttocks.

"Mmmmm," she moaned.

Wanting more, he brought his hand to the lips of her pussy that were held together by the twin ropes, and he slipped a finger up it. Looking at how slick his finger was he observed, "So wet, are we?"

"Yes, sir," she admitted.

Her body was shaking with excitement.

"What does sir want me to do?" she asked.

"Meow for me," Ray ordered.

Hedvig's head turned and looked at him. Her eyes were wide and staring at him. Even her slitted pupils went as wide as pennies. At first there was fear in Ray's heart at what her reaction was but then he saw the smile break across her face.

"M-m-m-m-m..." she stammered, "Meow!"

"Very good." Ray smiled, leaning forward, patting her white-haired head, and noticing how her ears moved against and away from his hand. He couldn't help but even bring a hand behind one of them and scratch it.

"Yes!" she moaned, "Oh my gods...mmmm...sir...I wanna cum again...please...I'll be your best little pussy."

"Then get on the bed, lay on your back and spread your legs," Ray said, "but you won't have my cock. You are going to get eaten out."

"Yes, sir," she acknowledged and bounded from where she was on her hands and knees to the bed. Ray let go of the leash so she could follow her instruction. She set her buttocks close to the edge of the bed while her hands came up under her thighs and spread them open while her tail snaked between the cheeks of her buttocks and waved back and forth.

The blue rope ran against the slit of her womanhood blocking Ray's access to it. He smiled knowing that the rope wasn't going to stop him. He got down onto his knees, set one hand on her pussy and pulled apart the twin ropes along with her lips of her lower half. In the light of the hotel room, he could see how pink and full she was and how wet she had become. Leaning down he took in the aroma of her sex and couldn't hold back anymore as he pushed his face into her and ate at her.

"NNNNNNN!" Hedvig yelped, thrashing her head back against the mattress. "Ffffffuuuuuuuuck...aaaaaahhh...fuck...oh my gods...yes...eat my pussy...aaaahhhhh..."

Ray ran his tongue up and down her slit before coming back to her clitoris and ran the tip around its tiny circumference. It was several rotations and hearing Hedvig moan more and more before he retracted his tongue and wrapped his lips around the organ and sucked on it.

"Ooooooo..." she moaned with her hands coming down into his hair and her thighs clenched at the sides of his head. "Ray...I'm..."

He heard her take a deep breath with her body clenching before she let out a low moan while her body relaxed, and her hands let go of Ray's hair. Pulling back from her pussy he could feel how damp and slick his face was from her orgasm. He reached up to wipe it away but then the look of Hedvig caught his attention.

Her thighs came up and were rubbing against each other while her arms were up and behind her head. With closed eyes she shook her head from side to side while she had a grand smile stretching across her face.

Ray could only smile as he climbed onto the bed and took the yule cat woman in his arms and kissed her.

"I hope that's not all we're going to be doing this evening," she whispered.

"What'd you have in mind?" Ray asked.

"I heard that you've drawn some very lewd art of Tuva and Maja," Hedvig said, while she brought her finger up and wagged it at Ray. "Now, you can have the complete set."

Without any other encouragement, Ray took out his sketchbook and drew Hedvig like he did with Tuva and Maja and the night continued with various types and positions of sex until sleep finally called for them to stop.

Chapter 13: A Group Discussion

It was the first day off in quite a while and Christmas was a week away. As Ray was lying awake in his bed, he tried to think over how long it had been since he encountered the three women who became his lovers.

"Going on three weeks now," he concluded upon doing the math in his head. "Who'd have thought? I lost everything and then I gained a lot more."

He had to admit to himself that it was a good thing that he had that Sunday to himself. The day of rest was needed as his legs and back were starting to ache from standing so much in spite of the stool that Maja allowed him to have. Then there was the fact that he needed to recharge other parts of himself as well. Both his cock and his balls felt sore from the excessive orgasms. Not since his adolescence had he had so many back-to-back climaxes.

Really am living a dream, Ray thought to himself.

He pulled the covers over himself snuggling in for a little longer, but then there was a familiar sound of his phone vibrating on his nightstand. Pulling the device up, Ray looked at the clock and saw that it was past ten o'clock in the morning but then he looked at the text.

MAJA: Good morning, sweetie. Would you mind if we talked?

Ray felt immediate apprehension. The sentence recalled all the various times that his ex-fiancé would say something similar. Then came the most uncomfortable of situations in which he felt like a child being scolded or as if he were being sent to the principal's office. What could Maja want to talk about that she needed to text him at ten in the morning? Was it something serious? Did he do something wrong? Was she breaking up with him? His mind's wheels spun its anxiety into the sand until either it would bury itself deeper or it would run out of gas.

RAY: Sure, what'd you want to talk about?

MAJA: I think it's time you came to our place.

RAY: Sure, what's the address?

Maja sent him the address and he let her know that he was getting dressed and cleaned up.

While in the shower, he couldn't help but think to the point of over-thinking and overanalyzing.

What does Maja want to talk to me about? He pondered as he sped up his pace of cleaning himself.

She didn't mention that it was something about them so there was that. And he was certain that she didn't want to break up with him because as he ruminated over the times he had with Maja, everything seemed to be good beyond all he could think of. There was no indication to suggest otherwise. If she did want to break up with him she would have taken the route that he had seen so many others take; break up over text or phone call or even email. Yet Maja wanted to talk to him face to face at the place that she shared with Tuva and Hedvig

It'll be my first time there, he thought upon finishing cleaning himself up and getting dressed.

He came down to the main floor and was greeted by the smells of breakfast being made along with the sounds of his mother working in the kitchen.

"Morning, Ray," his mother called out from the kitchen, "Are you working again today?"

"Not today, Mom," Ray answered. "I'm meeting with someone."

"New girlfriend?" she asked.

Ray could only smile. "You could say that."

"Don't stay out too late," she said. "But if you do, let us know, like last time."

"I will," Ray answered thankful that his father must have still been in bed watching his "news" and distracting him from his daily belittlement of his son.

Please, let this news be good, he thought as he headed out the door.

Coming outside to the car he followed the address to Maja's place. Getting there, road by road, he knew that the places were getting progressively more upscale. Every town and city had nicer areas and less nice areas. All one had to do was look at the houses and see how much more expensive they got. It was in the richer parts of the town where there were houses that probably had between four bedrooms or more and could only be afforded by the rich and wealthy along with their friends.

Maja's house was on a corner and Ray couldn't help but come to a stop and marvel at how big and luxurious it was. If he had to take a guess at it, it must have been three, maybe four, times bigger than his parents' place. The house was already decorated for the season with multitudes of Christmas lights at the edges, as well as on the trees and bushes in the front yard. More than the lights, there were the characters of Santa, his reindeer, elves, as well as snowmen.

This must be quite the sight at night, Ray thought parking his car at the curb.

After parking his car, he pushed his way through the snow and the cold, he looked at the number as well as the sign for the street at the corner. In some small way, he was wondering if he was at the right place because how could the three of them afford such a place in such times?

Only one way to find out, he concluded with a shrug.

He reached out for the doorbell and after less than a minute, the door opened, and there was Maja who smiled as if she had received the greatest news or present in her life. Coming out of the door she wrapped her arms around Ray's neck and kissed his lips. It must have been several seconds before she pulled back and nuzzled against him.

"Hey there," Ray said, hugging her waist and kissing her near her ear.

She pulled back looked him in the face with her signature sweet smile. "Welcome to our place."

After letting go, she stepped aside and held out an inviting hand to her lover.

"This is an amazing house," Ray observed while coming inside and taking off his coat.

"I think we made a good choice. But I'm certain you want to know why I-um...I mean *we*, invited you here today," Maja explained closing the door behind them.

"Right, because your roommates are Tuva and Hedvig," Ray reiterated.

"That's right," she said moving from the front door past a grand staircase to a grand kitchen where Tuva was busy making breakfast. Hedvig was sitting at the small bar that separated the kitchen from the breakfast nook and living room. The yule cat woman's ears turned towards him like a pair of radar dishes until they stopped, and she turned her head towards him.

"And here he is." Hedvig smiled getting off the barstool and coming up to her lover. She threw her loose sleeve encased arms around his neck, kissing his lips, and lifting herself off the ground into his arms.

"Hey there," Tuva called out, protesting Hedvig's action.

Hedvig pulled back and gave Ray another small peck on his lips. Turning her head towards the elf she said, "Couldn't resist him, am I right everyone?"

"Yes, yes." Tuva smiled coming out of the kitchen and cutting in between the yule cat woman and Ray. She cupped his face and gave him a very sweet loving kiss before turning back and heading back into the kitchen.

"What's all this about, everyone?" Ray asked.

"First, let's plate our breakfast, hon," Maja suggested. "Come."

She directed him over to the breakfast nook where there were already glasses of orange juice set out. Upon sitting down, Tuva was already plating the breakfast and bringing it over. He saw that she had made French toast with bacon and brought out a small bottle of maple syrup.

Everyone sat down and was about to eat. While Tuva and Hedvig began,

Maja was looking at Ray with a smile.

"The reason why we asked you here this morning," she began, "is because I felt that it was time for you to see our home. The three of us also wanted to discuss something with you."

"Okay," Ray said, trying to keep calm but feeling the rumblings and bubbling of anxiety with him as it were a dormant volcano that was about to erupt again.

"As of this moment," Maja continued, "you've been with all three of us in various sexual ways."

"Damn right," Hedvig said swallowing a mouthful of French toast. "Holy fuck Ray's got an amazing cock."

"Oh, don't forget his tongue too," Tuva added.

Hedvig nodded while looking at Ray and remembering what they had gotten up to on their date.

"And there's one added part to all of that," Maja pointed out to her lovers and roommates, "Ray's heart."

The elf and the yule cat woman agreed with a nod while they continued to eat.

Maja turned her attention back to Ray, "And as you've seen and been told, Ray, the three of us are already in a relationship with each other. What humans would call *polyamory* or a *polycue,* and we want *you* to join our relationship. Before now you've been our lover. Now we want you to officially become our boyfriend."

Ray didn't say anything. He looked at the faces of the women whom he had fucked in the past couple of weeks and shared some private details about himself. His eyes sunk down towards the French toast that he was certain were growing cold.

"Are you okay, sweetie?" Tuva asked, sounding as concerned as a truly loving and caring mother.

Ray cleared his throat. "I'm okay it's just-"

"Told you two it was too fast to spring this on him," Hedvig interrupted.

"Hedvig!" Maja snapped.

"No-no, it's okay," Ray assured while raising his hand. "Hedvig is right. It's a lot for me to take in. Only a few months ago, I had lost so much. My home, my job, and a woman I thought loved me. And now, in the span of a month, I not only got a job that I actually like in a place that I like. But I have three women that actually want me and are okay sharing with me with the others."

"Sounds like a really good porno, huh?" Hedvig asked with a smirk while munching on bacon.

Tuva giggled.

"It does," Ray agreed with a smile.

"So, are you saying 'no'?" Maja asked, her own anxiety and fear coming to the surface of her voice.

"No, not at all," Ray shook his head. "I'm just processing everything I'm hearing because...this is...it's a dream come true really. So, yeah, I'd love to be your boyfriend. And yours, Tuva. And yours, Hedvig."

"Oh, thank you, Ray." Hedvig smiled, sounding like she was about to let out tears of joy when she got up from her chair and went over to hug and kiss her new boyfriend.

"And you didn't ask him the better part," Tuva added.

"What's that?" Ray asked.

"We want you to move in with us," Hedvig answered, letting go of him and sitting back down.

"What?" Ray asked, wondering and hoping if he heard what he heard correctly.

"Yes." Tuva smiled. "We'd like you to move in with us."

"I'll pack my stuff," Ray answered without hesitation. "But do I get my own room or am I sharing a room...and a bed?"

"Let's have breakfast first, sweetie. Then we'll show you," Tuva suggested.

Ray didn't say another word. He reached for the slender bottle of maple syrup and poured it over the French toast and dug into it. The moment the piece of syrup and egg coated bread touched his lips and tongue he had to stop. Never before had he tasted the kind of French toast and syrup like he had in his mouth. Not even his mother's home cooking was that good.

"Oh my god," Ray mumbled through his full mouth.

"Gotta love *real* maple syrup." Hedvig shrugged.

Ray swallowed. "Really?"

"Why yes," Tuva answered, "This maple syrup is harvested from trees back from our home realm of Alfheimr."

"Really? Who else lives in Alfheimr?" Ray asked before digging into the rest of the food.

Maja answered. "All kinds of fae people from elves, cat people, reindeer people, goblins, gnomes, pixies, fairies, and other peoples that you humans probably never even heard of."

"And you all choose to live here?" Ray wondered aloud to them.

"Sure did," Hedvig said, finishing up her French toast.

"The human realm is just so interesting," Tuva agreed.

"And what's more, we got to meet you Ray," Maja added.

Ray had to smile at that sentiment. It made him think that perhaps all that he suffered through was worth something if he managed to have so much on the other side of it all. In eating breakfast there was a moment where he gave thanks to whoever or whatever had brought him to this path.

"But can I ask you all something?" he began.

"Sure, Ray," Hedvig premised.

"Why'd you all choose to do what you do? I mean, a bookstore, a candy shop and a game store?"

"Well, you know my reason, Ray," Maja began. "I've always admired humans for their capacity to imagine. There's also my love for books and I want to share that with others."

"The same goes for me," Tuva added. "I love sweet things and food in general. There are things here in the human realm that we can't get in Alfherimr and it always warms me to see the look on people's faces when they taste my creations."

"What about you, Hedvig?" Ray asked. "Why a game shop?"

"Games are fun." Hedvig shrugged. "Nothing complicated about that. The games here among humans are the most fun. And I like games and fun."

"Let's not forget sex," Maja added while bringing another forkful of breakfast to her lips.

"You bet your sweet fucking ass." Hedvig smirked, giving an alluring wiggle of her body at the reindeer woman.

Upon taking the last bite of his breakfast, Ray got up and gathered his plate. But before he could make one step away from his chair, he was stopped.

"What're you doing?" Tuva asked Ray, sounding confused as if he uttered a word she never heard before in her life.

"I'm taking my plate to the kitchen," Ray answered, feeling confused as to why someone who ask him such a question for his action.

Tuva laughed. "Gods bless you, sweet Ray. I'll take care of that. Leave it."

Hedvig pointed her fork towards the elf. "She is very controlling in the kitchen."

"I recall." Ray chuckled looking towards Tuva and remembering the first night that he and Tuva fucked. She in turn smiled, giving him a slight wink.

Ray set his plate back on the table.

"But it is sweet to see a man who knows how to clean up after himself," Tuva added.

"Thanks, Tuva." Ray smiled before he turned to Maja who was standing and waiting for him.

"Allow me show you around the place," Maja offered, leading the way.

From the kitchen and breakfast nook she showed him the living room, and then to the formal dining room where there was a round table with six chairs set around it. Then there was the backyard where the snow had laid a fresh white blanket over the landscape. Maja then took him up the grand staircase to the second floor. The first room she showed had a queen-sized bed with several bookcases around the room and posters of famous books.

"Here's my room," she said as she stepped to the side and presented the room with a wave of her arm.

"I like your taste," Ray complemented.

"Thanks, but I think you'll love the master bedroom much more," she predicted.

There were a couple other rooms that were empty or filled with taped up boxes. Then was also a room that was bare and had a treadmill in it.

"My exercise room," Maja explained. "I try to keep myself fit for running as you've seen."

"And am imagining," Ray flirted.

"Oh, stop imagining me naked. We'll get to that soon enough. Now those two rooms over there are Hedvig's and Tuva's."

She pointed to two doors that were closed before pointing to a room at the end of the hallway.

"And here's the master bedroom," she presented.

Compared to the other rooms, it was the biggest room of the second floor, but one feature that stood out the most to Ray was the bed. It was far wider than any bed he had ever seen in his life. It looked wide enough for four people to sleep comfortably in without disturbing each other. Opposite of it was a low and wide black dresser with a wide flatscreen sitting on top of it.

"And here," she said, bringing Ray over to the master bathroom where there was a separate tub and shower along with his and hers sinks.

"I like this bedroom already," Ray said, moving deeper into the bathroom leaving Maja behind, "but which room should be mine if I'm moving in?"

He asked his question as he looked over the tub that seemed to be big enough to be a hot tub. The other aspect that gave it the appearance of it were the small, jetted spouts along the bottom of the tub. Ray's mind began to think of spending nights luxuriating in it as he heard Maja's voice.

"You could use one of the other bedrooms that aren't being used," she answered, "but most of us sleep in here and...*fuck* in here."

Ray turned and came back into the bedroom to find Maja sitting on the edge of the bed without a single article of clothing on her body. Seeing him, she rolled over onto her stomach and got onto her hands and knees shaking her ass and wiggling her tail at her lover.

"Mmmmm." Ray smiled, enjoying the sight while he came closer and couldn't help but reach out and tug at Maja's shoulder. He rolled her over onto her back and leaned in to kiss her.

Maja's hands traveled over Ray's body from his shoulders, down his arms, over to his back before coming back up to his face and running through his hair. She brought her hands down from his hair to his face to caress his cheeks.

"I think you've been away from me a little too much," Maja whispered.

"How long has it been since we've...." Ray paused wondering the best way to describe what he did. On one hand he wanted to call it 'fucking', but with the recent development should it be called 'making love'?

"Make love to me," Maja begged, looking into Ray's eyes with hunger in them and a smile on her lips. "And *fuck* me."

Ray didn't say another word. He pushed himself off Maja and the bed and began to pull at his sweater and undershirt. Once it was off his head, he threw the garments onto the floor while his hands went to his pants, and he made the quick motions to get it off of his body. With it and his underwear off he only had his socks left, and he pulled them off as well.

"You are a sight for sore eyes. I love seeing your throbbing cock, eagerly waiting to claim my pussy again," Maja added spreading her legs wide by pointing her feet at the sides of the bed.

Bare and aroused, he climbed onto the bed, brought his lips to her angles and made slow licks from her ankles up her calves to her thighs with Maja beneath him, moaning with each touch of his tongue on her skin. His lips and tongue passed her mound and came up to her breasts but didn't stay as he made the quick move to her lips. After a passionate kiss, he then moved down her body and began to lick and suck at her breasts.

"You don't have to do any foreplay, Ray," Maja teased with a small moaning trailing at the end of her sentence. "This pussy has been ready for you since I woke up."

Pulling himself from her breasts with an audible pop as her nipple came out of his mouth, he looked up at his lover and new girlfriend. "Really?"

"Oh yes," Maja breathed. "I know that Christmas is a short time away, but I wanted to give myself to you as an early present. So, shall we get that magnificent cock of yours inside me?"

Ray pushed himself off Maja and got back onto his knees in between her spread legs. Giving a big, wide grin, his hands went to Maja's legs and lifted them up so they rested on his shoulders.

"Oooh!" she exclaimed, and her hands came up to cup her thighs to help Ray.

He let one hand go and brought it down to his cock to help guide it as he pushed it inside her.

"Mmmm," Maja moaned. "Oh, so delicious. I hope that Hedvig and Tuva didn't wear you out too much."

"Let me show you," Ray grunted planting his hands on either side of Maja body and began to thrust himself into her.

"Ah!" Maja yelped with each forward thrust inside her. "Ah! Ah! Ah!"

At first, Maja's hands were wrapped around his waist but at the moment of his thrusts inside his new and official girlfriend she brought them up to his back and held on tight.

He kept thrusting as she moved her waist trying to find the best spot. After a few moments, she said, "I need a different angle. Can I lower my legs?"

"Of course." He paused as she wrapped her legs around his lower half with her heels pressing against his buttock cheeks. He smiled as he started thrusting again, feeling her legs helping to pull him deeper into her.

"Ah!" she moaned again but then turned her head and looked into Ray's eyes. "Did you miss this pussy?"

"Oh yeah," Ray grunted in response giving one hard and fast thrust into her.

"MMM!" Maja responded, "That's right, Ray. *Fuck* me hard...oh fuck..."

"Maja!" Ray grunted feeling himself once again getting closer and closer to climax. He bit down on his lip, shut his eyes, and tried as hard as he could to hold it back and hold it in.

"It's okay, Ray," Maja said bringing her hands back up to Ray's face making him look at her. "Go ahead and cum inside me. You don't have to make me climax before you."

Ray slowed down his pace, "But I love it when you cum first."

"Oh you!" Maja sighed before leaning up to kiss him while her hips rocked against his. She took her lips away from his and uttered. "Make me cum, you fucking wonderful man!"

Ray wrapped his arms beneath Maja and sped up his thrusts harder and faster and faster and harder.

"Maja!" Ray grunted feeling himself coming closer to the edge.

"Ray!" Maja moaned, "*Please*...I'm gonna cum too...*cum* with me!"

At that moment, Ray felt his insides tighten and the release erupted inside of her while he heard Maja cry out with her arms holding tight and her thighs clenching at the side of his body. After a sharp breath in she let out a long exhale while her limbs let go of Ray and splayed out across the bed.

"Oh, sweet *merciful* fucks..." she uttered.

Ray pulled his cock out of her and lay beside her.

"You're telling me." he said while taking one winded breath after the other.

Maja rolled over onto her side and curled up next to Ray. He in turn, wrapped an arm around her body and looked down at her antlered head not minding them poking into his chest.

"Even though it's early in the morning but after that..." Maja exhaled a long breath before she muttered, "I could use a drink."

"Maybe some eggnog?" Ray laughed.

Maja laughed along with him and slapped his chest. "I think I've already had enough...for now."

"Hey, you two!" a voice called out from the door to the master bedroom.

Looking up, Ray looked to find Tuva stepping in and pulling off her clothes.

"You started without us?" she asked sounding annoyed as if a game had begun without her.

The moment she asked the question, Hedvig bounded into the bedroom as bare as Maja.

"Well," Maja answered sitting up. "You two had him a lot recently. I'm just making up for lost time."

"Don't be so greedy." Hedvig scowled. "We're all in this relationship together and we want some of that too."

"Well, ladies," Ray chimed in as he pushed himself out of Maja's intimate post-coital embrace. "Let's consummate this relationship."

He got up off the bed and pulled back the sheets. As he pulled back the comforter and the sheets back, Maja climbed off and he climbed back in looking at his three bare lovers. His heart raced so much that he thought it was going to pop in his chest. Holding out his hand to them he invited them in.

They first one to climb in was Tuva who came up to Ray's side of the bed. She set one knee on one side of him and threw one leg over his other side as if he were a horse that she wanted to ride.

"Did you miss these, Ray?" she asked bringing her hands up to her breasts and displaying them to him.

Ray could only answer with an utterance that made him sound so idiotic, "Ummmm...."

"Hah!" Tuva laughed turning her head over to the others. "Breast men, right?"

"Let's not be cruel, Tuva," Maja said coming over to the other side of the bed and climbed in. "Ray just had an orgasm. And a powerful one from what I felt. So, his head doesn't have the full blood supply yet, so words will be difficult."

The final one in the bed was Hedvig who climbed in on the side with Maja. Witnessing the action Ray couldn't help but notice just how large the bed was in terms of its width. With his two new girlfriends climbing in there was still enough room between him, Tuva, and them to include one more person. Yet, that thought, and amazement was pushed aside with Maja sitting in the bed with her back against the headboard while Hedvig straddled her lap. The yule cat woman brought the reindeer woman's head to her chest. Maja opened her mouth and took Hedvig's nipple into her mouth, and she began to suck.

"I think they have the right idea, sweetie," Tuva observed as her hand came to his cheek and turned him back into her warm voluptuousness.

Ray didn't need to think. He only acted when he brought his hands up to Tuva's massive breasts and massaged them while he looked up at her sweet face. Her red hair, green eyes, and the speckling of freckles across her face, her chest, and her arms.

"Don't hold back, sweetie," Tuva cooed her encouragement to her boyfriend. "Go on. Suckle. I know how much you love it."

Opening his mouth, he buried his face into her breast, latching onto one nipple and sucking hard. His tongue made a frenzied dance around her nipple and even his teeth gave light biting pressure and scraping against the sides.

"AH!" Tuva moaned. "Not so hard, Ray. Save that for Hedvig."

He could hear the concern in her voice, and he respected her want and pulled back a little before moving onto her other breast. Yet, her nipple wasn't inside his mouth for very long as she pushed herself off his lap and moved down his body.

The buxom elf was sitting on her knees in between Ray's legs looking down at his half-hard phallus, wet and shiny with a mix of his and Maja's cum. The appendage was rising once again and throbbing with his heartbeat as the sight of her pushed his buttons.

Tuva bent down and kissed his tip before getting off the bed and went to the bathroom. He could hear the water running as he wondered what she was doing. Before she came back, she took a small hand towel from the bathroom, ran it under a stream of hot water and came back to Ray. Taking the hot and damp cloth, she brought it to his cock and balls and began to run it up and over his length.

"Ah..." Ray exhaled, feeling the hot warmth making him shudder just a little and watched the way Tuva ran the cloth over him and undulated her body in an enticing show of hygienic affection.

"There," Tuva said, finishing up and drying his cock, balls and a little of his pubic hair. "All clean...for now."

She leaned down and gave the twitching member another small kiss on the head before turning to the bathroom and setting down the wet cloth near the sink. Ray couldn't help but watch the way she moved Her bare form looked delicious from her back to her shoulders, to her breasts, and buttocks. It made him grip his cock and stroke himself to the sweet sight of her while his ears kept hearing the moans, licks, and sucking from Maja and Hedvig.

"Oh no!" Tuva exclaimed as she turned around, climbing on the bed, lying down beside him, and pulling his hand from his cock. "You don't have to do that, Ray...I mean...you can if you want. But...isn't it more fun when we do it?"

"I..." Ray breathed, feeling Tuva's hand and watching her fingers encircle him while the want of her grew within him. "I didn't want to go soft."

"Oh sweetie." Tuva smiled before she leaned in and kissed him. "You'll never go soft for long with us around. Watch."

Tuva had let go of Ray's cock as she repositioned herself on the bed. She brought herself face down in between his legs with his cock at the side of her face. Her hand took hold of him and with an open mouth she devoured him. There was a flash of a moment when all he saw was her head bobbing up and down with her hair flailing at the sides and her ears twitching. But all that was only a flash as a wave of pleasure swept him away as Ray's eyes closed, and his head leaned back against the headboard.

"Oh, Jesus Christ..." he moaned as he brought his lower lip to bite upon.

There was a loud pop as Tuva's tight lips released his cock. Ray no longer felt her mouth on him, but he felt soft and delicate fingers around his shaft while the fingertips of her other hand tickled the tightened wrinkled surface of his scrotum. Bringing his head up he looked down and saw her take one hand away from his balls to brush her long red hair away from her face while her other hand began gentle strokes.

"This is why I cleaned your cock and balls, sweetie," she explained. "I wanted to just taste you. I like enjoying each flavor individually as well as thoroughly mixed."

The second she was done with her explanation she flicked out her tongue as if she were presenting her mouth to a doctor to check her through before she brought it down to his shaft and ran it up and down the sides. It was upon the fourth pass that she brought her tongue up to the head and ran the tip around the edge of his head.

"Mmmm," she cooed, bringing her tongue back into her mouth before kissing the head. "Such a gorgeous...*perfect*...cock...don't you agree, girls?"

The sight and sensation of Tuva's technique were so intense that Ray had forgotten about his other girlfriends at the other side of the bed having their own fun. He looked over and saw the two of them in an inverted position. Maja was lying on her back while Hedvig was on top of her with her head in between her legs and her white hair splayed out across the reindeer woman's thighs. All the while Maja had her head up against the yule cat woman's slit and licked at her while her lover's tail swished and flicked from side to side.

Tuva giggled while she held one hand to her face and the other still holding onto Ray's member. "Best not disturb them, Ray. When they get into that position, they get...oh...just so locked into eating each other out. But that just leaves your cock all to myself."

"I just hope I can satisfy all of you today," Ray huffed before biting down on his lower lip again as Tuva's hand became slick with the mixture of saliva and precum that not only oozed out but was milked out by her.

"If not today, sweetie," Tuva said giving his cock another kiss. "We have all the time in the world for you to fuck each one of us and satisfy us. And for us to satisfy you."

"Yes," Ray huffed, feeling the pressure grow once again,

"Please...*please*...I think I'm close."

"Very good," Tuva said sitting back up onto her knees and brushing away her exquisite strands of red hair so that they rested against her back. She looked down at Ray with a smile that grew smug and mischievous at the same time. "Time for me to ride you...just like our first night together."

"Come here," Ray begged as she brought her hips closer to his.

Her legs spread and her pussy just inches away, Ray grabbed her hip with one hand and the other gripped his manhood, before he shoved her down onto him.

"Ooooh, gonna be rough, are we?" Tuva teased as she ground her hips against him.

"Here's your answer," Ray grunted back in response, taking hold of her hips and thrusting himself hard upward.

"OOOF!" Tuva cried out as Ray's cock thrust inside her so quick that she fell forward against the headboard. Her hands caught herself just in time with her breasts hanging just inches away from her lover's face.

Taking the opportunity, he leaned in and took a nipple into his mouth. He clasped his lips, forming a good seal around one nipple and began to suck on her.

"Oh, Ray...mmmmmmmm..." she moaned. "I feel like I could cum just from you suckling on my tits...ahhh...I wish I were lactating...so...ah...I could hold you in my arms...and give you my milk..."

"Hmmmm-mmmm," Ray uttered his muffled agreement, while his hips came back down onto the mattress, and he made a gentler upward push to meet his elvish lover's pussy.

"Oooohhhnnnnnnn...yes, like that. You can be rough with me, but I like it more when you're gentle. Because I know how much of a sweetheart you are."

Tuva leaned down and kissed Ray's forehead.

"Mmmm,". Ray moaned as he continued to suck on her full and bountiful breasts.

"You don't have to rush, sweetie. Ah...You...ah...can take your time and don't worry about...me cumming just yet...ah...And you can cum...mm mm....as much as you want inside me...oh, Ray! Ah!"

Ray let go of Tuva's breast in favor of his labored breathing as if he were hard at work lifting weights. Yet it was the most joyous workout he knew as he held onto Tuva's hips and continued to thrust upward. He couldn't see her face. All he could see were her breasts that heaved back and forth against his face while her hair flowed over her like swaying branches in a breeze. There as a moment when she moved with such quickness that her breasts almost threatened to slap him in the face.

He didn't want it to stop.

"Ray!" Tuva squealed. "Fuck...fuck me, Ray! Ahhh! Fuuuuuck!"

It was then that Ray felt a trickling of liquid along his cock that was warm like tea that had been sitting on the counter for longer than intended.

There weren't any words from Tuva in the midst of her slow descent from her orgasm, but Ray's cock wasn't there just yet. There was the beginning tickle in his shaft but the pressure in him wasn't ready to burst.

"Here comes more." Ray smirked his grunt up at her while his hips went faster and faster inside her.

"OHH!" Tuva yelped as she fell forward a little further with her breasts pressing into Ray's face.

He didn't lose focus by being distracted by her wonderful breasts; there was only the sweet, wet, and slippery sensation of his cock inside her. It felt fantastic, and the pressure was starting to build and build and build. There was also the fatiguing sensation of thrusting his hips upward as if he were running a mile while lying down, but he knew his sweet release was coming.

"Cum for me, Ray," Tuva begged. "Pump your spunk inside me. Please! Cum in my pussy! Creampie my peach! Aaaaahhhh!"

"Hnnnnnnn!" Ray strained as he felt the sweet sensation bursting from inside him through his balls and out the tip of his cock.

"Ah...ah...ah..." Ray panted feeling his whole body start to go as limp as string cheese.

"Oh my...Ray..." Tuva huffed, "that was *amazing*..."

The elf's hands came to the side of Ray's face and turned it upward to her. She brought her dried lips to his and gave him a gentle kiss. He returned the kiss, not caring about the sensation. There was only the sweet want of kissing her and cuddling with her. With his arms holding her close, he rolled to his side so that they were lying down in the middle of the bed, facing each other. She rolled to her side as he relaxed his hold, causing Ray's cock to slip out of her along with his cum mixed with her own orgasmic juices. Ray caressed her cheek and began to kiss her, but the moment of intimate aftermath was broken by applause.

"Yay!" the voice of Hedvig called out. "Wooo! Fuck, that was *hot*!"

"Bravo!" Maja called out, "bravo you sweet lovers!"

Ray pulled away from Tuva and sat up along with the elf. At the other side of the bed, Maja was sitting up with her back against the headboard with Hedvig lying against her with her head in her lap. The two of them were smirking and nodding with approval as they applauded their lovers, their respective girlfriend and newly welcomed boyfriend.

"Oh stop, you two." Tuva blushed, flicking a hand at them.

"Fuck me, you're cute when you're embarrassed!" Hedvig squealed, while her hands came up to her face and she wiggled her body in her moment of cuteness overload.

"Did you two…". Ray asked, waving a slow finger from Hedvig to Maja and back again.

"Did we both have our mutual climax?" Maja asked. "Yes, we did, Ray. Hedvig is as adept as you with her tongue."

"But," Hedvig began her explanation as she broke out of her cuteness overload, "you two were so loud and into it that we finished right when Tuva had her first orgasm."

"Hedvig!" Tuva uttered.

"Aww, come on," Hedvig cooed sitting up and leaning in to give Tuva's buttocks and swift spanking strike on her thigh.

"Ooooohh…" Tuva moaned, "oh gods I love that."

"Then allow me," Ray volunteered leaning in to kiss Tuva while his hand came down to her voluptuous buttocks and spanked her.

"Mmm!" she squealed into his mouth but when Ray's lips pulled away from her, she whispered, "I'm such a lewd elf."

"And now it's my turn with Ray!" Hedvig proclaimed, as she got up and came over to Ray's side of the bed.

"Let's see if I have enough in me." Ray laughed as the orgy continued.

Chapter 14: Dances and Lights

Christmas was five days away and Ray was in his room wrapping presents. But the room wasn't at his parents' house. It was the room that Maja, Tuva, and Hedvig gave to him once he moved in. The move from his parents' house wasn't too arduous as the only things at his parents' place was a few personal items such as clothes and a couple of his electronics. Everything else was in a storage unit, so when Ray had finally moved in at the girls' house, all that was left at his parents' place was a desk and a bed.

It took him all of one day to unpack his stuff, such as his books, clothes, and his framed artwork that he had already covered all the available wall space in his room.

He was finishing wrapping up one more gift. He tapped up the ends and set the label onto it. Once he was done, he couldn't help but stop and look around the room. As he recalled the past few days it didn't take very long to move all his stuff from his parents' house to the new house. Thanks to the extra hands of help to get the stuff over; it only took part of a day to do it.

The room wasn't too small but with his bed, a few bookshelves, and his desk the space in the room certainly diminished. Still, there was the fact that he and the other ladies could share the massive bed in the master bedroom.

Whatever god gave this to me, he thought for a moment, *thank you!*

He looked back at the small pile of gifts that he had gotten together for Maja, Tuva, and Hedvig. With what they had already given to him, he started to wonder if his gifts were paltry compared to that. Despite that idea, he was going to make a sincere attempt at showing his appreciation for it all.

Alright, he thought while he went over the mental checklist of items for them. *The gifts for everyone. For Maja, I got her a couple smutty books. This year's best lesbian erotica and the manga of 'World's End Harem' and 'World's End Harem: Fantasia'. For Tuva, I got copies of 'Debbie Does Dallas' and 'Evil Dead'. For Hedvig, I got her a nice big comfy sweater and some bath bombs. I hope they'll like them...and the extra special items for each of them.*

Just then there was a knock at the door.

"Hon," the voice of Maja called out. "Breakfast is almost ready."

"Thanks, Maja," Ray called back. "Just finishing up wrapping some presents."

"Is that all you're doing?" she teased. "Cause I could come in there and help out."

Ray laughed. "I promise that's all I'm doing."

He loved how sexual the ladies were in their flirting and teasing with him. And in just a matter of a couple of days he noticed how at ease and open he had become with them. Such as how his hands would travel over each lady as he passed. This was true with Maja since she was the proudest of her exhibitionism. Though Hedvig always encouraged Ray to grab her ass while Tuva kept bringing his face into her breasts.

"Well, be sure to pull your pants up when you're finished," Maja joked.

"Okay." Ray laughed as he gathered up the presents in his arms and walked out of his room.

Making careful steps down the stairs, he came to the living room where Hedvig was watching an anime. He wasn't sure of the title, but he couldn't give his attention to it as there were presents to lay beneath the tree. The tree was set against the windows with the couches stretching into a u-shape around it with the television off to one side.

Looking at the presents that were already there, Ray noticed several from Hedvig to Maja, from Maja to Tuva, from Tuva to Ray, and so on in various combinations. Setting down the presents he looked over and saw that Maja was sitting on the couch reading. He had to admire the fact that she could read so easily with so much going on around her, from the sounds on the television to the clanking of various implements in the kitchen.

Ray had set down the final present when he turned to see Maja looking up from her book and smirking. It was easy to figure out what Maja was looking at given the angle she was at and where he was.

"Like what you see?" Ray smirked as he made his visual flirting with Maja.

"You know it, hon," Maja winked.

"Alright everyone, breakfast is ready," Tuva called out.

"Yay!" Hedvig cried out from the couch as she reached for the remote and paused her show.

Maja, on the other hand, set a bookmark into her book and set it on the arm of the couch and Ray followed behind both ladies as they came over to the breakfast area and saw what Tuva had made that morning.

Tuva had made pancakes. Seeing the small stacks of thin fluffy cake at each place setting made Ray smile. Maybe it was because there was something nostalgic about pancakes that harkened back to when he was a child or maybe it was because it was the way that Tuva made them. There was always a world of difference when one made pancakes at home in comparison to when one had them at a restaurant. It was a mystery that would come and go in Ray's mind, but the way Tuva made them was at a visual quality that rivaled professional chefs.

Set alongside the pancakes were sausage links and small glasses of orange juice. Around the table, there was Maja to Ray's right, Tuva to his left, and Hedvig across the table from him. Yet, the breakfast table was so small that he could easily reach out for Hedvig's hand if he wanted to.

"Mmmm," Hedvig vocalized from her side of the table. "I don't know which is more delicious, Tuva. Your cooking or your pussy."

"Hedvig." Maja laughed in her light scolding tone at her.

"Well, she's not wrong," Ray agreed as he reached for the maple syrup and began to pour it over his small stack. Once he was done, he looked up to the ladies who were all smiling at him. He looked at them and laughed, "What?"

"We're just so elated that you've joined us, Ray," Maja explained before she poured the syrup over her own stack.

"So am I, everyone," Ray said. "I just hope..."

The moment the words formed in his head and were about to head out of his mouth, he stopped himself.

"What is it, sweetie?" Tuva asked reaching out for his hand.

"Sorry, everyone," he apologized, while Tuva's hand gently held his. "I don't mean to spoil the mood."

"Not at all, Ray," Maja assured. "This is a safe place for you to say what you wish without fear of judgement or anything of the sort."

"I just hope that I'll be a good boyfriend to you all," Ray uttered the sentence that he stopped himself from saying.

"I know you will, Ray," Tuva said with her grip tightening around his hand. "As I told you before, we elves are very empathic, and I could tell on that first day we met that you're a good person. A good man. It's just unfortunate that most humans don't see a good thing when it's sitting in front of them."

"Fuckin' right," Hedvig agreed, reaching for the bottle of syrup.

Ray smiled and cut into the pancakes and ate them before the syrup would turn the fluffy stack into squishy mush. With it in his mouth, a sensation of elation came over him, and he couldn't help but hum his approval of it.

"So good," he said after his first bite.

Tuva got up from her chair and leaned in and kissed his syrup coated lips. Ray couldn't help but chuckle as he kissed her back.

"Oh, almost forgot," Maja exclaimed. "There's a little event we're going to be going to tonight."

"What's that?" Ray asked cutting more into his pancakes.

"There's a Christmas lights festival in the downtown vicinity," Maja explained. "It's something the three of us all go to along with seeing the Nutcracker Ballet performed by the local ballet school. And we got an extra ticket for you to come with us."

"You did?" Ray smiled, feeling a warmth coming to his face in the invitation.

"Of course, hon." Maja smiled leaning in and kissing his cheek. Upon sitting down, she explained, "The ballet will be at five and we'll be out in time to see the lights in their full luminous glory."

"Oh wait," he started, "should I dress up for the ballet?"

"What'd you mean?" Hedvig asked.

"Well, isn't that a rule when going to live performances? To dress up for it?"

"You won't have to dress to the nines, sweetie," Tuva explained. "Maybe just slacks and a nice sweater will do."

Ray nodded and finished his breakfast.

***

The four lovers didn't need to use a car to get to the event since everything in Northview was so clustered together that one just needed to walk from one place to the next.

The downtown of Northview was at the very center with the mall to the south of it. Ray's parents' house was to the east of it while his new home with Maja, Tuva, and Hedvig was to the west.

The walk from their house to the downtown area was a brisk affair with the sun setting behind them and the air temperature sinking further into the depths of the cold. Ray was thankful that he dressed in extra layers with a scarf wrapped around his neck and tucked into his jacket.

The others, as he observed, didn't need that. Hedvig was dressed in her regular pants with her oversized sweater and a long scarf that hung loose around her neck. The same for Maja but with the addition of a winter coat and knitted mittens. And yet the two of them looked like they would have been comfortable without them. Tuva, on the other hand, wore several layers along with a pair of earmuffs over her pointed ears. The sight of it made him smile at the cuteness since the muffs themselves looked like the shells of a macaron and making her face the sweet filling in the middle.

Within one block of the town center square, Ray could see the setups for the Christmas lights. In the light of the setting sun, he saw how skeletal and bare they were. Poking its head around the corner of one of the many red brick buildings was the head of a giant reindeer. Yet, its dark metal quality studded with unlit lights gave it the quality of a tree devoid of its leaves waiting for spring to come again.

Once the quartet rounded the corner, Maja couldn't help but look at the reindeer, shake her antlered head and laugh.

"What's funny, Maja?" Ray asked.

"The reindeer in these holiday stories about Santa," Maja said, pointing her mittened hand at the structure. "Everyone assumes by their names that they're all male."

"Yes?" Ray asked, wondering where Maja was going with her statement.

"Well, little secret, hon," she said, turning around with a wink and pointing her mittened hand to her own antlers. "The only reindeer that have their antlers in winter are females."

Ray looked at Maja and then back at the reindeer light structure and suddenly so much began to make sense.

Hedvig began to laugh. "She tells everyone that will listen every Christmas."

"Well, it's true, hon," Maja pointed out to Hedvig. "I just wish there would be proper representation done when it comes to this time of year."

Ray snorted. "People are hard to change, Maja. I mean people lost their minds when Starbucks changed the look of their cup for the holiday season."

"True," Tuva agreed. "Humans do tend to be stubborn and set in their ways. Especially human men."

The moment she made that sentence audible, she looked over at Ray and gave a grimaced smile and reached over to hug him and kiss his cheek.

"Not you, of course, sweetie," she apologized. "You are the sweetest exception of that."

"Thanks, Tuva," Ray said, kissing the elf back. He turned over to Maja and said, "What about that whole thing with Rudolph?"

"As far as reindeer are concerned?" Maja asked.

Ray nodded.

"Oh yes, if that one has antlers in winter, then Rudolph is female. But then again that one was a cereal box mascot that became part of the myth so, take it with a grain of salt."

Ray smirked but then added, "I used to like that story about Rudolph as a kid, but it hits differently as an adult."

"What'd you mean?" Hedvig asked.

"Well," Ray thought about it and strung together his verbal thesis, "think about this, Rudolph is born different. The red nose and all that, and everyone makes fun of him for it. And he was shunned because of it by everyone. But then when a crisis comes up where he's useful and suddenly they see him as worthy of inclusion. I think that's a horrible story to teach kids, that you won't be bullied if your difference becomes useful."

"Sounds like the story is very close to you, isn't it?" Tuva asked, reaching an arm around his shoulder and bringing him close.

"It does," Ray answered, feeling the memories of the past rising to the surface like ice cubes in a freshly poured drink.

Ray and Tuva stopped on the sidewalk and to share in their hug. That was when Hedvig and Maja came in and wrapped their arms around Tuva and Ray.

"We're nearly there," Maja informed as she broke away from the embrace.

The four lovers walked down the street past the unlit Christmas lights as well as the town hall and courthouse. The buildings of the old downtown Northview spoke of its old aesthetics with its red brick exteriors and signs that hung over the sidewalk like laundry on a clothesline. Ray had to look around and give it a small admiration that there was a certain charm to it all.

"We're here," Hedvig chimed in as they stopped at a street corner.

Ray looked across the street to find the Northview Valley Performing Arts Center. It was a wide squat but round building with the parked cars spread and scattered around it like marbles circling around a drain. Walking past the parked cars, Ray saw the line of people making their way inward.

"Is this your first time seeing this, sweetie?" Tuva asked, coming up to Ray's side wrapping her arms around his left arm and hugging her voluptuousness up against one side.

"I know the music," Ray explained. "But the ballet...I think I saw it years ago in grade school."

"Oh, you'll love this, hon," Maja explained. "Every year the classes just seem to get better and better."

There was a sigh of relief once the four of them were inside and experiencing the warmth of the theater's interior. But then there was also the minuscule claustrophobia that came from all the people being packed in as everyone tried to make their way through the lobby and to their respective seats.

As the four of them were led by Maja to their seats, they each loosened their winter wardrobe. First with the mittens, then the scarfs, and jackets. But once they were at their seats, Ray wasn't sure how or where to sit. When he was dating, he would sit on either side of his date but now he had three dates with him. He started to dart his gaze at the different seats wondering what to do.

"You okay, Ray?" Hedvig asked.

"Um, where should I sit?" he asked.

"Wherever you like, hon," Maja explained. "When you're in a polycue, you don't have to feel obliged to sit beside anyone in particular."

"Alright," Ray said, still reminding himself of how new the situation was. He sat in between Tuva and Maja while Hedvig sat next to Tuva.

Ray took a deep breath in sitting down while he felt the hands of Tuva and Maja reaching out and holding his. He turned to his left at Tuva and Hedvig, then to his right at Maja and smiled at them all.

Within minutes, the lights turned down, the curtain rose, and the ballet had begun.

***

All sense of time was lost.

When the ballet was over, the crowd began its standing ovation to the bowing performers whose ages ranged from six years old all the way up into teenagers and adults. Ray applauded along with Maja, Tuva, and Hedvig in the roaring wave of clapping hands, hollering, whistling, and cries of adulation of the performance. It didn't even bother him when his hands began to feel raw and pink from the action of admiration.

The performers bowed and waved to the audience before the curtain fell and the audience began to file out of the theater.

"Wow, that was amazing," Ray exclaimed to the others loud enough for them to hear over the loud conversations and muffled movements of the other audience members.

"I know, right?" Hedvig answered back.

"The show is like a fine wine," Maja added. "It keeps getting better every year."

"And just you wait, everyone," Tuva added. "The night has just begun."

Ray soon realized what Tuva meant. At the time when they went into the theater, the sun was still out, and everything looked so dull and bare. But all of that had changed when he and the ladies came to the front foyer and out into the dark winter air. The sky was black, and it was much colder, but there was a warm glow to the Christmas lights that were on.

There were multitudes of lights that were strung up on the streetlights as well as the various trees and bushes that lined the sidewalks. They were all white, but their glow gave an ethereal quality to the street and to the people that were walking down it. Of course, there weren't just humans to Ray's eyes. He saw various others including an elf man who was walking with an elf woman and two children that were running and laughing around them.

"Easy there, kids," the mother said as they walked past Ray, Tuva, Hedvig, and Maja.

"Wow..." Ray uttered, looking at it all.

He had seen the lights and decorations that were hung up at the mall and they always invoked a warm nostalgia in the stomach of his soul. Almost as if the simple and bold aesthetic had taken him back to a time when he was younger. Back when the world seemed so much simpler, and his wants and needs were simple as well.

"This is just the start," Hedvig said nudging him with her shoulder and some of her body. "Wait till you see what they got at the town square."

Ray looked down the street and saw what Hedvig was referring to. At the distance he was at it was as if he were looking at a bright ball of light that almost made Ray think of the lights at a baseball game but that changed as he was led by his polycue towards it.

Step by cold and steam breathing step they came close to it all. There was not only the sight of it, but there were also the sounds of Christmas carols being sung. It wasn't just the kind that one would think of where someone would just slap on music from a speaker. The sounds that Ray heard was an actual group, a choir, singing those carols.

He guessed that he was only a block away. The sounds were that much louder and sharper along with the images of the various structures of lights that were overlapping in their brightness and mixture of white, red, green, and blue.

Then came the smells.

Mixed with the sights of lights and the sounds of singing, there was a warm wafting smell of cooking food. It was difficult to discern one from the other, but he could smell the sweetness of baking treats as well as the oily saltiness of the savories among them.

They had arrived.

The town square had become an electric wonderland of Christmas trees, candy canes, snowflakes, reindeer, and arches. It was as if the town had brought a forest into its center and brought it to life with light. At the center of it, in front of the courthouse, there was a grand tree that was as tall as the courthouse itself and its branches shone in multiple colors with a star shining from the top. Off to the side of the grand tree there was a stage where there was a choir of people continuing to sing carols.

Hark how the bells,
Sweet silver bells,
All seem to say,
Throw cares away,
Christmas is here,
Bringing good cheer,
To young and old,

Meek and the bold,

"Wow…" Ray felt himself utter with the word rising out like the steam from his lips and then vanishing into the cold air.

"See what we meant, sweetie?" Tuva asked, leaning in to kiss his cold cheek. "Now, who's hungry? I'm buying."

"I move that we find something warm to drink first, hon," Maja suggested.

"I'm for that as well," Ray added.

"Then it's decided," Tuva said, leading the way.

Apart from the lights, decorations and the stage of carolers, there were also various stands set up around the town square and branching streets. Ray knew that there had to be a name for the event, but he couldn't quite place it. But then again, it didn't really matter because it was all such a sight to the eyes.

The quartet arrived at a stand that was dispensing cocktails and warm drinks to various people. There was a menu behind the registers that looked to be written in chalk on a chalkboard as if they were daily specials at a Starbucks.

"What would you all like?" Tuva asked, smiling.

"I'll have a hot chocolate, please," Maja stated.

"Same here but with peppermint," Hedvig added.

"And you, Ray?" Tuva asked.

He looked at the stand and the menu that was set above it and had a craving for a different kind of hot chocolate.

"You don't suppose they can do a hot white chocolate, would they?" Ray asked.

"Oh, I'm sure they can, sweetie," Tuva said.

"Hot white chocolate?" Hedvig asked, sounding confused. "Isn't that just hot milk?"

"Don't be rude, Hedvig," Maja cut into her question.

Ray laughed. "I know I have strange tastes. I just like white chocolate the most."

"And there's nothing wrong with that," Tuva said, kissing him again.

"Hey, don't hog him to yourself!" Hedvig protested as she squeezed in between Tuva and Ray. She turned to Tuva and gave her an over-the-top angry pout as she said, "I'm still trying to make up for lost time that you two have had with him."

Ray let out another laugh. "I don't intend to go anywhere, Hedvig."

He reached down to the yule cat woman's face, cupped it, turned her face to him where her angry pout melted as she looked up at him when he leaned in to kiss her. He pulled back and saw how glazed her eyes were. A look of love and lust that Ray had witnessed before, but seeing the way Hedvig did it brought a special brand and flavor to it.

"Kiss me again, Ray," Hedvig whispered.

Ray smiled and leaned in to give her a quick touch of his lips against her, but Hedvig wasn't satisfied. She wrapped her arms around him and she threw her body against his while her legs wrapped around him. Her face was pressed up against his.

"Me-yeow..." She smirked nuzzling her face against his.

"Down kitty!" Tuva called out, laughing and trying to get Hedvig off of Ray. "There'll be plenty of time for that when we get home."

"It would appear I missed some rather humorous actions," Maja observed with her signature humor, bringing over the warm drinks to her lovers.

"Hedvig was trying to...what's the word? 'Glomp' onto Ray," Tuva explained.

"Can't blame a kitty for trying," Hedvig said with a closed-eyed and toothy grin while her tail flicked from side to side.

"Of course not, hon," Maja said. "You do the same for all of us. But here's your drink."

She brought the warm cup over to Hedvig who took it with both hands and drunk it like she was slurping up a bowl of soup without a spoon. Tuva took hers and Ray took his. He began to drink his hot white chocolate and reveled in its creamy sweetness while the nearby choir began to sing another carol.

Silent night, holy night
All is calm. All is bright,
Round yon Virgin Mother and Child
Holy infant so tender and mild
Sleep in heavenly peace
Sleep in heavenly peace...

And that night after the four lovers took in the lights and left the festival for home, they all slept in such heavenly peace in each other's arms in their one big bed. All did seem calm and right with the world. Never had Ray Adler known such peace and love except in that bed and in the arms of Maja, Tuva, and Hedvig.

Chapter 15: The Yule Time Misunderstanding

Christmas was only three days away. Ray was sitting in the small breakfast nook with Maja, Tuva, and Hedvig. The situation was still the most incredulous thing that had ever happened to him. So much had changed in only one month. He ran his gaze over his lovers and girlfriends and couldn't help but smile. But the mood wasn't meant to last.

A message made his phone vibrate. Curious, he reached out, picked it up and his mood crashed.

"Ugh," Ray uttered, rolling his eyes.

"Everything alright, sweetie?" Tuva called from her side of the table while the others were eating.

"It's my mom," Ray answered. "She's reminding me that she's invited us to her Christmas party."

"Do you want to go?" Maja asked sipping on her orange juice.

"Not really." Ray shook his head.

"Why?" Tuva asked, scowling at him and sounding like a disappointed kid. "Are you *ashamed* of us?"

Ray looked at her while she made her fake pout and couldn't help but smile again and say, "I'm not ashamed of you ladies. I'm ashamed of my parents."

Hedvig laughed. "I don't blame you. I feel that way about my parents. Then again, they have over twenty-three kids, so whatever I do won't matter."

"Really?" Ray asked, trying to imagine the mother of Hedvig as a woman with the same color hair as hers but having that many kids all around her. The idea made him wonder if a yule cat woman gave birth to one child at a time or was it several at a time like regular cats.

"Before you ask," Hedvig said as if she heard his thought process on the issue. "Yule cat people have kids one at a time."

"Oh, your poor mom," Ray uttered, feeling his jaw drop.

"Nah, don't feel bad for her. She loves being a mom and my dad, as I found out, was one horny dude. But unlike most, he kept his dick in one woman and never pulled out."

"Hedvig!" Maja scolded at a comedic way. "Let's not be crass at the breakfast table."

"Well, I've always wanted to be eaten out at breakfast," Hedvig said while she winked at Ray. "Maybe I'll just get undressed and sit in front of him and have him eat out my pussy with a little maple syrup."

She further punctuated the point by holding up two fingers to either side of her mouth and flicked her tongue out at Ray while keeping one eye closed in her wink.

"Hedvig!" Maja snapped and laughed while she reached over to smack her hand.

Ray laughed. "This is why I love being here. I could never say such things at my parent's place or even around my dad's friends."

"I take it they're..." Maja asked while trailing off her sentence.

"A little too fucking *straight*," Ray finished her assessment of the people he mentioned.

"Ah, those types," Tuva observed while sipping her coffee.

"Yeah," Ray agreed. "But I know my mom will want me there, so let's go for a bit but let's try to curb ourselves, everyone."

"That goes double for you, Hedvig." Tuva pointed a finger holding her coffee cup.

"Yes, *mommy*." Hedvig winked and stuck her tongue out at her.

"Now, I won't hear that kind of talk out of bed, hon."

"Maybe later?"

"Promise."

Ray couldn't stop smiling at all of it, but he reminded himself to enjoy it for he knew how his smile would be lost later that night.

***

Coming to the front door of his parent's house, Ray still felt a swirling sensation in his head, his chest and gut. Still, he wasn't sure which was going to be colder, the night air or the reception from those at the Christmas party. He always knew how fake these people were. They pretend to be warm and inviting, but it was all a stiff facade like a microwave burrito that hadn't been warmed all the way through. The piping hot outside with the icicle core in the middle.

One such incident he remembered was when he was a young boy and there was a dinner party going on to welcome a neighbor. He remembered how the ladies were laughing and smiling with the new neighbor and his wife yet, that all changed the moment they left. At that moment they all turned to each other and began to pick her apart from how she spoke, what she wore, and what her husband did. That was the truth that Ray knew about these people, yet he wasn't going to give this band of assholes the satisfaction that he would simply crawl away in silence and never be heard from again.

The best form of revenge, he tried to remind himself, *is living a better life than what your enemies would want you to have.*

Turning to his left and his right, he saw Hedvig, Maja, and Tuva standing by his side. The source of his courage that night. He took a deep breath when he stepped up to the door and was about to ring the doorbell when he felt a hand come onto his shoulder. Turning his head he found the sweet mother-like face of Tuva who smiled at him along with the others. Returning a smile to them he turned his head back and pressed his finger to the doorbell.

It was within seconds that the door opened and there was Ray's mother wearing a bright red sweater and blue apron holding a tray of cookies.

"Ray!" she cried out. "Come in! Please. And you ladies come in too."

Ray stepped in and hugged his mother being sure not to upset the tray of cookies that she was no doubt bringing to the area of the party where the guests were about to devour them.

"Merry Christmas, Mom," Ray said, kissing her cheek.

"Oh, Merry Christmas, love," she said in return. "Now, who are these ladies?"

"This is Maja," Ray introduced. "And this is Tuva and Hedvig."

Ray's mother went around to each lady and hugged them. After she finished her embrace with Hedvig, she looked at Ray with puzzlement in her eyes.

"Now, Ray," she asked, "which one of these lovely ladies is your new girlfriend?"

Ray wanted to lie for a flash of a moment because he knew his mother wouldn't understand. But then he looked at them. Maja. Hedvig. And Tuva. Then the shame and hesitation vanished, and he answered, "They all are, Mom."

"What?" Mrs. Adler asked, looking at Ray confused, before looking at the ladies with suspicion. "Is my son *cheating* on any of you?"

Maja laughed and smiled, "I know this is a hard concept to understand, Mrs. Adler, but we all are Ray's girlfriends. We all love him. Our relationship is what you might call 'polyamorous'."

"Oh, these new things you millennials and Gen Z kids come up with." Mrs. Adler smiled dismissing the term outright. "You know you can only have *one* woman, Ray. So, don't you string any of them along. Now, come. The party is in full swing."

Without missing a beat or a step, she turned and headed into the living room where everyone was drinking their holiday beverages and eating whatever they wanted off the appetizer plates.

Ray, Maja, Tuva, and Hedvig began to mix and mingle among the various party guests. Each of them often would come to the questions of who they knew at the party and what they did. Overhearing a lot of it, he knew that each lady was basically a small business owner which he knew would garner points with them because *that's how you make it in America. With business, and hard work.* Yet, for him, there was one he knew that he wasn't looking forward to seeing.

Among the faces Ray's eyes gravitated towards one end of the couch where his father talking with Tim. As he predicted, his father had his drink in his hand and was already halfway in with how the liquid was sloshing around with each hard and jerky hand movement he made as if he forgot he had a beverage in the first place.

"Well, well," his father said as he stood up at a shambling pace while holding out his drink to make sure it didn't spill. "Look who came back, Tim. You know what I heard? I heard that not only did he get a job at a bookstore with a *female* boss, but he's moved into a house with three women. Relying on women? We really have raised a generation of men who are *pussies.* No surprise since there are men who fuckin' think that they can actually *have* pussies. You can't fight reality!"

"That's enough," Tim said trying to stop him. "At least he's moved out of the house and he's working. That's something to be proud of."

"Oh, I'm sorry, isn't this America? I thought this was America. Aren't I allowed to say what I want?"

"Well," Ray said narrowing his eyes upon his father, "Since it is America, Dad, here's what I have to say."

It was one thing to Ray to have his father insult and shame him but to insult the women that he had come to love was another matter entirely.

Ray moved with sure and heavy footsteps across the room towards his father and stared him in the eye. "I'm finally getting back on my feet and I'm finally making things better for myself. And I found three wonderful women who helped me actually feel better about myself. I'm in love and I'm happy, Dad! Can't you be happy for me? Just once? Just because your life is miserable doesn't give you license to make everyone else's miserable."

The moment had brought the room to a grinding halt, and he could feel all eyes looking at him, but he didn't give a single fuck about it all. With the want to punctuate it further, he took the glass from his dad's hand and said, "*This is America,* and while you can say what shit you want in your home, nobody has to stick around and listen."

With the drink in his hand, he emptied it onto the floor at his dad's feet. The pale eyes of his father went wide, and his jaw went slack as he looked at the audacity of his son.

"Merry Christmas, Dad," Ray added giving extra bitterness in his voice while he set the glass down, "and *fuck you.*"

Turning on his heel he made his way out towards the front door and out of the house and to the wicker chairs on the brick deck.

Taking a deep breath, he tried to remind himself that at least he didn't have to live in that house with his father anymore.

The front door opened and out came Ray's mother. "Oh, Ray," she called out.

"I am *not* apologizing to Dad, if that's what you're going to ask me," Ray interrupted. "The old man can frankly go to hell and rot in pieces."

"That's not why I came out here," she said, sitting down next to him, "I'm actually proud of you, love."

Ray looked at his mother who smiled in a way that showed her motherly love and pride in her son.

"Why?"

"Ever since you were young, you've always been so kind-spirited, big hearted and soft spoken," she began, reaching out her hand to his shoulder. "It's a wonderful thing for you to have. After all, you have three women that love you. I may not understand it, but I see the way you look at them and the way they look at you and each other. That's love. But the way you are, it leaves you vulnerable to people like your father who has always been far too hard on you. I always hoped that you wouldn't turn out like him."

"Like him? How?"

"Embittered and hardened, but you haven't become like that. Don't *ever* lose that, no matter how cruel the world has been to you."

"Thanks, Mom," Ray smiled.

"But you're happy, aren't you?"

"I am," Ray answered. "I am living with Maja…Tuva…and Hedvig…they all love me without any condition."

"Of course, we do, Ray," Maja's voice called out.

Ray looked and saw that Tuva, Hedvig, and Maja had all come out onto the porch with him and his mother.

"She's right," Hedvig added. "So much in this world is easy to attain but you…you're not as easy to get as money."

The yule cat woman came in close and kissed his cheek while her arms wrapped around his neck.

The four lovers began to wrap their arms around each other for their embrace.

"Let's all go back inside then," Ray's mother insisted.

The four lovers got up and headed back inside where they continued to mingle and eat and enjoy themselves. Ray saw that his father was nowhere to be seen but then again that was a good thing to him. He didn't want the night to be ruined by his presence or anything else.

Everything in his world was as he had hoped and wanted it to be.

Merry Christmas to me, he thought as the conversations around him had faded into low level nothing.

But then there was a ring at the doorbell and the voice of his mother broke through.

"Ray!" she called, "there's someone at the front door for you."

Ray broke the embrace with his loves, "I'll be right back everyone."

The three ladies nodded while Ray went to handle the business at the front door.

He came to the door and found a face that he hoped to never see again: *Angela,* his ex-fiancé. She stood dressed in thick winter coat with a knitted winter hat over her shoulder length blonde hair. Her arms were crossed over her chest as if she were bracing herself from the cold or maybe it was because no one else would hold her except herself. At first, her face was downturned but then it made a slow upward tilt to show her blue eyes that were reddened from tears.

"Hello, Ray," she said, trying to smile in her toothpaste commercial worthy way but only managed a weak upward twinge at the corners of her mouth.

"What do *you* want?" Ray asked, feeling sour as the familiar feelings of anger, resentment and betrayal had risen back up like a dead and forgotten body rising to the surface of a bog.

"I came back to say I'm sorry," she said. "Can we talk?"

Ray stepped outside and onto the brick deck once again, "We can talk out here and before you say anything, the answer is no."

"You don't even know what I'm going to ask."

"*I shouldn't have to.* Remember all those times you said that to me?"

"I'm sorry, Ray," she began to cry, blubber and made her make-up run even more like ice cream in the hot sun. "The man I cheated on you with ran off with a yoga instructor. I made a mistake, okay?" She sniffled hard trying to wipe away the tears as she smeared her mascara even more. "I should have...I should have known what a good man I had before I threw it all away. I don't care how much money you *earn*. I just want *you* in my life."

"I was just a facilitator of *your* wants and dreams," Ray answered back showing no sway to her tears. "I hope your new guy gave you *everything* you wanted because I gave you everything I had. It was always about what *you* wanted. You wanted everything and you wanted me to want what you want making it seem like it was my actual desires. I loved you without want of anything else. I just wanted you but your love always at a price."

"Please, Ray," she begged pleading louder than before. "I know I messed up, but I'll do anything to have you back."

"And yet your timing of showing up here is pretty damn suspicious."

"I know that I was bad to you, but I know I can change if we work together," she answered back.

But Ray had been burnt to a crisp in the past by her. He was no longer a fool. He had been with her long enough to know her tell-tale signs that she was lying. The biggest was the way that her eyes would make rapid blinks, and it wasn't because she was crying. Her body betrayed her lies. Just like how he knew that she was faking when she had orgasms. Knowing that and still remembering the scene that he walked in on when she betrayed him. Coming into that bedroom that they shared with her riding another man as if he were a bull at a rodeo and showing joy and ecstasy like she never showed him in their intimate moments. The memory of that only gave rise to his disgust for her.

"*Get out*," Ray sneered shaking his head. "I have something far better now, and I don't need you. I don't need your controlling. Your mind games. Your drama. I no longer need to bend over backwards to please you anymore."

"Please, Ray," she begged again. "I'll do all those things that I know you love but I would never do."

She came up to him, wrapping her arms around his neck, her hand coming down to his groin.

"Come on, Ray," she coaxed.

"No," Ray rebuffed.

"Oh, shut up, Ray," she said pushing aside his arms and forcing her lips upon his mouth.

Ray struggled and shoved her away and before he could say another word, he heard a sharp cry, but it wasn't from her. It came from his right.

He turned and saw Maja. She was standing in the doorway looking at him and his ex with her eyes wide, but filled with tears ready to pour over her cheeks. Her ears were down. A sign that Ray knew that she had whenever she was saddened with a hand at her chest that was gripping into the material of her sweater.

"I see…" she cried and in one blink her tears flowed. "We were just a good time, weren't we? We were just a good time until you got her back. Well, you have your money and her….so there's no point in staying with us…is there?"

"*Who* is *this*, Ray?"

"Maja," Ray uttered.

Without another word, Maja dashed out of the door and into the night.

"Maja!" Ray cried out pushing his ex out of his arms.

"What in the name of Santa's Jingle balls is going on out here?" the voice of Hedvig called out, coming to the front doorstep with Tuva at her side.

"Maja just ran off," Ray explained.

"And who's this?" Tuva asked pointing at the woman who caused it all.

"My ex-fiancé," Ray answered, sneering the words in a loathing tone.

"This is the one who cheated on you?" Hedvig asked, cocking her eyebrow and looking the woman up and down.

"Yeah, but that's not important right now," Ray pointed out. "We need to find Maja."

"I'll call her phone," Tuva volunteered, going back inside to look for her phone.

"I'm going to try to find her," Ray said reaching inside to grab his coat and take off into the night.

"Ray, wait!" Angela called out.

"You lost him once," Hedvig said. "Compared to you, I think he upgraded. Which is something *you* should know about."

Chapter 16: The Christmas Tree Confession

Ray tried to follow Maja through the snow from his parents' house. At first, he kept track of a running antlered headed shape in the dark at the far edge of his vision. A shape that had an antlered head. He tried to push as hard as he could to catch up with her, but he knew that Maja was a faster runner than he was. But he didn't care...he kept running when the burning acidic feeling came into his mouth and his veins pounded with each running stride he made until it felt as if he was moving through thick mud. With his body screaming for him to stop, he found himself leaning against one of the streetlamps huffing and coughing into the cold air. Once he caught his breath, he went for his phone. What he found were a few messages from Hedvig and Tuva.

TUVA: We tried calling Maja but she's not answering her phone.

HEDVIG: I tried texting her too, she's not answering that either.

Seeing that, Ray couldn't stop himself from trying.

He called Maja's phone.

There was the ringing.

Once.

Twice.

Thrice.

"Come on, Maja," Ray begged while he wheezed. "Please, pick up. Please."

The ringing stopped and there came the voice message.

"Greetings," the message started. "This is Maja. Please leave me a message, and I'll get back to you after I finish this next chapter."

There was the tone from the phone that signaled to start recording his message.

"Maja," Ray began. "Please pick up. I *need* to talk to you."

He hung up and tried to text the same message to her.

But no reply came back.

"Ugh," he cried out in exasperation of the situation while his head turned upward and in his moment of frustration he asked, "I don't suppose anyone up there can give me a hand with this?"

He had hoped in the face of all the magical things that had happened to him and around him in the past month that maybe there'd be a deus ex machina moment. It would have been fitting for the holiday season. But there was none. There was only silence, the black sky, and the radiant light of the nearby Christmas decorations.

"Thanks a lot," Ray said, making sure his dejection was laid on thicker than a frozen milkshake.

Turning his head towards his left and down the road he saw a brighter glow of light. It was towards the town's central square where the courthouse and town square were located. The place where the four of them had their group date. The lights and decorations were still up sending out the bold glow into the dark night.

Ray shrugged and said to himself, "Worth a try."

Walking towards the towns square, he found that the Christmas Market was still setup with the various stands and decorations. The most prominent that his eyes kept coming to was the grand Christmas Tree near the courthouse that was like a tree shaped shadow covered in the strings of lights. A small town's attempt to recreate the tree at the Rockafeller Center. Ray had to admit that the way it glowed amid the streetlights and streetlamps gave it such a warm ethereal quality. A piece of heavenly light in a dark and cold world. Among the stands, there were still people out and enjoying the food, shops, and sights.

Taking a deep breath, he took a moment to remember how so much of his life had changed once again. Finding that job, finding Maja, Tuva, and Hedvig. Moving in with them and so much more.

"I don't deserve them," he acknowledged in a low whisper. "But Maja *deserves* to know the truth."

His eyes came down from the tree, and he saw a pair of reindeer antlers among the small crowd that gathered around the tree. While most were bundled up in their coats, scarves and hats but this one just wore a sweater.

"Maja!" Ray cried out as he broke into a dash to her not caring that his shoes were kicking up snow or even a mild risk of slipping. He wanted to *run* to *her*.

The person who had the antlers turned, and Ray saw the sweet face of Maja. Her expression held such mourning and melancholia while her arms were crossed holding her tight as if she were the only one who would hug her at that a moment.

"Hey, Ray," she answered while he came up to him. "I was just admiring this Christmas tree here. I wanted to have one more look at it. I mean...you've gotten back with your ex...and you have money...and...maybe...I'll go back to the Alfheimr and-"

"Maja, please stop," Ray said placing his hands on her shoulder and making her turn to face him. "It's all a big misunderstanding. I'm *not* getting back with my ex. I want to stay here with you. With Hedvig and Tuva as well. *I love you*. I love *all* of *you*. For god's sakes, Maja, I chased you down through the cold, and you know I'm not the best runner. I know it's been a short time, but I've come to care for all of you as you've done so much for-"

Maja's hand reached up to his cheek. The touch of her cold fingers and palms against his skin made him stop talking to gaze his love in the face. The expression Maja held had transformed from mourning and melancholia to one of tearful jubilation. In the light of the Christmas tree, it almost looked like her eyes were sparkling when it filled with tears.

"You said that you love me," she said while shaking her head. "That's all I needed to hear. Ray...I love you so much."

She took her hand away from his face and wrapped her arms around his neck, bringing him in tight while her chilled lips pressed against his. For Ray, nothing else mattered. He had Maja, Tuva, and Hedvig. Nothing more could be asked for.

Then something happened. Something miraculous, but something so silly at the same time.

Ray started to feel something icy and cold on his cheek. Pulling back from Maja's kiss and embrace he saw white flakes landing on her hair. Looking up and around he discovered that it was starting to snow.

Maja began to laugh. "Seriously?"

"What?"

"It's *snowing* at a time like *this*," Maja observed still laughing and making a light slap on his shoulder. "This is like one of those insipid Christmas movies."

"Well, shall we head back before it gets any cheesier?"

Maja nodded while her ears flapped away the snowflakes that landed on them. She wrapped her arms around his left arm.

No sooner had Ray uttered the sentence that the moment had reached a far greater level of insipidness.

Several dozen feet away, there was a stage that was still set up for singers. It was a place that Ray had remembered a choir singing Christmas Carols. For the moment that Ray had with Maja, the singer and musicians were taking a break but then the players took up their instruments and a blonde woman in an ice blue dress stepped up to the microphone.

The band began to play, and she began to sing.

The song that was Mariah Carey's "All I want for Christmas is You."

"*Oh, my gods!*" Maja laughed while rolling her eyes. "It happened!"

"Let's run then." Ray laughed with her.

"I love you, Ray," Maja declared as she continued to laugh and held onto his arm tighter while they made their way back.

***

"Maja!" Hedvig cried when the pair came through the door of Ray's parents' house. The yule cat woman dashed to her and wrapped her arms around her.

"I'm quite alright, hon," Maja said, petting her lover's long white hair and patting her back.

Hedvig pulled away and slapped her on the shoulder. "*What the hell!?*" she demanded. "Running away like that!"

"My apologies, hon," Maja said, turning down her face and her ears. "I didn't mean to worry everyone. It was just...a bad moment."

"We all have those, sweetie," Tuva said, coming up to her and kissing her lips. "But you really shouldn't run off without telling us like that. We were worried about you."

"I'm quite alright, everyone," Maja reassured. "Especially now that I know how Ray here feels about me and all of us."

She leaned in and kissed his lips.

"There you are, Ray," an unwelcome and familiar voice called out.

Angela came over with her arms wide open as if she was about to hug him as well, but Ray held up a hand to stop her. There was rich satisfaction of revenge in the action. It was a move that she had done to him so many times in the past. Whenever she was upset with him and he would try to hug her to show her that he was sorry, even though it was never his fault, she would push him away as if he meant nothing to her.

At that moment *she* meant *nothing* to him.

"*Don't even try,*" he said sounding colder than the outside winter air. "You wouldn't have even thought about coming back to me if you hadn't wanted me to pay your way and support your selfish lifestyle."

"That's not true," Angela refuted.

"Yes, it is. I was nothing but a means to fulfill *your* dreams. You wanted *everything* all at once. When all I wanted was to be *loved* and *cared* for but all you cared about was you. You turned every conversation, action and emotion into the means to gratify yourself. But now, I have these three wonderful women who actually love and care for me, just like I love and care for them."

"It's just a sex thing, Ray. You'll get bored and find your way back to me. Your life is *empty* and *meaningless* without me."

"Oh, fuck you," Hedvig interjected.

"Ray, *darling*," Angela said sounding disgusted while she sneered at Hedvig and pointed at her as if she were a turd that needed to be scooped up. "Could you *please* leash your *whore*?"

Ray raised his eyebrows and cocked a smile towards her. "Are you the pot or the kettle here?"

"And fuck you and eat my ass," Hedvig said, stepping forward and shoving her finger into Angela's chest. "Fuck you, fuck the high horse you rode in on, fuck your privileged and spoiled ass, fuck your entitlement and fuck the cunt that farted you out."

Angela's eyes went wide, and her mouth went wider as if she never heard anyone speak to her in such a way in her entire life.

"Hedvig!" Tuva scolded.

"What?" Hedvig shrugged. "We were all thinking it. I just had the ovaries to say it."

"She's right," Ray said addressing his ex. "After all you did to me and all you put me through, you're lucky I'm talking to you. So, kindly fuck off."

"No," she refuted. "I'm the *best* thing that happened to *you*. You'll see it one way or another."

"I doubt that and since kindly didn't work...so *fuck off*." Ray said, before turning to his loves. "What'd you all say we just go home?"

"I would agree to that," Maja agreed.

"Well, at least the food was good," Tuva conceded.

"Wish the same could be said of the people," Hedvig said before looking at Ray's ex-fiancé to get one last word in. "You know the American Kennel Club called; they want you back home...with your *mom*."

"Hedvig!" Tuva called out.

"Oh, come on!" Hedvig protested. "You gotta let me have at least that one."

The four of them left and Maja couldn't help but give an encouraging wink to Hedvig for her most excellent of eloquence insults.

***

"Alright, sweeties," Tuva called out, "get ready for a real holiday treat."

Ray, Maja, and Hedvig were waiting at the breakfast nook for the newest culinary creation of the elf. Once they had arrived back home after all the excitement that happened at the Christmas party it was decided, on Tuva's part, that she make something special for the group. What it was, she wouldn't say other than it was going to be a surprise.

The three waited until it came out, and their eyes widened at the sheer massiveness of the creation. Tuva had brought over four large sized mugs that had a small mountain of whipped cream on top with a candy cane pushed through on one side and a miniature chocolate covered doughnut on the other. The miniature baked good sat at the edge of the cup as if it were a garnish.

"Holy shit," Hedvig uttered, looking at the thing. "This has to be your most outrageous creation, Tuva."

"I think this beats out last year's creation of the peppermint and mocha cupcakes," Maja said, moving in her seat to look at the creation from various angles.

"What exactly is this?" Ray asked, feeling curious and hungry at the sight of it.

"Oh, that's right, this will be your first of my Christmas creations," Tuva said. "What you have here is a very special hot chocolate."

"What's the special part?" Ray asked but then amended, "Apart from the sheer delight of the sight of it with the candy cane and doughnut."

"The special part, sweetie." Tuva said as she winked at him, while her finger tapped her chin, "is that this is made with some very special ingredients that are only found in Alfheimr."

"*No*," Maja uttered, looking at the elf, then to her own mug and back to the elf again. "You managed to get a hold of *Alfheimr chocolate*?"

"A relative of a relative managed to find some for me." Tuva nodded. "Don't let it get too cold, sweeties."

"Well then, bottoms up," Maja said before taking her mug and lifting it up and tasting the hot beverage. After several sips, she sat it down not caring about the whipped cream that had pasted itself on her nose and cheeks. "Sweet Christmas, that's good."

Ray looked at the drink and reached with delicate fingers and a careful grip for the doughnut and ate it. He expected, at first, for it to be akin to the grocery store bought mini doughnuts but when the thing hit his mouth and tongue, he felt sensations he never thought such a miniature creation would give. There was an engulfing wave of goodness that started from his mouth, combed over his head, down his back, though his legs and back up into his groin where he felt the first tingles of arousal. It was as if he were being caressed by silken feathers both inside and outside of his body.

"Wow," he uttered before devouring the rest of the doughnut.

"Be careful, Ray," Tuva warned, "Alfheimr chocolate is quite something to humans."

Ray shrugged. "Okay then, but don't care; this is fantastic!"

He took the mug and began to take careful and light sips of it. The temperature of it was just right. It wasn't too hot that it would burn the tip of the tongue, thus ruining the rest of the drink, but at the same time it wasn't too cold that would leave the drinker wishing it to be warmer. Yet, when he took those sips, he felt the same ecstasy of sensation brushing over him in waves from his lips and mouth all through his body.

"Oh my god, that's *amazing*," Ray uttered, feeling the tingle in his groin begin to grow. When his eyes looked over his lovers, he started to feel arousal for them, and he wanted them then and there. "Tuva? When you said that this chocolate is quite something to humans. What'd you mean?"

"Oh, are you starting to feel it, Ray?" Tuva asked with a wink. Her hands nestled her mug and running her tongue over the remnants of whipped cream at the edges while she kept eye contact with her lover.

"Feeling what?" Ray asked, being coy but knowing full well the fire that was starting to smolder inside him.

"Alfheimr chocolate, hon," Maja said, reaching under the table to his thigh. Her palm moving towards his groin. "It's an...*aphrodisiac.*"

Ray chuckled. "As if I need an aphrodisiac for you ladies."

It was true after all from Ray's point of view. He had three wonderful, loving, and beautiful ladies. The day that he needed anything like that for them was the day that he knew that he had left the mortal world. He took another sip of the hot chocolate feeling his arousal and desire growing stronger and stronger. It made itself known by the fact that he was rock-hard to the point of pain and his desire crying to be released.

After another sip his eyes looked over at Maja who developed that signature look of hers that she wanted to fuck, and she wanted it then and there.

Ray pushed himself away from the table, reached down for the button and zipper of his pants, and opened them up for his lover as if it were an early Christmas present. His cock popped up but was still covered by his underwear. He adjusted himself, freeing his cock from his boxers so it was ready to greet the woman he proclaimed his love for.

"Want another sweet treat, Maja?" Ray asked gripping his cock for her and spreading his legs wide.

"Oh, yes, please," Maja agreed while her fingers went for the whipped cream of her drink. She scooped up a little and set it on top of Ray's cock before she got down on her knees in between his legs. She opened her mouth, stuck out her tongue and ran it over his cock as she licked at the whipped cream.

"Mmmmm...." Ray moaned leaning back his head.

Ray wanted to watch Maja, but the pleasure was so much that it made his eyes roll into the back of his head. The motion was usually a telltale sign of his own orgasm and yet he didn't ejaculate just yet. Maybe it was a different kind of orgasm, one that didn't end with anything erupting from him. Pulling his head forward he willed himself to look down and saw Maja's antlered head bobbing up and down on him to the point that her antlers were lightly touching him sometimes. As he enjoyed the sensations, suddenly her movements changed, and her antlers scratched against his chest.

"Ah!" he uttered as the antlers came away.

"Are you okay, hon?" Maja asked pulling back while her hand continued the motions that her mouth was making.

"I'm okay," Ray answered. "Just your antlers hit me."

"Oh!" Maja said, bringing both hands to her face. "I'm so sorry, hon."

"It's okay." Ray laughed. "Don't let that stop you."

"Well, for hitting you with these," she said, pointing to her antlers. "I think that warrants a punishment."

She got to her feet and turned around giving a good view of her toned ass as she bent over.

"I believe you know what to do, hon," she said, wiggling her ass at him.

"Yes, I do," Ray said standing up letting his boxers and pants fall to his ankles. He reached for the waistband of Maja's pants and pulled them down along with her panties over her exquisite ass. Once they were down to her thighs, he pushed the hem of the sweater up her back to get a good look at her cute and sweet tail that wiggled over her sweet vertical crevice.

Looking up he saw that Hedvig and Tuva were doing something similar. The elf was lying back on the table, her legs spread wide open, and her feet set on the table's edge. Her pants were completely off, and her sweater was pushed up, along with her bra, to expose her breasts that she was massaging with both hands. In between her legs was the white-haired-cat-eared head of Hedvig who was taking her sweet time in eating out her elvish lover.

"Yes..." Tuva moaned. "Don't stop, sweetie. Oh fuck...your tongue is delicious...please, don't stop...ah..."

Ray watched Hedvig's head move with a rapidity that signified how excited and aroused she was to eat out the elf. He could even hear sounds of slurping coming from Hedvig's lips.

"Unnnngggg..." Tuva moaned, her back arching as she pinched her nipples and thrashed her head left and right, "Eat this pussy! Fucking eat it! AHHH!"

"Mmmm," Maja cooed before she turned her head and looked over at Ray. "Come on, Ray...let's not just watch."

"Right...ummm..." he uttered, rubbing his hands over her ass and giving each cheek a squeeze.

"You can fuck me while you spank me this time," Maja encouraged.

"Yeah?"

"I'm ready, and I *need* it," Maja encouraged. "And I want to feel you *inside* me...but first...I need a *punishment*..."

Ray smiled, cupping one cheek of her buttocks and brought his hand back before letting it loose against the skin over her sweet ass.

CRACK!

The echo reverberated through the living room and kitchen.

"AH!" Maja squealed. "Oooh, that's so good..."

Ray leaned against Maja and kissed her shoulder while he whispered in her ear, "And here comes something else."

"Ray..." she whispered back.

But Ray didn't stop, he took one cheek of her, spread it to the side to show her waiting womanhood and pushed his cock against her lips and shoved it deep down into her.

"Fuuuuuuuuccck...". Maja moaned out, gripping the side of the tables while she let her head down on the table turning it to one side.

Ray gripped onto her thighs, pulled back and thrust again, and again, and again until the table was rocking forward to which Hedvig held onto it to keep their sexual platform in one spot. She started using the extra movement to tease Tuva even more.

"Ah...ah...ah!" Maja moaned.

"Mmmm...." Tuva moaned in accompaniment to Maja's sexual utterances.

"Maja!" Ray grimaced while he bit down on his lip feeling the building tension inside him and knowing that it wouldn't take long before his essence would be let loose. He let go of his lip and bit down on his tongue then bit into his cheek. But none of it was working.

"Ray...ah...Ray..." Maja begged, "don't cum inside me...I want you to cum on my face!"

Maja held onto the edge of the table and gave a good push back against Ray's cock making him take a step back. With his cock slipping out of her and with just enough room to move, she got up, turned around and got down on her knees in front of her lover. Her arms wrapped around his legs while her head tilted back with her mouth wide open.

"Mark me as yours, Ray!" she begged. "Cum in my mouth, on my face, on my tits...cum on me, my love!"

Ray reached down for his cock and began to stroke it while Maja's face was tilted upward towards him with her eyes closed, mouth open, and her tongue sticking out ready to receive its gooey treat. There was a sensation of weakness in his knees and Ray reached out for the table to support his body while his hand stroked himself.

Out of the side of his eye he could still see Hedvig eating out Tuva, and the elf was continuing her exquisite flavor of dirty talk.

"Suck on my clit, Hedvig!" she begged. "Suck on my clit and make me cum! Please! Please make me cum!"

"Hnnnnn...". Ray grunted feeling the cum rising and ready to burst from within. He turned and saw some of it had erupted from the tip of his cock and landed on Maja's tongue. And then it spurted more. Some of it hit her upper lip and leaked down into Maja's open mouth but some jumped over her mouth and landed on her nose. As the shot oozed down to her cheek, his spurt landed on her chin and dropped onto her breasts.

Maja reached up, scooped it down to her mouth and slurped it all up like the whipped cream of her hot chocolate.

"Mmm..." she hummed her delight. "Sweeter than ambrosia."

Ray took a deep breath and leaned against the table.

"Easy there, hon," Maja said, reaching out to Ray to help him steady himself.

"That was one of the more powerful orgasms I've had in a while," Ray remarked and was about to go further in his statement but then he looked down to his cock. Under most circumstances he would have already gone soft and flaccid after cumming, but he saw that he was as rock hard as he was before Maja started sucking him.

"Ooooooo..." Tuva cooed. "I love all of you...you all eat my pussy so well."

Ray looked over and saw how Tuva had her back arched against the table and was slowly going lax while her hands cupped her breasts.

"Well..." Ray laughed. "Each of you had such a delicious pussy."

"Fucking right," Hedvig agreed, pulling herself from Tuva's groin. Her expression was one of smug satisfaction with how her eyes were closed, a toothy grin spread wide across her face and her hand coming up to wipe away the thick layer of Tuva's juices. "Mmmm-mmmm, puss-say! It's delicious!"

"And I don't know about you, lovers," Tuva said sitting up and taking her sweater off completely. "I want some more."

"In that case," Ray said, taking off the rest of his clothes and leaving them on the floor, "Let's go to our big bed."

"And I can whole heartedly agree to that,"

Maja seconded the motion as she got to her feet, pulling off her sweater and tossing it aside before she went for her pants. In her nudity she looked over at Tuva and Hedvig and began to run her hands together. "I wonder which of our ladies I should have first, Ray."

"Well, I think Tuva could use some of this cock," Ray said, teasing a little.

"Oh yes please," Tuva concurred, getting off the table. "To our bedroom."

The four lovers went up to the bedroom and on and on the rounds of love went. Ray with Tuva while Maja had Hedvig. Then Ray fucked

Hedvig while Tuva and Maja got it on.

It was just after midnight when the four lovers felt their collective fatigue and pulled the covers over themselves and slept in each other's arms.

Chapter 17: Christmas Morning

R ay remembered other times that he awoke on Christmas morning. From the times when he was a kid when there was excitement and anticipation to go downstairs and open the Christmas presents in the hopes of something that he had been waiting for all year long. Then there were the times as an adult when it was just another day. This was especially true during his time with his ex-fiancé when he had spent so much of his money to fulfill her wishes throughout the year that he barely had enough for the holiday.

This Christmas morning Ray awoke but kept his eyes closed and he could feel the smile on his face. It was from knowing that his life wasn't just some wonderful dream that was going to end at any moment. He felt the warm bodies of his loves and lovers next to him. Maja. Tuva. Hedvig. Each one was sleeping in such peaceful and heavenly sleep next to him, naked and sated from the night before.

Maja was sleeping at Ray's left with her horns poking up against the headboard. Behind her was Tuva whose massive breasts were pressed up against Maja's back while her arm was draped over the reindeer woman. To Ray's right was Hedvig who was curled up against his side and snoring at a light volume. She was also doing that one thing he found adorable about her: she was purring in her sleep while her ears twitched.

The three of them were all comfortable and warm beneath the thick down blanket and exquisite sheets.

If I could spend all Christmas in this bed with all three of you, Ray thought, *I'd be okay with that.*

But of course, something interrupted the idea.

The urge to use the bathroom.

Shit, Ray cursed not wanting to get up but knowing that he had to.

He pulled himself from Hedvig's embrace and the yule cat woman simply rolled over onto one side not knowing that Ray was getting up. After making the careful maneuver to pull himself out of the massive bed, he made ginger steps towards the bathroom. There was a sharp chill to the air despite the heater kicking on but despite the cold, Ray turned to look back at the massive bed that he shared with them.

Leaning against the doorway to the bathroom, he smiled.

Turning around, he went to the bathroom and came back out. He smirked, knowing that he needed to crawl back into bed with all of them. Taking his position, he crawled into the spot between Hedvig and Maja. Once at the spot he wiggled himself under the covers and curled up in their shared warmth.

"Mmmm," Maja uttered, sounding like a combination of a yawn and low moan. "You're cold, Ray."

"You're awake?" Ray whispered.

"On and off for a while," she answered, opening her eyes to her lover. "Come here and let me warm you up."

Smiling, Ray scooted himself over and brought himself into Maja's embrace feeling how warm her body was compared to his. He pulled the covers up to his face and snuggled in with the reindeer woman.

"Aww, no fair," a voice meowed from behind them as Hedvig came up, wrapped her arms around Ray and pressed her body up against him.

"Oh, ladies," Ray said, "I'm not going anywhere. You can each have me to yourselves."

"Especially this," Hedvig said bringing her warm hand down Ray's front until she was cupping his cock and balls and caused a stirring as he started growing hard in her gentle digits.

"Mmmm," Ray moaned with a smile on his face while his hips began to gyrate into Hedvig's palm.

"Easy there, sweetie," Tuva called out, sounding half asleep. "Ray gave us all a good pounding last night. Let him rest a little."

"It's okay, Tuva," Ray countered with his eyes closed and his cock growing hard. "I just love the way you all touch me."

"Well," Tuva said throwing off the covers. "Since we're all awake, I shall start on breakfast."

Ray sat up feeling Hedvig's hand come away from his crotch. "Are you sure you want to cook today, Tuva? I mean, you cook for us so much."

Tuva was at the door standing as bare as the day Ray first had sex with her at the soup kitchen. She turned, crossed her arms, and smiled at her love and lover before she got onto the bed and crawled her way to him.

He watched the way she moved. Each step of her arms and legs while her movement gave special emphasis to her massive breasts and how they swayed with each motion. Ray wanted so much to stare at them, but he brought his gaze up to Tuva's sweet green eyes.

"Oh, Ray." She smiled closing the distance between them and bent over to him. Her hands coming up on either side of him before her lips met with his. "You're *such* a sweetheart, and I love you dearly. But the kitchen is my domain, you should know that by now. So, I'll go make breakfast. And by the way, sweetie, my tits are down here."

Pulling herself from Ray, she stood back up and headed out the door and Ray's gaze followed every inch of her bare body as she left.

"And I think we should all get dressed," Maja said, kissing Ray's cheek and bouncing and bounding her way off the bed and out the door. "As much as I'd like to stay naked and show off for you, lovers, it's pretty chilly and I'd hate to catch cold."

"Or we could just stay in bed," Hedvig suggested, pulling Ray back into her embrace.

"Not for what we have planned for today, Hedvig." Maja smirked waving her finger at the yule cat woman. "We do have presents."

Hedvig paused for a moment and then pulled away from Ray. "You got me there."

With that, Hedvig sat up, rolled out of the bed, and making a graceful landing on her feet just like a cat would, and breezed past Maja. The reindeer woman watched her lover move past her before she looked back at Ray and gave a smirking shrug.

"I guess we're all up now," she surmised before heading out behind her.

"I guess we are." Ray smiled before getting up and getting himself dressed in his pajamas and his thick slipper socks. While he did, he noticed how much whiter the light was at the edge of the curtains.

After pulling on his sweater, he came up to the window and pushed aside the black out curtains and saw the fresh blanket of snow that covered the landscape of the neighborhood. Seeing it made him feel cold on the outside, but at the same time, it warmed his heart to see such a picture-perfect sight of fresh snow without a single footprint made in it. The sight made him feel like a kid again, wanting to go outside and play in the cascading white powder.

But there were other things to do that day.

He let go of the curtain and headed downstairs where he not only heard the television playing a Christmas movie, but there was the magical wafting smoky smell of Tuva cooking bacon and sausage. Coming to the kitchen and peeking in, he saw that Tuva was preparing a breakfast feast. Ray knew this since she had all four of the gas burners on, one had the sausage cooking in it, the other had bacon, and another she was making eggs, and the fourth had hashbrowns sizzling in it.

It was a sight that always amazed Ray that Tuva had skills that would put most professionally trained chefs to shame. Yet he couldn't help but just look at the elf and smile. He turned to the living room to find Hedvig lying on the couch watching "How the Grinch Stole Christmas" with Maja curled up next to her and reading. The Christmas tree itself was plugged in with the lights giving off its multicolored glow, and the fireplace had its roaring fire going.

The sight warmed Ray even more on the inside than the outside as he came to the living room and joined Hedvig and Maja on the couch. Seeing him coming over, Maja scooted to one side so that Ray could sit in between her and Maja. Once he sat down, Maja reached out and took his hand while the other held open the book that she was reading. He looked over at the reindeer woman and leaned in to kiss her cheek while he looked over at Hedvig who was engrossed in the TV. Leaning over he kissed her cat-like ear that twitched against his face.

"Hey," Hedvig whispered as she turned, rubbing her ear. She smiled and leaned up to kiss him as well.

"Alright, sweeties!" Tuva called from the kitchen. "Christmas Breakfast is almost ready."

"Yay!" Hedvig squealed, as she leaped up from the couch and headed into the kitchen where she picked up a plate from a stack that Tuva had set out.

Maja placed a bookmark into her book and set it aside before getting up to get her breakfast as well while Ray followed behind.

That morning was a little different from the others. Under other circumstances, Ray noticed how Tuva would be the one to setup the plating as if she were a chef in a five-star restaurant. But that morning things were set up more like a buffet where she had setup a small stack of plates on one counter while there were serving dishes and bowls filled with hash browns, bacon, sausage, eggs, slices of bread not yet toasted, and a decanter of orange juice with four glasses set around it.

The sight brought a grin to Ray's face in how it made him think of how his mom was in the kitchen, but at the same time Tuva had her own uniqueness when it came to her culinary magic.

Hedvig had gotten a plate with a little bit of eggs but a lot of bacon and hash browns. She skipped the toast but got a glass of orange juice. Maja, on the other hand, was a little more equal and precise when she got her portions. The same could be said of Tuva only she got a little portion of each.

Once the toast was ready, the polycue headed to the table and began to eat.

"Mmmm." Ray smiled and hummed in his gratitude. "So good but really, Tuva, if you ever want a break from the kitchen, don't hesitate to ask."

"Oh, sweetie," Tuva cooed, leaning over to kiss his forehead. "I never tire of this. But if I'm ever sick or anything, I'll be sure to ask."

"Has that ever happened?" he asked the others.

"Once," Hedvig answered. "Last year. It was actually during Autumn's End."

"Autumn what?" Ray asked.

"Autumn's End," Maja explained. "It's a festival roughly around November similar to what humans call Thanksgiving. Poor Tuva was sick and couldn't cook even though she wanted to, but she had a bad fever and couldn't get out of bed. So, Hedvig and I stepped in and tried to make her something hearty."

"Old fashioned Chicken Noodle soup," Tuva recalled and smiled as she munched on sausage. "It was the sweetest thing you two had done for me."

"That's not the only thing." Hedvig winked bringing up two fingers to either side of her mouth and flicked out her tongue at the elf.

Tuva blushed. "Of course, sweetie. There's that."

"Now you have a third to help out in the kitchen when the need comes up," Ray added. "But I can't wait to see how you three will like the presents I got for you."

"I'm sure we'll all love it, Ray," Maja assured in her smile.

***

After breakfast was done, Tuva gathered up the plates and brought them over to the sink where she set them in and came back out into the living room where Ray, Hedvig and Maja were congregating.

"Alright," Tuva said coming in, "who'll be in charge of handing out the gifts?"

Ray made the immediate interjection. "Since I'm the new guy. I'll do it."

"That makes you our Santa," Hedvig teased as she poked Ray in his belly. "Ho...ho...ho..."

Ray chuckled as he leaned in and kissed Hedvig before he went over to the pile of presents under the tree. The first one he picked up was an oblong one that had the elegant script written on its tag "To Maja, from Ray."

He handed the gift over to Maja then he went specifically for the gifts that he got for each lady. By the time that he gave the final gift to Hedvig, the ladies were already starting to rip at the packaging.

"Oh, Ray!" Maja cried out in her surprised bliss. "I love it!"

Ray turned and saw the gift that he had gotten for her. It was a hardcover copy of the year's best sapphic erotica. Maja held it up and then hugged it close to her chest and even lay halfway down on the couch with it as if it were a pillow.

"For this gift, Ray," she stated, "I'd have you on this couch right now, but there are other gifts to give."

"Let's see what Ray got me," Tuva said, ripping off more of the gift paper. She was smiling but when she saw the gift her smile melted, and her hand came up to her face. "Oh...oh sweetie..."

Fear gripped onto Ray's stomach as his guts twisted, and face felt cold.

"Is...um...Tuva?"

Tuva held onto the gift, got up from the couch and came over the Ray and wrapped her arms around him and squeezed him in her hug.

"Sweetie, I absolutely love it," she whispered.

"What'd he get you?" Hedvig asked.

Tuva held up the item. It was a DVD copy of the limited-edition director's cut of the movie "Army of Darkness" by Sam Raimi with rare behind-the-scenes footage, director and star's commentary.

"Only forty-thousand of these were released," Tuva explained. "Look it even has a serial number on it."

She mentioned this as she turned the case around and showed the number of 27842/40000

"I don't know how you got this, Ray," Tuva said coming back to her lover and squeezing him tight. "But I love it. Thank you...thank you so much."

"Tuva!" Maja cried out, "I don't think Ray can breathe."

Ray was having trouble breathing but being held so tight in Tuva' voluptuousness was always a welcomed event. But being told about Ray, she let go.

"Oh, I'm sorry, Ray," she said, patting his cheek. "Are you alright?"

"I'm alright," Ray laughed. "Just didn't know if you'd like the gift that much. I figured a horror movie buff like you would have something like this in their collection already."

"I do, but not this one," Tuva said leaning in to kiss his lips. "Thank you, Ray."

"My turn!" Hedvig cried out with her gift as she ripped it open and found a small box inside. Opening the box, she reached in and pulled out a special collar. It was made of dragon scale-like metallic pieces in the colors of pink and purple with a simple ring at the front and metal buckle at the back. "Wow..."

"You like it?" Ray asked.

"I fucking love it!" Hedvig cried holding it out for Ray. "Collar me, please?"

"Shouldn't we all do that?" Ray asked.

"Perhaps, hon," Maja answered. "But out of the three of us, I think you're the most dominant one so, I think you should collar Hedvig."

Without saying a word, Ray went over to Hedvig's spot on the couch.

She got up from the couch, knelt in front of him, still offering up the collar to her dominant. As he unbuckled it, the yule cat woman took her long white hair and held it up as best as she could to offer her neck to her lover. Ray brought the thing up and wrapped it around her neck and buckled it in place with the buckle under her chin. Once set, he twisted it around her neck so that the buckle was at the back of her neck while the ring was under her chin.

"There," Ray said pulling back his hands and admiring how the dragon scales reflected the Christmas lights but still held their anodized aluminum colors of pink and purple that contrasted against her tan skin and white hair.

"Thank you, Ray," Hedvig said letting down her hair. Ray leaned down and gave her a sweet touch of his lips against hers. She got up and looked at her loves, bringing her hand to the collar. "How do I look, everyone?"

"You look submissively sexy, Hedvig," Maja answered.

"The next thing we need for you is a leash," Tuva stated.

Hearing that Ray tried his best to hide a smirk on his face.

"And now we have gifts for you, Ray," Maja announced coming over to the tree. She knelt and gathered up three wrapped gifts and brought them over to her boyfriend, lover, and friend.

Ray sat down on the couch with the wrapped gifts in hand and saw there was one gift from each of the ladies. He reached out for one from Maja and began to rip at the paper. He could already feel that it was a book given its thickness, weight, and the fact that he could feel a slight indent through the wrapping paper along the edges. But what book, he wasn't sure. Once the paper was off, he only saw the backside of it, but he turned it over and saw the title.

"Art of Spider-man: Across the Spider-Verse".

Ray smiled. "I love it, Maja."

He began to open the book and flip through the multitude of pages showing every scene, character, and shot from the film. From the concept sketches, storyboards and on and on until the finished product.

"Thank you," he said, holding it to his chest the way that Maja did.

"My turn," Tuva added holding up her hand.

"Alright then," Ray said shoving aside the ripped wrapping paper for the gift from Tuva. He could already feel that it was a book as well just like the first one, but there was something else on top of it given the pronounced bulge in it. He ripped it open and saw two black covered books with a pack of his favorite brand of pens he used for his sketches. He flipped open the books to find that the pages were blank and unlined.

"We each saw that you're really filling up your sketchbook, " Tuva explained. "So, we each thought that you needed a new one and some new pens too."

"Thank you, Tuva," Ray beamed his thanks to the elf and the others.

"And that leaves mine," Hedvig added.

Hedvig's was wider and thicker than the others but there was a certain heaviness to it. Feeling that weight, Ray started to wonder what kind of gift the yule cat woman got for him. Tearing open the paper he found a plain white box underneath it all that one would find when one bought clothes from high end clothing stores. He opened the box and found pink and purple tissue paper inside. He pushed through it and found a sweater inside.

Reaching in for the garment, Ray immediately felt that was something more to the sweater. First, he set the box and wrapping paper aside and set the sweater on his lap. Pulling at it, he found it was an ugly Christmas sweater that read, "Merry Christmas, ya filthy animal."

Ray began to burst out laughing at it.

"Wouldn't be a yule cat if I didn't make sure someone got some clothes," Hedvig remarked. "But wait till you see what's inside."

Following his lover's instructions, he pulled open the sweater and found something else inside. A great book that read, "Dungeons and Dragons:

Player's Handbook" and next to it was a set of red opaque dice in a small plastic container.

"I remembered you mentioned wanting to play," Hedvig said. "Now, you have something to start a character with before we get you into a group."

"Can't wait to get started," Ray said, looking at his gifts.

"But there's one more form all of us," Maja began as she went over and brought out one final gift to Ray.

Holding it out, Ray set aside Hedvig's gifts and received the wrapped package from Maja. He tore open the wrapping paper and found another book but the title on the front read, "How to write a graphic novel".

"You told all of us how you want to write a graphic novel, so we'd like to encourage you to start and if you don't know how then this will help."

Looking at it and all the gifts, Ray couldn't help but feel a stinging in his eyes. He reached up and started to rub at his eyes with the back of his hand.

"Are you okay, sweetie?" Tuva asked coming to his side.

"I'm sorry, everyone," Ray sniffled. "It's just…it's all so good. It's still so amazing that in the span of one month, not only have you all taken me on as your lover, but also your boyfriend and had me move into your home. It's like I became a member of the family so quickly."

"Well, of course you did, hon," Maja said, coming over to Ray and taking him in his arms. "We all love you."

"We certainly do," Tuva said, coming over and hugging Ray from one side.

"Yeah," Hedvig said, coming to the other side and taking in the impromptu group hug.

After a moment the group hug broke apart and Ray looked at his loves and said, "But I know this season isn't about the giving or getting. Because I know what the best part of this season is."

"What's that?" Hedvig asked.

Ray smiled and reached into the pile of torn up wrapping paper and found three bows. He reached out and placed one on Hedvig's sweater, then onto Tuva's and finally onto Maja's.

"All three of you," he said. "That's the greatest gift of all is all of you coming into my life and being showered with your love."

"Such a sweetheart you are," Tuva said, leaning in to kiss him.

Maja said nothing and kissed him as well.

At that moment, Hedvig giggled.

"What's funny?" Ray asked.

The yule cat woman stopped her giggling and leaned in and kissed Ray before pulling back and laughed, "Tuva's right. You're a sweetheart, Ray, but this moment feels like a holiday movie of our own."

Ray let out a balking laugh. "You're right. Only our Christmas movie has a lot more sex in it."

"And there is one thing missing," Hedvig added. "We need someone from royalty in this."

"How could you have forgotten, Hedvig?" Maja asked sounding offended. "Let's not forget that Tuva is royalty."

"She is?!" Ray asked shocked by the news turning to face Tuva to confirm what his ears had told him.

The elf woman was blushing and giving a sheepish grin as she shrugged.

"I suppose you would have found out sooner or later, Ray," Tuva said, sounding like a surprise had been spoiled. "But it is true. I am of elvish royalty. My full title is Princess Tuva of House Orimaris."

"If you're royalty…" Ray asked, trying to come to terms and understand the reality of such a bombshell. "What in the world are you doing in the human realm?"

Tuva smiled. "I already told you why, Ray. Besides…I may be of royalty, but I have several brothers and sisters so there's no shortage of heirs. Plus I renounced my royalty when I came to the human realm. All I want to do is cook, make sweet treats, and have amazing sex with all of you. I just hope you don't think less of me because of this."

Her face became downturned and, Ray wasn't sure of it, but he thought that even her ears became downcast.

"I never would, Tuva," he said, coming closer and hugging her and kissing her and even laying multiple quick kisses on her ears.

"Hey now." She giggled while giving him a playful shove, "I'm sure there will be plenty of time for that later, sweetie."

"Quite so," Maja agreed. "And we still have some more gifts."

On and on the giving of gifts went. Maja had received an illustrated copy of the Kama Sutra as well as several manga from a series called "World's End Harem: Fantasia". In addition to that she had also received a very high-end remote-controlled vibrator and a new pair of running shoes. To which she replied, "Can't wait to try them both out."

For Tuva, she received a DVD copy of such adult film classics as *Deep Throat* and *Debbie Does Dallas*. Sure, one could get them on streaming, but streaming adult films was always a hassle. She also received special copies of *Tales from the Crypt*, *The Vault of Horror*, and *Tales from the Hood*. Then there were a couple of fine baking pans from Sur La Table.

Hedvig's gifts consisted of a basket of assorted bath bombs as well as more plushies for her ever-growing collection. On top of that were some more comfortable sweaters with various designs on them. One had a pair of twenty-sided dice with text saying "Yes, they're natural". But the final piece was something that Tuva, Maja and Ray put together. It was a build a bear that they made to look like it was gaming with a stitched-on headset and game controller in its hand. Yet, that still wasn't the end of it. They told Hedvig to squeeze it and it played an audio message from the three of them saying, "We love you, Hedvig!" The yule cat woman hugged it and said how much she loved it in a tone that bordered upon crying.

But things were not over yet.

"And I have one more gift each for you," Ray said reaching to the back side of the tree where he pulled out three rectangular gifts. He gave one to Maja, Hedvig, and Tuva. As if on cue, the three of them opened up the gifts together, and they each saw what they were.

Their gifts were framed pieces of artwork that Ray had created of each lady. The first was of Maja posed among books as if she were an antlered patron goddess of books. The same could be said of the piece of Tuva where she was posed in a kitchen wearing nothing but a chef's hat, oven mitts and holding a tray of freshly baked cookies. Finally, there was the one of Hedvig where she was posed in a gamers chair holding a controller and wearing a headset as if she were some kind of gaming streamer.

"Hope you all like them," Ray said smiling.

"I love it," Hedvig stated.

"So do I," Maja added.

"Oh, sweetie," Tuva said, standing up and coming over to Ray and hugging him. "It's one of the sweetest gifts you've given me."

And she kissed him.

And on the kisses came from them all.

But things were still not over.

***

Ray surveyed the landscape of gifts and torn up paper and smiled to himself as he said, "What a lovely Christmas."

"But there's more," Hedvig said as she looked over at Tuva and Maja and gave a jerk of her head to follow her.

The two lovers followed the yule cat woman and Ray stayed behind to gather up the ripped wrapping paper for the trash. It didn't take him too long and he was already putting away the last bit into the trash bag when he heard the ladies coming back. He was tying up the trash bag when he heard the voice of Maja.

"Oh, hon?" she called with a tone that carried layers upon inviting layers of seduction.

Ray looked up from his work and found Maja, Tuva, and Hedvig all standing in the living room completely naked, but each was wearing a massive Christmas bow wrapped around their chests. Maja's was red, Tuva's was green, and Hedvig's was blue. Each of them wore such a wide smile waiting for their new boyfriend to come open his gifts.

"Merry Christmas, Ray!" they all called out in unison.

Ray stood up and smiled feeling the arousal beginning to stir within him. He first came up to Maja, pulled at her bow and let it fall off of her body. With her body bare before him, he leaned in and kissed her. Pulling away, he did the same act to Tuva and then to Hedvig.

"Let's go to our bedroom," Tuva whispered, coming in close while her hand reached underneath his shirt.

"We could always...fuck...here under the Christmas tree," Maja suggested, "but our bed is much better."

"Yeah, I say bed."

"Then let's go," Ray said pulling at his shirt, tossing it aside, and then yanking down his pajama pants and underwear making his cock spring outward, voting to go upstairs to bed, Ray didn't care about leaving behind his clothes on the floor.

He then made his way up the stairs with his lovers following behind him until he came to the Master bedroom and climbed into their shared bed.

***

"Oh my god," Ray huffed, collapsing onto the bed with the others. "This has got to be the best Christmas of my life."

"Only one thing to make this complete," Hedvig said, coming up to her boyfriend and cupping his flaccid cock and tightening balls. She then began to bounce his scrotum in her hand and sang, "Jingle Balls! Jingle Balls! All in my puss-say!"

"Hedvig!" Tuva scolded, half smiling and laughing herself.

Maja on the other hand was holding back a small sniggering behind her hand.

Hedvig pulled back her hand and couldn't stop herself laughing.

"That's too good," Ray commented still chuckling. "But after all that we did, I think that joke should be allowed."

With the laughter dying down, the four lovers embraced one another and pulled the covers over themselves, but there was one who continued to sing.

"Oh Christmas Tree," Tuva began to sing, "Oh Christmas Tree."

Her singing voice was unlike anything that Ray had heard. It was on par with the most well-trained vocalists that he had heard through the years.

"I had no idea you could sing," Ray said.

"Most elves can," Tuva said. "We're all trained to do so. Some keep it up and others don't."

"Well, I encourage you to keep on doing that."

"Thank you, sweetie," Tuva said. leaning up to kiss him. "And Merry Christmas, my love."

"Merry Christmas, sweet elf," Ray said. kissing her back. The elf pulled back and smiled and tapped him on the nose.

"Let's not forget about me, hon," Maja said. pushing in and kissing him. "Merry Christmas, Ray."

"Merry Christmas, Maja," Ray smiled.

"God bless us everyone," Hedvig said. in a humorous voice with a slight lisp before pushing in to kiss Ray.

"And Merry Christmas to you as well, Hedvig," Ray laughed, kissing her. "I love you all, so very much."

Epilogue

Ray sat at a table at the Paper Playground signing another copy of his graphic novel "My Journeys in Alfheimr".

"Who should I make this out to?" he asked.

"Alicia," she said. "Absolutely love this book. You drew everyone so beautiful, and it's not just mindless smut."

"I'm glad you like it." Ray smiled, not looking up from making his signature. He closed the book and looked up at the last person in line for his book. She smiled and kissed the cover of his book before she walked away.

"Hard to believe," Ray said to himself in awe of what had happened to him. He looked at his table and the book that he had propped up that had the main character on the front with three women smiling around him as they hugged him. Next to it was the sign that said, "Special sale with author signing. Today only!"

Ray looked at his phone and saw that it was nearly lunch time. He got up and brought up a sign that read, "Author will be back."

"Hey, Maja," Ray called over to his love, "I'm gonna get some lunch. Do you want anything?"

"Do you mean besides you, hon?" Maja called from the register, leaning forward and winking at him.

"Could you two *not, please*?" Danielle asked from her register as she smiled and rolled her eyes while her long rabbit-like ears folded downward against her head.

"I can't help it, Danielle," Maja said, giving her a slight and playful shove. "You've seen him, right?"

"Yes," Danielle said with a sigh as her ears perked up and a slight blush came to her cheek. "I have..."

Danielle was a new hire that Maja had taken on thanks to the booming business. Danielle, like Maja and the others, was one of the Fey people. In her case she was what one might call a "Rabbit Woman", though her people prefer to call themselves "the Coinin".

Ray still remembered when Maja hired her and how much flirting there was. But Ray, Hedvig, and Tuva weren't jealous types. Besides with how much the four of them were getting it on nearly every day there wasn't much need to bring in anyone else. Still, Ray and Maja did talk about having a threesome with Danielle but only as a joking hypothetical.

"If you're heading to the food court," Maja asked, "I wouldn't say no to some fried rice."

"Chinese it is then," Ray acknowledged and headed out to the food court.

He still couldn't believe that a year had passed since he not only came back home to Northview Valley but came into that very mall for a job and found so much more as a result. The decorations for the holiday season were already up and the holiday season stands were already set up in the middle walkways of the mall. And Ray felt like he was walking on air.

"If this is a dream," he said to himself as he got in line at Panda Express, "please don't let me wake up from it."

"Hey there, brother," a voice said from behind him. "Merry Christmas to you."

Ray turned and came face to face with a man who was dressed as Santa. Though he was much skinner than what most Santa's would be. Yet there was something oddly familiar about the man.

"I hope you remember me," he said. "Last year, you gave me some Thanksgiving food?"

Ray thought back to that time and that Thanksgiving party before he met Maja and the others, and the lights connected just like the stringed Christmas decorations.

"Nicholas?" Ray asked.

"That be me," the man said, opening his arms and giving a jovial smile behind his clean white beard.

"How have you been?" Ray asked, excited to see the man and shook his hand.

"The year has gotten better for me," Nicholas mentioned. "I even got this gig as a mall Santa."

"That's marvelous to hear," Ray answered. "Hope the guests aren't giving you any grief."

"Well, you know how it is." Nichola shrugged. "You get some good ones, some real good ones and a few bad ones, but hey, what can you do?"

"Yeah," Ray said, looking over his shoulder to move along with the line.

He made his order and moved along with Nicholas behind him.

"How about you?" he asked. "Did the year get better for you?"

Ray smiled. "Oh, like you wouldn't believe. For one, I got a great job and met three wonderful women. I moved out of my parents' house and in with them. I'm in love and love all three of them so much. We even got rings for each other."

Ray showed his left hand and a simple black metal band on his third finger.

"Congratulations, kid."

"Thanks, and what's more, I won a good-sized check in a wrongful termination lawsuit. Some friends of mine at the company helped file a suit along with several others and we won. But right now, I have a graphic novel that I published. I'm doing signings for it today."

"What'd I tell you, brother?" Nicholas laughed, patting Ray on the back. "You keep your head up and good things will happen."

"No question," Ray said, coming up to the counter and was about to pay for his and Maja's food but then when Nicholas came up he looked at the cashier and said, "I'll pay for his as well."

"Oh, you don't have to do that," Nicholas said.

"I insist."

"Alright then," Nicholas relented. "But I guess you're doing pretty well if you're buying this Santa his lunch."

"Oh yes," Ray answered. "With the settlement I won last year, I had more than enough, and so do the others. The three of them wanted to quit their jobs in favor of married life with me. But I said I wouldn't ask any of them to give up their careers. They love working the shops that they do, and I didn't want to take that away from them."

Ray looked up and saw that they were approaching The Paper Playground.

"This is my stop." Ray smiled and looked at Nicholas. "Take care of yourself, Nicholas."

"Keep being a good man," Nicholas said, waving his white gloved hand. "And Merry Christmas."

"Merry Christmas to you too, Nicholas."

Ray turned and saw Maja coming out and looking towards the mall Santa with an open mouth and wide eyes.

"I didn't know Santa was here this year," she remarked.

"Isn't there always a Santa in this mall every hear?"

"Of course, hon, but not the true Santa Claus."

Ray's mind connected the dots. From what Maja said to Nicholas. The Santa suit. Thanksgiving the year before. Him in that tattered knitted red hat and red backpack. He turned his head towards the mall Santa Claus, and he smiled.

"Are you alright, hon?" Maja asks.

"I'm quite alright," Ray said as he walked with Maja back into the store. "Everything is right with the world."

Author's Notes

Hello, my dear reader. If you've made it this far then you probably have read the whole book. I do hope that you really like what you've read in it. And now, to tell you a small story about how this book came to be. Once again, if you're interested, stick around, if not, you won't hurt my feelings.

The idea for this book came about around Christmas of 2022 and the love of my life, Luna, and I had gotten tickets to this event sponsored by Hallmark called "Enchant". If I were to describe it to be like anything to you, it'd be Hallmark's version of a Christmas Market. It was held at a local baseball field with various vendors in the stands, but the real crown of it was on the baseball field itself. It was a maze of Christmas lights where there was a small game set up to find all of Santa's reindeer, including Rudolph, stamp a card and turn it in for a chance to be in a Hallmark Christmas movie.

During this whole adventure, Luna and I discussed a lot of tropes and clichés that were done in those movies. Such as how it often involves a blonde woman leaving the big city for small town America and rediscovering its charm. Then she falls in love with some guy who was either an old flame or someone who had a "glow up" in her time away. Then it all ends in a wedding. And various other things tacked onto that but that's usually the core story.

It's because of how laughable and repetitive Hallmark is that I wanted to parody that in my own way much like how I parodied Harlequin in my book 'The Sanguine Elf'. So, I started with something that hits close to home for a lot of people, a failed job and having to move back in with their parents.

As far as the ladies that come into the main character's life, I wanted each of them to have some kind of connection to Christmas. The first two that came to mind were Tuva, the elf, but I wanted her to be a mixture of the two extremes of thought in popular culture when it came to elves. The second was Maja where, thanks to inspiration from old mythology, I came up with the idea of a reindeer woman. The real hard part was designing the third because I didn't want to do something that had been done before. But the irony of that came when I heard of the stories of the "Yule cat". A Yule cat is from Icelandic folklore and is essentially a massive cat that lurks around during Christmas and eats people who have not received any new clothes to wear before Christmas Eve.

And so, with all these pieces in place for this Christmas story I went ahead and started crafting the story. Just like working on any other long book, the journey has been arduous, but I don't think I could have accomplished this without the people closest to me who encouraged me all along the way.

And now, dear reader, I hope that you've enjoyed this book, and I hope you'll come back to read more of my books.